THE MERMAID

A Love Tale

LILY DOUGALL

CONTENTS

BOOK I

CHAPTER 1. THE BENT TWIG

Caius Simpson was the only son of a farmer who lived on the north-west coast of Prince Edward's Island. The farmer was very well-to-do, for he was a hard-working man, and his land produced richly. The father was a man of good understanding, and the son had been born with brains; there were traditions of education in the family, hence the name Caius; it was no plan of the elder man that his son should also be a farmer. The boy was first sent to learn in what was called an "Academy," a school in the largest town of the island. Caius loved his books, and became a youthful scholar. In the summer he did light work on the farm; the work was of a quiet, monotonous sort, for his parents were no friends to frivolity or excitement.

Caius was strictly brought up. The method of his training was that which relies for strength of character chiefly upon the absence of temptation. The father was under the impression that he could, without any laborious effort and consideration, draw a line between good and evil, and keep his son on one side of it. He was not austere—but his view of righteousness was derived from puritan tradition.

A boy, if kindly treated, usually begins early to approve the only teaching of which he has experience. As a youth, Caius heartily endorsed his father's views, and felt superior to all who were more lax. He had been born into that religious school which teaches that a man should think for himself on every question, provided that he arrives at a foregone conclusion. Caius, at the age of eighteen, had already done much reasoning on certain subjects, and proved his work by observing that his conclusions tallied with set models. As a result, he was, if not a reasonable being, a reasoning and a moral one.

We have ceased to draw a distinction between Nature and the forces of education. It is a great problem why Nature sets so many young people in the world who are apparently unfitted for the battle of life, and certainly have no power to excel in any direction. The subjective religion which Caius had been taught had nourished within him great store of

I

noble sentiment and high desire, but it had deprived him of that rounded knowledge of actual life which alone, it would appear, teaches how to guide these forces into the more useful channels. Then as to capacity, he had the fine sensibilities of a poet, the facile intro-spection of the philosophical cast of mind, without the mental power to write good verse or to be a philosopher. He had, at least in youth, the conscience of a saint without the courage and endurance which appear necessary to heroism. In mockery the quality of ambition was bestowed upon him but not the requisites for success. Nature has been working for millions of years to produce just such characters as Caius Simpson, and, char-acter being rather too costly a production to throw away, no doubt she has a precise use for every one of them.

It is not the province of art to solve problems, but to depict them. It is enough for the purpose of telling his story that a man has been endowed with capacity to suffer and rejoice.

CHAPTER 2. THE SAD-EYED CHILD

One evening in early summer Caius went a-fishing. He started to walk several miles to an inlet where at high tide the sea-trout came within reach of the line. The country road was of red clay, and, turning from the more thickly-settled district, Caius followed it through a wide wood of budding trees and out where it skirted the top of low red cliffs, against which the sea was lapping. Then his way led him across a farm. So far he had been walking indolently, happy enough, but here the shadow of the pain of the world fell upon him.

This farm was a lonesome place close to the sea; there was no appearance of prosperity about it. Caius knew that the farmer, Day by name, was a churl, and was said to keep his family on short rations of happiness. As Caius turned off the public road he was not thinking specially of the bleak appearance of the particular piece of farmland he was crossing, or of the reputation of the family who lived upon the increase of its acres; but his attention was soon drawn to three children swinging on a gate which hung loosely in the log fence not far from the house. The eldest was an awkward-looking girl about twelve years of age; the second was a little boy; the youngest was a round-limbed, blond baby of two or three summers. The three stood upon the lowest bar of the gate, clinging to the upper spars. The eldest leaned her elbows on the top and looked over; the baby embraced the middle bar and looked through. They had set the rickety gate swinging petulantly, and it latched and unlatched itself with the sort of sound that the swaying of some dreary wind would give it. The children seemed to swing there, not because they were happy, but because they were miserable.

As Caius came with light step up the lane, fishing gear over his shoulder, the children looked at him disconsolately, and when he approached the gate the eldest stepped down and pulled it open for him.

"Anything the matter?" he asked, stopping his quick tread, and turning when he had passed through.

The big girl did not answer, but she let go the gate, and when it jerked forward the baby fell.

She did not fall far, nor was she hurt; but as Caius picked her up and patted her cotton clothes to shake the dust out of them, it seemed to him that he had never seen so sad a look in a baby's eyes. Large, dark, dewy eyes they were, circled around with curly lashes, and they looked up at him out of a wistful little face that was framed by a wreath of yellow hair. Caius lifted the child, kissed her, put her down, and went on his way. He only gave his action half a thought at the time, but all his life afterwards he was sorry that he had let the baby go out of his arms again, and thankful that he had given her that one kiss.

His path now lay close by the house and on to the sea-cliff behind. The house stood in front of him—four bare wooden walls, brown painted, and without veranda or ornament; its barns, large and ugly, were close beside it. Beyond, some stunted firs grew in a dip of the cliff, but on the level ground the farmer had felled every tree. The homestead itself was ugly; but the land was green, and the sea lay broad and blue, its breast swelling to the evening sun. The air blew sweet over field and cliff, add the music of the incoming tide was heard below the pine-fringed bank. Caius, however, was not in the receptive mind which appreciates outward things. His attention was not thoroughly aroused from himself till the sound of harsh voices struck his ear.

Between the farmhouse and the barns, on a place worn bare by the feet of men and animals, the farmer and his wife stood in hot dispute. The woman, tall, gaunt, and ill-dressed, spoke fast, passion and misery in all her attitude and in every tone and gesture. The man, chunky in figure and churlish in demeanour, held a horsewhip in his hand, answering his wife back word for word in language both profane and violent.

It did not occur to Caius that the whip was in his hand otherwise than by accident. The men in that part of the world were not in the habit of beating their wives, but no sooner did he see the quarrel than his wrath rose hot against the man. The woman being the weaker, he took for granted that she was entirely in the right. He faltered in his walk, and, hesitating, stood to look. His path was too far off for him to hear the words that were poured forth in such torrents of passion. The boy's strong sentiment prompted him to run and collar the man; his judgment made him doubt whether it was a good thing to interfere between man and wife; a certain latent cowardice in his heart made him afraid to venture nearer. The sum of his emotions caused him to stop, go on a few paces, and stop to look and listen again, his heart full of concern. In this way he was drawing further away, when he saw the farmer step nearer his wife and menace her with the whip; in an instant more he had struck her, and Caius had run about twenty feet forward to interfere, and halted again, because he was afraid to approach so angry and powerful a man.

Caius saw the woman clearly now, and how she received this attack. She stood quite still at her full stature, ceasing to speak or to gesticulate, folded her arms and looked at her husband. The look in her hard, dark face, the pose of her gaunt figure, said more clearly than any passionate words, "Hold, if you value your life! you have gone too far; you have heaped up punishment enough for yourself already." The husband understood this language, vaguely, it might be, but still he understood enough to make him draw back, still growling and menacing with the whip. Caius was too young to understand what the woman expressed; he only knew strength and weakness as physical things; his mind was surging with pity for the woman and revenge against the man; yet even he gathered the knowledge that for the time the quarrel was over, that interference was now needless. He walked on, looking back as he went to see the farmer go away to his stables and the wife stalk past him up toward the byre that was nearest the sea.

As Caius moved on, the only relief his mind could find at first was to exercise his imagination in picturing how he could avenge the poor woman. In fancy he saw himself

3

holding Day by the throat, throwing him down, belabouring him with words and blows, meting out punishment more than adequate. All that he actually did, however, was to hold on his way to the place of his fishing.

The path had led him to the edge of the cliff. Here he paused, looking over the bank to see if he could get down and continue his walk along the shore, but the soft sandy bluff here jutted so that he could not even see at what level the tide lay. After spending some minutes in scrambling half-way down and returning because he could descend no further, he struck backwards some paces behind the farm buildings, supposing the descent to be easier where bushes grew in the shallow chine. In the top of the cliff there was a little dip, which formed an excellent place for an outside cellar or root-house for such farm stores as must be buried deep beneath the snow against the frost of winter. The rough door of such a cellar appeared in the side of this small declivity, and as Caius came round the back of the byre in sight of it, he was surprised to see the farmer's wife holding the latch of its door in her hand and looking vacantly into the dark interior. She looked up and answered the young man's greeting with apathetic manner, apparently quite indifferent to the scene she had just passed through.

Caius, his mind still in the rush of indignation on her behalf, stopped at the sight of her, wondering what he could do or say to express the wild pity that surged within him.

But the woman said, "The tide's late to-night," exactly as she might have remarked with dry civility that it was fine weather.

"Yes," said Caius, "I suppose it will be."

She was looking into the cellar, not towards the edge of the bank.

"With a decent strong tide," she remarked, "you can hear the waves in this cave."

Whereupon she walked slowly past him back toward her house. Caius took the precaution to step after her round the end of the byre, just to see that her husband was not lying in wait for her there. There was no one to be seen but the children at a distance, still swinging on the gate, and a labourer who was driving some cows from the field.

Caius slipped down on to the red shore, and found himself in a wide semicircular bay, near the point which ended it on this side. He crept round the bay inwards for half a mile, till he came to the mouth of the creek to which he was bound. All the long spring evening he sat angling for the speckled sea-trout, until the dusk fell and the blue water turned gray, and he could no longer see the ruddy colour of the rock on which he sat. All the long spring evening the trout rose to his fly one by one, and were landed in his basket easily enough, and soft-throated frogs piped to him from ponds in the fields behind, and the smell of budding verdure from the land mingled with the breeze from the sea. But Caius was not happy; he was brooding over the misery suggested by what he had just seen, breathing his mind after its unusual rush of emotion, and indulging its indignant melancholy. It did not occur to him to wonder much why the object of his pity had made that quick errand to the cellar in the chine, or why she had taken interest in the height of the tide. He supposed her to be inwardly distracted by her misery. She had the reputation of being a strange woman.

CHAPTER 3. LOST IN THE SEA

There was no moon that night. When the darkness began to gather swiftly, Caius swung his basket of fish and his tackle over his shoulder and tramped homeward. His preference

4

was to go round by the road and avoid the Day farm; then he thought it might be his duty to go that way, because it might chance that the woman needed protection as he passed. It is much easier to give such protection in intention than in deed; but, as it happened, the deed was not required. The farmstead was perfectly still as he went by it again.

He went on half a mile, passing only such friendly persons as it was natural he should meet on the public road. They were few. Caius walked listening to the sea lapping below the low cliff near which the road ran, and watching the bats that often circled in the dark-blue dusk overhead. Thus going on, he gradually recognised a little group walking in front of him. It was the woman, Mrs. Day, and her three children. Holding a child by either hand, she tramped steadily forward. Something in the way she walked, in the way the children walked—a dull, mechanical action in their steps—perplexed Caius.

He stepped up beside them with a word of neighbourly greeting.

The woman did not answer for some moments; when she did, although her words were ordinary, her voice seemed to Caius to come from out some far distance whither her mind had wandered.

"Going to call on someone, I suppose, Mrs. Day?" said he, inwardly anxious.

"Yes," she replied; "we're going to see a friend—the children and me."

Again it seemed that there was some long distance between her and the young man who heard her.

"Come along and see my mother," he urged, with solicitude. "She always has a prime welcome for visitors, mother has."

The words were hearty, but they excited no heartiness of response.

"We've another place to go to to-night," she said. "There'll be a welcome for us, I reckon."

She would neither speak to him any more nor keep up with his pace upon the road. He slackened speed, but she still shrank back, walking slower. He found himself getting in advance, so he left her.

A hundred yards more he went on, and looked back to see her climbing the log fence into the strip of common beside the sea.

His deliberation of mind was instantly gone. Something was wrong now. He cast himself over the low log fence just where he was, and hastened back along the edge of the cliff, impelled by unformulated fear.

It was dark, the dark grayness of a moonless night. The cliff here was not more than twenty feet above the high tide, which surged and swept deep at its base. The grass upon the top was short; young fir-trees stood here and there. All this Caius saw. The woman he could not see at first. Then, in a minute, he did see her—standing on the edge of the bank, her form outlined against what light there was in sea and sky. He saw her swing something from her. The thing she threw, whatever it was, was whirled outwards, and then fell into the sea. With a splash, it sank.

The young man's mind stood still with horror. The knowledge came to him as he heard the splash that it was the little child she had flung away. He threw off his basket and coat. Another moment, and he would have jumped from the bank; but before he had jumped he heard the elder girl groaning as if in desperate fear, and saw that mother and daughter were grappled together, their figures swaying backwards and forwards in convulsive struggle. He did not doubt that the mother was trying to drown this child also. Another low wild groan from the girl, and Caius flung himself upon them both. His strength released the girl, who drew away a few paces; but the woman struggled terribly to get to her again. Both the girl and little boy stood stupidly within reach.

"Run—run—to the road, and call for help!" gasped Caius to the children, but they only stood still.

He was himself shouting with all his strength, and holding the desperate woman upon the ground, where he had thrown her.

Every moment he was watching the dark water, where he thought he saw a little heap of light clothes rise and sink again further off.

"Run with your brother out of the way, so that I can leave her," he called to the girl. He tried with a frantic gesture to frighten them into getting out of the mother's reach. He continued to shout for aid as he held down the woman, who with the strength of insanity was struggling to get hold of the children.

A man's voice gave answering shout. Caius saw someone climbing the fence. He left the woman and jumped into the sea.

Down under the cold black water he groped about. He was not an expert swimmer and diver. He had never been under water so long before, but so strong had been his impulse to reach the child that he went a good way on the bottom in the direction in which he had thought he saw the little body floating. Then he knew that he came up empty-handed and was swimming on the dark surface, hearing confused cries and imprecations from the shore. He wanted to dive and seek again for the child below, but he did not know how to do this without a place to leap from. He let himself sink, but he was out of breath. He gasped and inhaled the water, and then, for dear life's sake, he swam to keep his head above it.

The water had cooled his excitement; a feeling of utter helplessness and misery came over him. So strong was his pity for the little sad-eyed child that he was almost willing to die in seeking her; but all hope of finding was forsaking him. He still swam in the direction in which he thought the child drifted as she rose and sank. It did not occur to him to be surprised that she had drifted so far until he realized that he was out of hearing of the sounds from the shore. His own swimming, he well knew, could never have taken him so far and fast. There was a little sandy island lying about three hundred yards out. At first he hoped to strike the shallows near it quickly, but found that the current of the now receding tide was racing down the channel between the island and the shore, out to the open sea. That little body was, no doubt, being sucked outward in this rush of water—out to the wide water where he could not find her. He told himself this when he found at what a pace he was going, and knew that his best chance of ever returning was to swim back again.

So he gave up seeking the little girl, and turned and swam as best he could against the current, and recognised slowly that he was making no headway, but by using all his strength could only hold his present place abreast of the outer point of the island, and a good way from it. The water was bitterly cold; it chilled him. He was far too much occupied in fighting the current to think properly, but certain flashes of intelligence came across his mind concerning the death he might be going to die. His first clear thoughts were about a black object that was coming near on the surface of the water. Then a shout reached him, and a stronger swimmer than he pulled him to the island.

"Now, in the devil's name, Caius Simpson!" The deliverer was the man who had come over the fence, and he shook himself as he spoke. His words were an interrogation relating to all that had passed. He was a young man, about the same age as Caius; the latter knew him well.

"The child, Jim!" shivered Caius hoarsely. "She threw it into the water!"

"In there?" asked Jim, pointing to the flowing darkness from which they had just scrambled. He shook his head as he spoke. "There's a sort of a set the water's got round this here place——" He shook his head again; he sat half dressed on the edge of the grass, peering into the tide, a dark figure surrounded by darkness.

It seemed to Caius even then, just pulled out as he was from a sea too strong for him, that there was something horribly bad and common in that they two sat there taking breath, and did not plunge again into the water to try, at least, to find the body of the child who a few minutes before had lived and breathed so sweetly. Yet they did not move.

"Did someone else come to hold her?" Caius asked this in a hasty whisper. They both spoke as if there was some need for haste.

"Noa. I tied her round with your fish-cord. If yo'd have done that, yo' might have got the babby the same way I got yo'."

The heart of Caius sank. If only he had done this! Jim Hogan was not a companion for whom he had any respect; he looked upon him as a person of low taste and doubtful morals, but in this Jim had shown himself superior.

"I guess we'd better go and look after them," said Jim. He waded in a few paces. "Come along," he said.

As they waded round to the inner side of the island, Caius slowly took off some of his wet clothes and tied them round his neck. Then they swam back across the channel at its narrowest.

While the water was rushing past their faces, Caius was conscious of nothing but the animal desire to be on the dry, warm shore again; but when they touched the bottom and climbed the bank once more to the place where he had seen the child cast away, he forgot all his fight with the sea, and thought only with horror of the murder done—or was there yet hope that by a miracle the child might be found somewhere alive? It is hope always that causes panic. Caius was panic-stricken.

The woman lay, bound hand and foot, upon the grass.

"If I couldn't ha' tied her," said Jim patronizingly, "I'd a quietened her by a knock on the head, and gone after the young un, if I'd been yo'."

The other children had wandered away. They were not to be seen.

Jim knelt down in a business-like way to untie the woman, who seemed now to be as much stunned by circumstances as if she had been knocked as just suggested.

A minute more, and Caius found himself running like one mad in the direction of home. He cared nothing about the mother or the elder children, or about his own half-dressed condition. The one thought that excited him was a hope that the sea might have somewhere cast the child on the shore before she was quite dead.

Running like a savage under the budding trees of the wood and across his father's fields, he leaped out of the darkness into the heat and brightness of his mother's kitchen.

Gay rugs lay on the yellow painted floor; the stove glistened with polish at its every corner. The lamp shone brightly, and in its light Caius stood breathless, wet, half naked. The picture of his father looking up from the newspaper, of his mother standing before him in alarmed surprise, seemed photographed in pain upon his brain for minutes before he could find utterance. The smell of an abundant supper his mother had set out for him choked him.

When he had at last spoken—told of the blow Farmer Day had struck, of his wife's deed, and commanded that all the men that could be collected should turn out to seek for the child—he was astonished at finding sobs in the tones of his words. He became oblivious for the moment of his parents, and leaned his face against the wooden wall of the room in a convulsion of nervous feeling that was weeping without tears.

It did not in the least surprise his parents that he should cry—he was only a child in their eyes. While the father bestirred himself to get a cart and lanterns and men, the mother soothed her son, or, rather, she addressed to him such kindly attentions as she supposed were soothing to him. She did not know that her attention to his physical comfort hardly entered his consciousness.

Caius went out again that night with those who went to examine the spot, and test the current, and search the dark shores. He went again, with a party of neighbours, to the same place, in the first faint pink flush of dawn, to seek up and down the sands and rocks left bare by the tide. They did not find the body of the child.

CHAPTER 4. A QUIET LIFE

In the night, while the men were seeking the murdered child, there were kindly women who went to the house of the farmer Day to tend his wife. The elder children had been found asleep in a field, where, after wandering a little while, they had succumbed to the influence of some drug, which had evidently been given them by the mother to facilitate her evil design. She herself, poor woman, had grown calm again, her frenzy leaving her to a duller phase of madness. That she was mad no one doubted. How long she might have been walking in the misleading paths of wild fancy, whether her insane vagaries had been the cause or the result of her husband's churlishness, no one knew. The husband was a taciturn man, and appeared to sulk under the scrutiny of the neighbourhood. The more charitable ascribed his demeanour to sorrow. The punishment his wife had meted out for the blow he struck her had, without doubt, been severe.

As for Caius Simpson, his mind was sore concerning the little girl. It was as if his nature, in one part of it, had received a bruise that did not heal. The child had pleased his fancy. All the sentiment in him centred round the memory of the little girl, and idealized her loveliness. The first warm weather of the year, the exquisite but fugitive beauties of the spring, lent emphasis to his mood, and because his home was not a soil congenial to the growth of any but the more ordinary sentiments, he began at this time to seek in natural solitudes a more fitting environment for his musings. More than once, in the days that immediately followed, he sought by daylight the spot where, in the darkness, he had seen the child thrown into the sea. It soon occurred to him to make an epitaph for her, and carve it in the cliff over which she was thrown. In the noon-day hours in which his father rested, he worked at this task, and grew to feel at home in the place and its surroundings.

The earth in this place, as in others, showed red, the colour of red jasper, wherever its face was not covered by green grass or blue water. Just here, where the mother had sought out a precipice under which the tide lay deep, there was a natural water-wall of red sandstone, rubbed and corrugated by the waves. This wall of rock extended but a little way, and ended in a sharp jutting point.

THE MERMAID

The little island that stood out toward the open sea had sands of red gold; level it was and covered with green bushes, its sandy beach surrounding it like a ring.

On the other side of the jutting point a bluff of red clay and crumbling rock continued round a wide bay. Where the rim of the blue water lay thin on this beach there showed a purple band, shading upward into the dark jasper red of damp earth in the lower cliff. The upper part of the cliff was very dry, and the earth was pink, a bright earthen pink. This ribbon of shaded reds lay all along the shore. The land above it was level and green.

At the other horn of the bay a small town stood; its white houses, seen through the trembling lens of evaporating water, glistened with almost pearly brightness between the blue spaces of sky and water. All the scene was drenched in sunlight in those spring days.

The town, Montrose by name, was fifteen miles away, counting miles by the shore. The place where Caius was busy was unfrequented, for the land near was not fertile, and a wooded tract intervened between it and the better farms of the neighbourhood. The home of the lost child and one other poor dwelling were the nearest houses, but they were not very near.

Caius did not attempt to carve his inscription on the mutable sandstone. It was quite possible to obtain a slab of hard building-stone and material for cement, and after carting them himself rather secretly to the place, he gradually hewed a deep recess for the tablet and cemented it there, its face slanting upward to the blue sky for greater safety. He knew even then that the soft rock would not hold it many years, but it gave him a poetic pleasure to contemplate the ravages of time as he worked, and to think that the dimpled child with the sunny hair and the sad, beautiful eyes had only gone before, that his tablet would some time be washed away by the same devouring sea, and that in the sea of time he, too, would sink before many years and be forgotten.

The short elegy he wrote was a bad mixture of ancient and modern thought as to substance, figures, and literary form, for the boy had just been dipping into classics at school, while he was by habit of mind a Puritan. His composition was one at which pagan god and Christian angel must have smiled had they viewed it; but perhaps they would have wept too, for it was the outcome of a heart very young and very earnest, wholly untaught in that wisdom which counsels to evade the pains and suck the pleasures of circumstance.

There were only two people who discovered what Caius was about, and came to look on while his work was yet unfinished.

One was an old man who lived in the one poor cottage not far away and did light work for Day the farmer. His name was Morrison—Neddy Morrison he was called. He came more than once, creeping carefully near the edge of the cliff with infirm step, and talking about the lost child, whom he also had loved, about the fearful visitation of the mother's madness, and, with Caius, condemning unsparingly the brutality, known and supposed, of the now bereaved father. It was a consolation to them both that Morrison could state that this youngest child was the only member of his family for whom Day had ever shown affection.

The other visitor Caius had was Jim Hogan. He was a rough youth; he had a very high, rounded forehead, so high that he would have almost seemed bald if the hair, when it did at last begin, had not been exceedingly thick, standing in a short red brush round his head. With the exception of this peculiar forehead, Jim was an ordinary freckled, healthy young man. He saw no sense at all in what Caius was doing. When he came he sat himself down on the edge of the cliff, swung his heels, and jeered unfeignedly.

When the work was finished it became noised that the tablet was to be seen. The neighbours wondered not a little, and flocked to gaze and admire. Caius himself had never told of its existence; he would have rather no one had seen it; still, he was not insensible to the local fame thus acquired. His father, it was true, had not much opinion of his feat, but his mother, as mothers will, treasured all the admiring remarks of the neighbours. All the women loved Caius from that day forth, as being wondrously warm-hearted. Such sort of literary folk as the community could boast dubbed him "The Canadian Burns," chiefly, it seemed, because he had been seen to help his father at the ploughing.

In due course the wife of the farmer Day was tried for murder, and pronounced insane. She had before been removed to an asylum: she now remained there.

CHAPTER 5. SEEN THROUGH BLEAR EYES

It was foreseen by the elder Simpson that his son would be a great man. He looked forth over the world and decided on the kind of greatness. The wide, busy world would not have known itself as seen in the mind of this gray-haired countryman. The elder Simpson had never set foot off the edge of his native island. His father before him had tilled the same fertile acres, looked out upon the same level landscape—red and green, when it was not white with snow. Neither of them had felt any desire to see beyond the brink of that horizon; but ambition, quiet and sturdy, had been in their hearts. The result of it was the bit of money in the bank, the prosperous farm, and the firm intention of the present farmer that his son should cut a figure in the world.

This stern man, as he trudged about at his labour, looked upon the activities of city life with that same inward eye with which the maiden looks forth upon her future; and as she, with nicety of preference, selects the sort of lover she will have, so he selected the sort of greatness which should befall his son. The stuff of this vision was, as must always be, of such sort as had entered his mind in the course of his limited experience. His grandfather had been an Englishman, and it was known that one of the sons had been a notable physician in the city of London: Caius must become a notable physician. His newspaper told him of honours taken at the University of Montreal by young men of the medical school; therefore, Caius was to study and take honours. It was nothing to him that his neighbours did not send their sons so far afield; he came of educated stock himself. The future of Caius was prearranged, and Caius did not gainsay the arrangement.

That autumn the lad went away from home to a city which is, without doubt, a very beautiful city, and joined the ranks of students in a medical school which for size and thorough work is not to be despised. He was not slow to drink in the new ideas which a first introduction to modern science, and a new view of the relations of most things, brought to his mind.

In the first years Caius came home for his summer vacations, and helped his father upon the farm. The old man had money, but he had no habit of spending it, and expenditure, like economy, is a practice to be acquired. When Caius came the third time for the long summer holiday, something happened.

He did not now often walk in the direction of the Day farm; there was no necessity to take him there, only sentiment. He was by this time ashamed of the emblazonment of his poetic effort upon the cliff. He was not ashamed of the sentiment which had prompted it, but he was ashamed of its exhibition. He still thought tenderly of the little child that was lost, and once in a long while he visited the place where his tablet was, as he would have visited a grave.

One summer evening he sauntered through the wood and down the road by the sea on this errand. Before going to the shore, he stopped at the cottage where the old labourer, Morrison, lived.

There was something to gossip about, for Day's wife had been sent from the asylum as cured, and her husband had been permitted to take her home again on condition that no young or weak person should remain in the house with her. He had sent his two remaining children to be brought up by a relative in the West. People said he could get more work out of his wife than out of the children, and, furthermore, it saved his having to pay for her board elsewhere. The woman had been at home almost a twelvemonth, and Caius had some natural interest in questioning Morrison as to her welfare and general demeanour. The strange gaunt creature had for his imagination very much the fascination that a ghost would have had. We care to hear all about a ghost, however trivial the details may be, but we desire no personal contact. Caius had no wish to meet this woman, for whom he felt repulsion, but he would have been interested to hear Neddy Morrison describe her least action, for Neddy was almost the only person who had constant access to her house.

Morrison, however, had very little to tell about Mrs. Day. She had come home, and was living very much as she had lived before. The absence of her children did not appear to make great difference in her dreary life. The old labourer could not say that her husband treated her kindly or unkindly. He was not willing to affirm that she was glad to be out of the asylum, or that she was sorry. To the old man's imagination Mrs. Day was not an interesting object; his interest had always been centred upon the children. It was of them he talked chiefly now, telling of letters that their father had received from them, and of the art by which he, Morrison, had sometimes contrived to make the taciturn Day show him their contents. The interest of passive benevolence which the young medical student gave to Morrison's account of these children, who had grown quite beyond the age when children are pretty and interesting, would soon have been exhausted had the account been long; but it happened that the old man had a more startling communication to make, which cut short his gossip about his master's family.

He had been standing so far at the door of his little wooden house. His old wife was moving at her household work within. Caius stood outside. The house was a little back from the road in an open space; near it was a pile of firewood, a saw-horse and chopping-block, with their accompanying carpet of chips, and such pots, kettles, and household utensils as Mrs. Morrison preferred to keep out of doors.

When old Morrison came to the more exciting part of his gossip, he poked Caius in the breast, and indicated by a backward movement of his elbow that the old wife's presence hampered his talk. Then he came out with an artfully simulated interest in the weather, and, nudging Caius at intervals, apparently to enforce silence on a topic concerning which the young man as yet knew nothing, he wended his way with him along a path through a thicket of young fir-trees which bordered the road.

The two men were going towards that part of the shore to which Caius was bound. They reached the place where the child had been drowned before the communication was made, and stood together, like a picture of the personification of age and youth, upon the top of the grassy cliff.

"You'll not believe me," said the old man, with excitement obviously growing within him, "but I tell you, young sir, I've sat jist here behind those near bushes like, and watched the creatur for an hour at a time."

"What was it you watched?" asked Caius, superior to the other's excitement.

"I tell you, it was a girl in the sea; and more than that—she was half a fish."

The mind of Caius was now entirely scornful.

"You don't believe me," said the old man, nudging him again.

But Caius was polite.

"Well, now"—good-humouredly—"what did you see?"

"I'll tell you jist what I saw." (The old man's excitement was growing.) "You understand that from the top here you can see across the bay, and across to the island and out to sea; but you can't see the shore under the rocky point where it turns round the farm there into the bay, and you can't see the other shore of the island for the bushes on it."

"In other words, you can see everything that's before your eyes, but you can't see round a corner."

The old man had some perception that Caius was humorous. "You believe me that far," he said, with a weak, excited cackle of a laugh. "Well, don't go for to repeat what I'm going to tell you further, for I'll not have my old woman frightened, and I'll not have Jim Hogan and the fellows he gets round him belabouring the thing with stones."

"Heaven forbid!" A gleam of amusement flitted through the mind of Caius at the thought of the sidelight this threw on Jim's character. For Jim was not incapable of casting stones at even so rare a curiosity as a mermaid.

"Now," said the old man, and he laughed again his weak, wheezy laugh, "if *you* told *me*, I'd not believe it; but I saw it as sure as I stand here, and if this was my dying hour, sir, I'd say the same. The first time it was one morning that I got up very early—I don't jist remember the reason, but it was before sun-up, and I was walking along here, and the tide was out, and between me and the island I saw what I thought was a person swimming in the water, and I thought to myself, 'It's queer, for there's no one about these parts that has a liking for the water.' But when I was younger, at Pictou once, I saw the fine folks ducking themselves in flannel sarks, at what they called a 'bathing-place,' so the first thing I thought of was that it was something like that. And then I stood here, jist about where you are now, and the woman in the water she saw me—"

"Now, how do you know it was a woman?" asked Caius.

"Well, I didn't know for certain that day anything, for she was a good way off, near the island, and she no sooner saw me than she turned and made tracks for the back of the island where I couldn't see her. But I tell you this, young sir, no woman or man either ever swam as she swam. Have you seen a trout in a quiet pool wag its tail and go right ahead —*how*, you didn't know; you only knew that 'twasn't in the one place and 'twas in t'other?"

Caius nodded.

"Well," asked the old man with triumph in his voice, as one who capped an argument, "did you ever see man or woman swim like that?"

"No," Caius admitted, "I never did—especially as to the wagging of the tail."

"But she *hadn't* a tail!" put in the old man eagerly, "for I saw her the second day—that I'm coming to. She was more like a seal or walrus."

"But what became of her the first day?" asked Caius, with scientific exactitude.

"Why, the end of her the first day was that she went behind the island. Can you see behind the island? No." The old man giggled again at his own logical way of putting things. "Well, no more could I see her; and home I went, and I said nothink to nobody, for I wasn't going to have them say I was doting."

"Yet it would be classical to dote upon a mermaid," Caius murmured. The sight of the dim-eyed, decrepit old man before him gave exquisite humour to the idea.

Morrison had already launched forth upon the story of the second day.

"Well, as I was telling you, I was that curious that next morning at daybreak I comes here and squats behind those bushes, and a dreadful fright I was in for fear my old woman would come and look for me and see me squatting there." His old frame shook for a moment with the laugh he gave to emphasize the situation, and he poked Caius with his finger. "And I looked and I looked out on the gray water till I had the cramps." Here he poked Caius again. "But I tell you, young sir, when I saw her a-coming round from behind the bank, where I couldn't see jist where she had come from, like as if she had come across the bay round this point here, I thought no more of the cramps, but I jist sat on my heels, looking with one eye to see that my old woman didn't come, and I watched that 'ere thing, and it came as near as I could throw a stone, and I tell you it was a girl with long hair, and it had scales, and an ugly brown body, and swum about like a fish, jist moving, without making a motion, from place to place for near an hour; and then it went back round the head again, and I got up, and I was that stiff all day I could hardly do my work. I was too old to do much at that game, but I went again next morning, and once again I saw her; but she was far out, and then I never saw her again. Now, what do you think of that?"

"I think"—after a moment's reflection—"that it's a very remarkable story."

"But you don't believe it," said the old man, with an air of excited certainty.

"I am certain of one thing; you couldn't have made it up."

"It's true, sir," said the old man. "As sure as I am standing here, as sure as the tide goes in and out, as sure as I'll be a-dying before long, what I tell you is true; but if I was you, I'd have more sense than to believe it." He laughed again, and pressed Caius' arm with the back of his hard, knotted hand. "That's how it is about sense and truth, young sir—it's often like that."

This one gleam of philosophy came from the poor, commonplace mind as a beautiful flash may come from a rough flint struck upon the roadside. Caius pondered upon it afterwards, for he never saw Neddy Morrison again. He did not happen to pass that place again that summer, and during the winter the old man died.

Caius thought at one time and another about this tale of the girl who was half a fish. He thought many things; the one thing he never happened to think was that it was true. It was clear to him that the old man supposed he had seen the object he described, but it puzzled him to understand how eyes, even though so dim with age, could have mistaken any sea-creature for the mermaid he described; for the man had lived his life by the sea, and even the unusual sight of a lonely white porpoise hugging the shore, or of seal or small whale, or even a much rarer sea-animal, would not have been at all likely to deceive him. It would certainly have been very easy for any person in mischief or malice to have played the hoax, but no locality in the wide world would have seemed more unlikely to be the scene of such a game; for who performs theatricals to amuse the lonely shore, or the ebbing tide, or the sea-birds that poise in the air or pounce upon the fish when the sea is gray at dawn? And certainly the deception of the old man could not have been the object of the play, for it was but by chance that he saw it, and it could matter to no one what he saw or thought or felt, for he was one of the most insignificant of earth's sons. Then Caius would think of that curious gleam of deeper insight the poor old mind had displayed in the attempt to express, blunderingly as it might be, the fact that truth exceeds our understanding, and yet that we are bound to walk by the light of understanding. He came, upon the whole, to the conclusion that some latent faculty of imagination, working in the old man's mind, combining with the picturesque objects so familiar to his eyes, had produced in him belief in this curious vision. It was one of those things that seem to have no reason for coming to pass, no sufficient cause and no result, for Caius never heard that Morrison had related the tale to anyone but himself, nor was there any report in the village that anyone else had seen an unusual object in the sea.

CHAPTER 6. "FROM HOUR TO HOUR WE RIPE——"

The elder Simpson gradually learned to expend more money upon his son; it was not that the latter was a spendthrift or that he took to any evil courses—he simply became a gentleman and had uses for money of which his father could not, unaided, have conceived. Caius was too virtuous to desire to spend his father's hardly-gathered stores unnecessarily; therefore, the last years of his college life in Montreal he did not come home in summer, but found occupation in that city by which to make a small income for himself.

In those two years he learned much of medical and surgical lore—this was of course, for he was a student by nature; but other things that he learned were, upon the whole, more noteworthy in the development of his character. He became fastidious as to the fit of his coat and as to the work of the laundress upon his shirt-fronts. He learned to sit in easy attitude by gauzily-dressed damsels under sparkling gaslight, and to curl his fair moustache between his now white fingers as he talked to them, and yet to moderate the extent of the attention that he paid to each, not wishing that it should be in excess of that which was due. He learned to value himself as he was valued—as a rising man, one who would do well not to throw himself away in marriage. He had a moustache first, and at last he had a beard. He was a sober young man: as his father's teaching had been strict, so he was now strict in his rule over himself. He frequented religious services, going about listening to popular preachers of all sorts, and critically commenting upon their sermons to his friends. He was really a very religious and well-intentioned man, all of which stood in his favour with the more sober portion of society whose favour he courted. As his talents and industry gained him grace in the eyes of the dons of his college, so his good life and good understanding made him friends among the more worthy of his companions. He was conceited and self-righteous, but not obviously so.

When his college had conferred upon him the degree of doctor of medicine, he felt that he had climbed only on the lower rungs of the ladder of knowledge. It was his father, not himself, who had chosen his profession, and now that he had received the right to practise medicine he experienced no desire to practise it; learning he loved truly, but not that he might turn it into golden fees, and not that by it he might assuage the sorrows of others; he loved it partly for its own sake, perhaps chiefly so; but there was in his heart a long-enduring ambition, which formed itself definitely into a desire for higher culture, and hoped more indefinitely for future fame.

Caius resolved to go abroad and study at the medical schools of the Old World. His professors applauded his resolve; his friends encouraged him in it. It was to explain to his father the necessity for this course of action, and wheedle the old man into approval and consent, that the young doctor went home in the spring of the same year which gave him his degree.

Caius had other sentiments in going home besides those which underlay the motive which we have assigned. If as he travelled he at all regarded the finery of all that he had acquired, it was that he might by it delight the parents who loved him with such pride. Though not a fop, his hand trembled on the last morning of his journey when he fastened a necktie of the colour his mother loved best. He took an earlier train than he could have been expected to take, and drove at furious rate between the station and his home, in order that he might creep in by the side door and greet his parents before they had thought of coming to meet him. He had also taken no breakfast, that he might eat the more of the manifold dainties which his mother had in readiness.

For three or four days he feasted hilariously upon these dainties until he was ill. He also practised all the airs and graces of dandyism that he could think of, because he knew that the old folks, with ill-judging taste, admired them. When he had explained to them how great a man he should be when he had been abroad, and how economical his life would be in a foreign city, they had no greater desire than that he should go abroad, and there wax as great as might be possible.

One thing that consoled the mother in the heroism of her ambition was that it was his plan first to spend the long tranquil summer by her side. Another was that, because her son had set his whole affection upon learning, it appeared he had no immediate intention of fixing his love upon any more material maid. In her timid jealousy she loved to come across this topic with him, not worldly-wise enough to know that the answers which reassured her did not display the noblest side of his heart.

"And there wasn't a girl among them all that you fancied, my lad?" With spotless apron round her portly form she was serving the morning rasher while Caius and his father sat at meat.

"I wouldn't say that, mother: I fancied them all." Caius spoke with generous condescension towards the fair.

"Ay," said the father shrewdly, "there's safety in numbers."

"But there wasn't one was particular, Caius?" continued the dame with gleeful insinuation, because she was assured that the answer was to be negative. "A likely lad like you should marry; it's part of his duty."

Caius was dense enough not to see her true sentiment. The particular smile that, in the classification of his facial expressions, belonged to the subject of love and marriage, played upon his lips while he explained that when a man got up in the world he could make a better marriage than he could when comparatively poor and unknown.

Her woman's instinct assured her that the expression and the words arose from a heart ignorant of the quality of love, and she regarded nothing else.

The breakfast-room in which they sat had no feature that could render it attractive to

Caius. Although it was warm weather, the windows were closely shut and never opened; such was the habit of the family, and even his influence had not strength to break through a regulation which to his parents appeared so wise and safe. The meadows outside were brimful of flowers, but no flower found its way into this orderly room. The furniture had that desolate sort of gaudiness which one sees in the wares of cheap shops. Cleanliness and godliness were the most conspicuous virtues exhibited, for the room was spotless, and the map of Palestine and a large Bible were prominent objects.

The father and mother were in the habit of eating in the kitchen when alone, and to the son's taste that room, decorated with shining utensils, with its door open to earth and sky, was infinitely more picturesque and cheery; but the mother had a stronger will than her son, and she had ordained that his rise in the world should be marked by his eating in the dining-room, where meals were served whenever they had company. Caius observed also, with a pain to which his heart was sensitive, that at these meals she treated him to her company manners also, asking him in a clear, firm voice if he "chose bread" or if he would "choose a little meat," an expression common in the country as an elegant manner of pressing food upon visitors. It was not that he felt himself unworthy of this mark of esteem, but that the bad taste and the bad English grated upon his nerves.

She was a strong, comely woman, this housemother, portly in person and large of face, with plentiful gray hair brushed smooth; from the face the colour had faded, but the look of health and strong purpose remained. The father, on the other hand, tended to leanness; his large frame was beginning to be obviously bowed by toil; his hair and beard were somewhat long, and had a way of twisting themselves as though blown by the wind. When the light of the summer morning shone through the panes of clean glass upon this family at breakfast, it was obvious that the son was physically somewhat degenerate. Athletics had not then come into fashion; Caius was less in stature than might have been expected from such parents; and now, after his years of town life, he had an appearance of being limp in sinew, nor was there the same strong will and alert shrewdness written upon his features. He was a handsome fellow, clear-eyed and intelligent, finer far, in the estimation of his parents, than themselves; but that which rounded out the lines of his figure was rather a tendency to plumpness than the development of muscle, and the intelligence of his face suggested rather the power to think than the power to utilize his thought.

After the first glad days of the home-coming, the lack of education and taste, and the habits that this lack engendered, jarred more and more upon Caius. He loved his parents too well to betray his just distress at the narrow round of thought and feeling in which their minds revolved—the dogmatism of ignorance on all points, whether of social custom or of the sublime reaches of theology; but this distress became magnified into irritation, partly because of this secrecy, partly because his mind, wearied by study, had not its most wholesome balance.

Jim Hogan at this time made overtures of renewed friendship to Caius. Jim was the same as of old—athletic, quick-witted, large and strong, with his freckled face still innocent of hair; the red brush stood up over his unnaturally high forehead in such fashion as to suggest to the imaginative eye that wreath of flame that in some old pictures is displayed round the heads of villains in the infernal regions. Jim was now the acknowledged leader of the young men of that part who were not above certain low and mischievous practices to which Caius did not dream of condescending. Caius repulsed the offer of friendship extended to him.

The households with which his parents were friendly made great merrymakings over his return. Dancing was forbidden, but games in which maidens might be caught and kissed were not. Caius was not diverted; he had not the good-nature to be in sympathy with the sort of hilarity which was exacted from him.

CHAPTER 7. "A SEA CHANGE"

In the procession of the swift-winged hours there is for every man one and another which is big with fate, in that they bring him peculiar opportunity to lose his life, and by that means find it. Such an hour came now to Caius. The losing and finding of life is accomplished in many ways: the first proffer of this kind which Time makes to us is commonly a draught of the wine of joy, and happy is he who loses the remembrance of self therein.

The hour which was so fateful for Caius came flying with the light winds of August, which breathed over the sunny harvest fields and under the deep dark shade of woods of fir and beech, waving the gray moss that hung from trunk and branch, tossing the emerald ferns that grew in the moss at the roots, and out again into light to catch the silver down of thistles that grew by the red roadside and rustle their purple bloom; then on the cliff, just touching the blue sea with the slightest ripple, and losing themselves where sky and ocean met in indistinguishable azure fold.

Through the woods walked Caius, and onward to the shore. Neddy Morrison was dead. The little child who was lost in the sea was almost forgotten. Caius, thinking upon these things, thought also upon the transient nature of all things, but he did not think profoundly or long. In his earlier youth he had been a good deal given to meditation, a habit which is frequently a mere sign of mental fallowness; now that his mind was wearied with the accumulation of a little learning, it knew what work meant, and did not work except when compelled. Caius walked upon the red road bordered by fir hedges and weeds, amongst which blue and yellow asters were beginning to blow, and the ashen seeds of the flame-flower were seen, for its flame was blown out. Caius was walking for the sake of walking and in pure idleness, but when he came near Farmer Day's land he had no thought of passing it without pausing to rest his eyes for a time upon the familiar details of that part of the shore.

He scrambled down the face of the cliff, for it was as yet some hours before the tide would be full. A glance showed him that the stone of baby Day's tablet yet held firm, cemented in the niche of the soft rock. A glance was enough for an object for which he had little respect, and he sat down with his back to it on one of the smaller rocks of the beach. This was the only place on the shore where the sandstone was hard enough to retain the form of rock, and the rock ended in the small, sharp headland which, when he was down at the water's level, hid the neighbouring bay entirely from his sight.

The incoming tide had no swift, unexpected current as the outgoing water had. There was not much movement in the little channel upon which Caius was keeping watch. The summer afternoon was all aglow upon shore and sea. He had sat quite still for a good while, when, near the sunny island, just at the point where he had been pulled ashore on the adventurous night when he risked his life for the child, he suddenly observed what appeared to be a curious animal in the water.

There was a glistening as of a scaly, brownish body, which lay near the surface of the waves. Was it a porpoise that had ventured so near? Was it a dog swimming? No, he knew well that neither the one nor the other had any such habit as this lazy basking in sunny shallows. Then the head that was lying backwards on the water turned towards him, and he saw a human face—surely, surely it was human!—and a snow-white arm was lifted out of the water as if to play awhile in the warm air.

The eyes of the wonderful thing were turned toward him, and it seemed to chance to see him now for the first time, for there was a sudden movement, no jerk or splash, but a fish-like dart toward the open sea. Then came another turn of the head, as if to make sure that he was indeed the man that he seemed, and then the sea-maid went under the surface, and the ripples that she left behind subsided slowly, expanding and fading, as ripples in calm waters do.

Caius stood up, watching the empty surface of the sea. If some compelling fate had said to him, "There shalt thou stand and gaze," he could not have stood more absolutely still, nor gazed more intently. The spell lasted long: some three or four minutes he stood, watching the place with almost unwinking eyes, like one turned to stone, and within him his mind was searching, searching, to find out, if he might, what thing this could possibly be.

He did not suppose that she would come back. Neddy Morrison had implied that the condition of her appearing was that she should not know that she was seen. It was three years since the old man had seen the same apparition; how much might three years stand for in the life of a mermaid? Then, when such questioning seemed most futile, and the spell that held Caius was loosing its hold, there was a rippling of the calm surface that gave him a wild, half-fearful hope.

As gently as it had disappeared the head rose again, not lying backward now, but, with pretty turn of the white neck, holding itself erect. An instant she was still, and then the perfect arm which he had seen before was again raised in the air, and this time it beckoned to him. Once, twice, thrice he saw the imperative beck of the little hand; then it rested again upon the rippled surface, and the sea-maid waited, as though secure of his obedience.

The man's startled ideas began to right themselves. Was it possible that any woman could be bathing from the island, and have the audacity to ask him to share her sport?

He tarried so long that the nymph, or whatever it might be, came nearer. Some twelve feet or so of the water she swiftly glided through, as it seemed, without twist or turn of her body or effort; then paused; then came forward again, until she had rounded the island at its nearest point, and half-way between it and his shore she stopped, and looked at him steadily with a face that seemed to Caius singularly womanly and sweet. Again she lifted a white hand and beckoned him to come across the space of water that remained.

Caius stood doubtful upon his rock. After a minute he set his feet more firmly upon it, and crossed his arms to indicate that he had no intention of swimming the narrow sea in answer to the beckoning hand. Yet his whole mind was thrown into confusion with the strangeness of it. He thought he heard a woman's laughter come across to him with the lapping waves, and his face flushed with the indignity this offered.

The mermaid left her distance, and by a series of short darts came nearer still, till she stopped again about the width of a broad highroad from the discomforted man. He knew now that it must be truly a mermaid, for no creature but a fish could thus glide along the surface of the water, and certainly the sleek, damp little head that lay so comfortably on the ripple was the head of a laughing child or playful girl. A crown of green seaweed was on the dripping curls; the arms playing idly upon the surface were round, dimpled, and exquisitely white. The dark brownish body he could hardly now see; it was foreshortened to his sight, down slanting deep under the disturbed surface. If it had not been for the indisputable evidence of his senses that this lovely sea thing swam, not with arms or feet, but with some snake-like motion, he might still have tried to persuade himself that some playful girl, strange to the ways of the neighbourhood, was disporting herself at her bath.

It was of no avail that his reason told him that he did not, could not, believe that such a creature as a mermaid could exist. The big dark eyes of the girlish face opened wide and looked at him, the dimpled mouth smiled, and the little white hand came out from the water and beckoned to him again.

He was suffering from no delirium; he had not lost his wits. He stamped his foot to make sure that the rock was beneath him; he turned about on it to rest his eyes from the water sparkles, and to recall all sober, serious thought by gazing at the stable shore. His eye stayed on the epitaph of the lost child. He remembered soberly all that he knew about this dead child, and then a sudden flash of perception seemed to come to him. This sweet water-nymph, on whom for the moment he had turned his back, must be the baby's soul grown to woman in the water. He turned again, eager not to lose a moment of the maiden's presence, half fearful that she had vanished, but she was there yet, lying still as before.

Of course, it was impossible that she should be the sea-wraith of the lost child; but, then, it was wholly impossible that she should be, and there she was, smiling at him, and Caius saw in the dark eyes a likeness to the long-remembered eyes of the child, and thought he still read there human wistfulness and sadness, in spite of the wet dimples and light laughter that bespoke the soulless life of the sea-creature.

Caius stooped on the rock, putting his hand near the water as he might have done had he been calling to a kitten or a baby.

"Come, my pretty one, come," he called softly in soothing tones.

The eyes of the water-nymph blinked at him through wet-fringed lids.

"Come near; I will not hurt you," urged Caius, helpless to do aught but offer blandishment.

He patted the rock gently, as if to make it by that means more inviting.

"Come, love, come," he coaxed. He was used to speak in the same terms of endearment to a colt of which he was fond; but when a look of undoubted derision came over the face of the sea-maiden, he felt suddenly guilty at having spoken thus to a woman.

He stood erect again, and his face burned. The sea-girl's face had dimpled all over with fun. Colts and other animals cannot laugh at us, else we might not be so peaceful in our assumption that they never criticise. Caius before this had always supposed himself happy in his little efforts to please children and animals; now he knew himself to be a blundering idiot, and so far from feeling vexed with the laughing face in the water, he wondered that any other creature had ever permitted his clumsy caresses.

Having failed once, he now knew not what to do, but stood uncertain, devouring the beauty of the sprite in the water as greedily as he might with eyes that were not audacious, for in truth he had begun to feel very shy.

"What is your name?" he asked, throwing his voice across the water.

The pretty creature raised a hand and pointed at some object behind him. Caius, turning, knew it to be the epitaph. Yes, that was what his own intelligence had told him was the only explanation.

Explanation? His reason revolted at the word. There was no explanation of an impossibility. Yet that the mermaid was the lost child he had now little doubt, except that he wholly doubted the evidence of his senses, and that there was a mermaid.

He nodded to her that he understood her meaning about the name, and she gave him a little wave of her hand as if to say good-bye, and began to recede slowly, gliding backward, only her head seen above the disturbed water.

"Don't go," called Caius, much urgency in his words.

But the slow receding motion continued, and no answer came but another gentle wave of the hand.

The hand of Caius stole involuntarily to his lips, and he wafted a kiss across the water. Then suddenly it seemed to him that the cliff had eyes, and that it might be told of him at home and abroad that he was making love to a phantom, and had lost his wits.

The sea-child only tossed her head a little higher out of the water, and again he saw, or fancied he saw, mirth dancing in her eyes.

She beckoned to him and turned, moving away; then looked back and beckoned, and darted forward again; and, doing this again and again, she made straight for the open sea.

Caius cursed himself that he had not the courage to jump in and swim after her at any cost. But then he could not swim so fast—certainly not in his clothes. "There was something so wonderfully human about her face," he mused to himself. His mind suggested, as was its wont, too many reasonable objections to the prompt, headlong course which alone would have availed anything.

While he stood in breathless uncertainty, the beckoning hand became lost in the blur of sparkling ripples; the head, lower now, looked in the water at a distance as like the muzzle of a seal or dog as like a human head. By chance, as it seemed, a point of the island came between him and the receding creature, and Caius found himself alone.

CHAPTER 8. BELIEF IN THE IMPOSSIBLE

Caius clambered up the cliff and over the fence to the highroad. A man with a cartload of corn was coming past. Caius looked at him and his horse, and at the familiar stretch of road. It was a relief so to look. On a small green hillock by the roadside thistles grew thickly; they were in flower and seed at once, and in the sunshine the white down, purple flowers, and silver-green leaves glistened—a little picture, perfect in itself, of graceful lines and exquisite colour, having for its background the hedge of stunted fir that bordered the other side of the road. Caius feasted his eyes for a minute and then turned homeward, walking for awhile beside the cart and talking to the carter, just to be sure that there was nothing wild or strange about himself to attract the man's attention. The cart raised no dust in the red clay of the road; the monotonous creak of its wheels and the dull conversation of its owner were delightful to Caius because they were so real and commonplace.

Caius felt very guilty. He could not excuse himself to himself for the fact that he had not only seen so wild a vision but now felt the greatest reluctance to make known his strange adventure to anyone. He could not precisely determine why this reluctance was guilty on his part, but he had a feeling that, although a sensible man could not be much blamed for seeing a mermaid if he did see one, such a man would rouse the neighbour-hood, and take no rest till the phenomenon was investigated; or, if that proved impossible, till the subject was at least thoroughly ventilated. The ideal man who acted thus would no doubt be jeered at, but, secure in his own integrity, he could easily support the jeers. Caius would willingly have changed places with this model hero, but he could not bring himself to act the part. Even the reason of this unwillingness he could not at once lay his hand upon, but he felt about his mind far it, and knew that it circled round and round the memory of the sea-maid's face.

That fresh oval face, surrounded with wet curls, crowned with its fantastic wreath of glistening weed—it was not alone because of its fresh girlish prettiness that he could not endure to make it the talk of the country, but because, strange as it seemed to him to admit it, the face was to him like the window of a lovely soul. It was true that she had laughed and played; it was true that she was, or pretended to be, half a fish; but, for all that, he would as soon have held up to derision his mother, he would as soon have derided all that he held to be most worthy in woman and all that he held to be beautiful and sacred in ideal, as have done despite to the face that looked at him out of the waves that afternoon. His memory held this face before him, held it lovingly, reverently, and his lips shut firmly over the tale of wonder he might have told.

At the gate of one of the fields a girl stood waiting for him. It was his cousin Mabel, and when he saw her he knew that she must have come to pay them a visit, and he knew too that she must have come because he was at home. He was not attached to his cousin, who was an ordinary young person, but hitherto he had always rather enjoyed her society, because he knew that it was her private ambition to marry him. He did not attribute affec-tion to Mabel, only ambition; but that had pleased his vanity. To-day he felt exceedingly sorry that she had come.

Mabel held the gate shut so that he could not pass.

"Where have you been?" asked she, pretending sternness.

"Just along by the shore." He noticed as he said it that Mabel's frock had a dragged look about the waist, and that the seams were noticeable because of its tightness. He remembered that her frocks had this appearance frequently, and he wished they were not so ill-made.

"I shan't let you in," cried Mabel sportively, "till you tell me exactly what you've been doing for this age."

"I have not been serving my age much," he said, with some weariness in his tone.

"What?" said Mabel.

"You asked me what I had been doing for this age," said he. It was miserably stupid to explain.

When Caius and Mabel had sauntered up through the warm fields to the house, his mother met them in the front parlour with a fresh cap on. Her cap, and her presence in that room, denoted that Mabel was company. She immediately began to make sly remarks concerning Mabel's coming to them while Caius was at home, about her going to meet him, and their homeward walk together.

The mother was comparatively at ease about Mabel; she had little idea that Caius would ever make love to her, so she could enjoy her good-natured slyness to the full. What hurt Caius was that she did enjoy it, that it was just her natural way never to see two young people of opposite sex together without immediately thinking of the subject of marriage, and sooner or later betraying her thought. Heretofore he had been so accustomed to this cast of mind that, when it had tickled neither his sense of humour nor his vanity, he had been indifferent to it. To-night he knew it was vulgar; but he had no contempt for it, because it was his mother who was betraying vulgarity. He felt sorry that she should be like that—that all the men and women with whom she was associated were like that. He felt sorry for Mabel, because she enjoyed it, and consequently more tender-hearted towards her than he had ever felt before.

He had not, however, a great many thoughts to give to this sorrow, for he was thinking continually of the bright apparition of the afternoon.

When he went to his room to get ready for tea he fell into a muse, looking over the fields and woods to the distant glimpse of blue water he could see from his window. When he came down to the evening meal, he found himself wondering foolishly upon what food the child lost in the sea had fed while she grew so rapidly to a woman's stature. The present meal was such as fell to the daily lot of that household. In homely blue delft cups a dozen or more eggs were ranged beside high stacks of buttered toast, rich and yellow. The butter, the jugs of yellow cream, the huge platter heaped with wild raspberries —as each of these met his eye he was wondering if the sea-maid ever ate such food, or if her diet was more delicate.

"Am I going mad?" he thought to himself. The suspicion was depressing.

Three hours after, Caius sough his father as the old man was making his nightly tour of the barns and stables. By way of easing his own sense of responsibility he had decided to tell his father what he had seen, and his telling was much like such confession of sins as many people make, soothing their consciences by an effort that does not adequately reveal the guilt to the listener.

Caius came up just as his father was locking the stable door.

"Look here, father; wait a minute. I have something to say. I saw a very curious thing down at the shore to-day, but I don't want you to tell mother, or Mabel, or the men."

The old man stood gravely expectant. The summer twilight just revealed the outline of his thin figure and ragged hair and beard.

"It was in the water swimming about, making darts here and there like a big trout. Its body was brown, and it looked as if it had horny balls round its neck; and its head, you know, was like a human being's."

"I never heard tell of a fish like that, Caius. Was it a porpoise?"

"Well, I suppose I know what a porpoise is like."

"About how large was it?" said the elder man, abandoning the porpoise theory.

"I should think about five or six feet long."

"As long as that? Did it look as if it could do any harm?"

"No; I should think it was harmless; but, father, I tell you its head looked like a person's head."

"Was it a shark with a man stuck in its throat?"

"N—n—no." Not liking to deny this ingenious suggestion too promptly, he feigned to consider it. "It wasn't a dead man's head; it was like a live woman's head."

"I never heard of sharks coming near shore here, any way," added the old man. "What distance was it off—half a mile?"

"It came between me and the little island off which we lost baby Day. It lay half-way between the island and the shore."

The old man was not one to waste words. He did not remark that in that case Caius must have seen the creature clearly, for it went without saying.

"Pity you hadn't my gun," he said.

Caius inwardly shuddered, but because he wished to confide as far as he might, he said outwardly: "I shouldn't have liked to shoot at it; its face looked so awfully human, you know."

"Yes," assented the elder, who had a merciful heart "it's wonderful what a look an animal has in its eyes sometimes." He was slowly shuffling round to the next door with his keys. "Well, I'm sure, my lad, I don't know what it could ha' been, unless 'twas some sort of a porpoise."

"We should be quite certain to know if there was any woman paying a visit hereabout, shouldn't we? A woman couldn't possibly swim across the bay."

"Woman!" The old man turned upon him sternly. "I thought you said it was a fish."

"I said she *swam* like a fish. She might have been a woman dressed in a fish-skin, perhaps; but there isn't any woman here that could possibly be acting like that—and old Morrison told me the same thing was about the shore the summer before he died."

His father still looked at him sharply. "Well, the question is, whether the thing you saw was a woman or a fish, for you must have seen it pretty clear, and they aren't alike, as far as I know."

Caius receded from the glow of confidence. "It lay pretty much under the water, and wasn't still long at a time."

The old man looked relieved, and in his relief began to joke. "I was thinking you must have lost your wits, and thought you'd seen a mermaid," he chuckled.

"I'd think it was a mermaid in a minute"—boldly—"if there were such things."

Caius felt relieved when he had said this, but the old man had no very distinct idea in his mind attached to the mythical word, so he let go the thought easily.

"Was it a dog swimming?"

"No," said Caius, "it wasn't a dog."

"Well, I give it up. Next time you see it, you'd better come and fetch the gun, and then you can take it to the musee up at your college, and have it stuffed and put in a case, with a ticket to say you presented it. That's all the use strange fish are that I know of."

When Caius reflected on this conversation, he knew that he had been a hypocrite.

CHAPTER 9. THE SEA-MAID'S MUSIC

At dawn Caius was upon the shore again, but he saw nothing but a red sunrise and a gray sea, merging into the blue and green and gold of the ordinary day. He got back to breakfast without the fact of his matutinal walk being known to the family.

He managed also in the afternoon to loiter for half an hour on the same bit of shore at the same hour as the day before without anyone being the wiser, but he saw no mermaid. He fully intended to spend to-morrow by the sea, but he had made this effort to appear to skip to-day to avoid awaking curiosity.

He had a horse and buggy; that afternoon he was friendly, and made many calls. Wherever he went he directed the conversation into such channels as would make it certain that he would hear if anyone else had seen the mermaid, or had seen the face of a strange woman by sea or land. Of one or two female visitors to the neighbourhood within a radius of twenty miles he did hear, but when he came to investigate each case, he found that the visit was known to everyone, and the status, lineage and habits of the visitors all of the same humdrum sort.

He decided in his own mind that ten miles was the utmost length that a woman could possibly swim, but he talked boldly of great swimming feats he had seen in his college life, and opined that a good swimmer might even cross the bay from Montrose or from the little port of Stanhope in the other direction; and when he saw the incredulity of his listeners, he knew that no one had accomplished either journey, for the water was overlooked by a hundred houses at either place, and many a small vessel ploughed the waves.

When he went to sleep that night Caius was sure that the vision of the mermaid was all his own, shared only by old Morrison, who lay in his grave. It was perhaps this partnership with the dead that gave the matter its most incredible and unreal aspect. Three years before this lady of the sea had frequented this spot; none but the dead man and himself had been permitted to see her.

"Well, when all's said and done," said Caius to himself, rolling upon a sleepless bed, "it's a very extraordinary thing."

Next morning he hired a boat, the nearest that was to be had; he got it a mile and a half further up the shore. It was a clumsy thing, but he rowed it past the mouth of the creek where he used to fish, all along the water front of Day's farm, past the little point that was the beginning of the rocky part of the shore, and then he drew the boat up upon the little island. He hid it perfectly among the grass and weeds. Over all the limited surface, among the pine shrubs and flowering weeds, he searched to see if hiding-place for the nymph could be found. Two colts were pastured on the isle. He found no cave or hut. When he had finished his search, he sat and waited and watched till the sun set over the sea; but to-day there was no smiling face rearing itself from the blue water, no little hand beckoning him away.

"What a fool I was not to go where she beckoned!" mused Caius. "Where? Anywhere into the heart of the ocean, out of this dull, sordid life into the land of dreams."

For it must all have been a dream—a sweet, fantastic dream, imposed upon his senses by some influence, outward or inward; but it seemed to him that at the hour when he seemed to see the maid it might have been given him to enter the world of dreams, and go on in some existence which was a truer reality than the one in which he now was. In a deliberate way he thought that perhaps, if the truth were known, he, Dr. Caius Simpson, was going a little mad; but as he sat by the softly lapping sea he did not regret this madness: what he did regret was that he must go home and—talk to Mabel.

He rowed his boat back with feelings of blank disappointment. He could not give another day to idleness upon the shore. It was impossible that such an important person as himself could spend long afternoons and evenings thus without everyone's knowledge. He had a feeling, too, born, as many calculations are, of pure surmise, that he would have seen the mermaid again that afternoon, when he had made such elaborate arrangements to meet her, if Fate had destined them to meet again at all. No; he must give her up. He must forget the hallucination that had worked so madly on his brain.

Nevertheless, he did not deny himself the pleasure of walking very frequently to the spot, and this often, in the early hours before breakfast, a time which he could dispose of as he would without comment. As he walked the beach in the beauty of the early day, he realized that some new region of life had been opened to him, that he was feeling his way into new mysteries of beatified thought and feeling.

A week passed; he was again upon the shore opposite the island at the sunrise hour. He sat on the rock which seemed like a home to his restless spirit, so associated it was with the first thoughts of those new visions of beauty which were becoming dear to him.

He heard a soft splashing sound in the water, and, looking about him, suddenly saw the sea-child's face lifted out of the water not more than four or five yards from him. All around her was a golden cloud of sand; it seemed to have been stirred up by her startled movement on seeing him. For a moment she was still, resting thus close, and he could see distinctly that around her white shoulders there was a coil of what seemed like glistening rounded scales. He could not decide whether the brightness in her eye was that of laughing ease or of startled excitement. Then she turned and darted away from him, and having put about forty feet between them, she turned and looked back with easy defiance.

His eyes, fascinated by what was to him an awful thing, were trying to penetrate the sparkling water and see the outlines of the form whose clumsy skin seemed to hang in horrid folds, stretching its monstrous bulk under the waves. His vision was broken by the sparkling splash which the maiden deliberately made with her hands, as if divining his curiosity and defying it. He felt the more sure that his senses did not play him false because the arrangement of the human and fishy substance of the apparition did not tally with any preconceived ideas he had of mermaids.

Caius felt no loathing of the horrid form that seemed to be part of her. He knew, as he had never known before, how much of coarseness there was in himself. His hands and feet, as he looked down at them, seemed clumsy, his ideas clumsy and gross to correspond. He knew enough to know that he might, by the practice of exercises, have made his muscles and brain the expression of his will, instead of the inert mass of flesh that they now seemed to him to be. He might—yes, he might, if he had his years to live over again, have made himself noble and strong; as it was, he was mutely conscious of being a thing to be justly derided by the laughing eyes that looked up at him from the water, a man to be justly shunned and avoided by the being of the white arms and dimpled face.

And he sat upon the rock looking, looking. It seemed useless to rise or speak or smile; he remembered the mirth that his former efforts had caused, and he was dumb and still.

Perhaps the sea-child found this treatment more uninteresting than that attention he had lavished on her on the former occasion; perhaps she had not so long to tarry. As he still watched her she turned again, and made her way swift and straight toward the rocky point. Caius ran, following, upon the shore, but after a minute he perceived that she could disappear round the point before, either by swimming or wading, he could get near her. He could not make his way around the point by the shore; his best means of keeping her in sight was to climb the cliff, from which the whole bay on the other side would be visible.

Like a man running a race for life, he leaped back to a place where it was possible to climb, and, once on the top, made his way by main force through a growth of low bushes until he could overlook the bay. But, lo! when he came there no creature was visible in the sunny sea beneath or on the shelving red bank which lay all plain to his view. Far and wide he scanned the ocean, and long he stood and watched. He walked, searching for anyone upon the bank, till he came to Day's barns, and by that time he was convinced that the sea-maid had either vanished into thin air or sunk down and remained beneath the surface of the sea.

The farm to which he had come was certainly the last place in which he would have thought to look for news of the sportive sea-creature; and yet, because it stood alone there in that part of the earth, he tarried now to put some question to the owner, just as we look mechanically for a lost object in drawers or cupboards in which we feel sure it cannot be. Caius found Day in a small paddock behind one of the barns, tending a mare and her baby foal. Day had of late turned his attention to horses, and the farm had a bleaker look in consequence, because many of its acres were left untilled.

Caius leaned his elbows on the fence of the paddock. "Hullo!"

Day turned round, asking without words what he wanted, in a very surly way.

At the distance at which he stood, and without receiving any encouragement, Caius found a difficulty in forming his question.

"You haven't seen anything odd in the sea about here, have you?"

"What sort of a thing?"

"I thought I saw a queer thing swimming in the water—did you?"

"No, I didn't."

It was evident that no spark of interest had been roused in the farmer by the question. From that, more than anything else, Caius judged that his words were true; but, because he was anxious to make assurance doubly sure, he blundered into another form of the same inquiry:

"There isn't a young girl about this place, is there?"

Day's face grew indescribably dark. In an instant Caius remembered that, if the man had any feeling about him, the question was the sorest he could have asked—the child, who would now have been a girl, drowned, her sister and brother exiled, and Day bound over by legal authority to see to it that no defenceless person came in the way of the wife who had killed her child! A moment more, and Day had merely turned his back, going on with his work. Caius did not blame him; he respected the man the more for the feeling he displayed.

Vexed with himself, and not finding how to end the interview, Caius waited a minute, and then turned suddenly from the fence, without knowing why he turned until he saw that the constraining force was the presence of Day's wife, who stood at the end of the barn, out of sight of her husband, but looking eagerly at Caius. She made a sign to him to come. No doubt she had heard what had been said.

Caius went to her, drawn by the eagerness of her bright black eyes. Her large form was slightly clad in a cotton gown; her abundant black hair was fastened rather loosely about her head. Her high-boned cheeks were thinner than of old, and her face wore a more excited expression; otherwise, there was little difference in her. She had been sent from the asylum as cured. Caius gave her a civil "Good-day."

"She has come back to me!" said the woman.

"Who?"

"My baby as you've put up the stone to. I've allers wanted to tell you I liked that stone; but she isn't dead—she has come back to me!"

Now, although the return of the drowned child had been an idea often in his mind of late, that he had merely toyed with it as a beautiful fancy was proved by the fact that no sooner did the mother express the same thought than Caius recognised that she was mad.

26

"She has come back to me!" The poor mother spoke in tones of exquisite happiness. "She is grown a big girl; she has curls on her head, and she wears a marriage-ring. Who is she married to?"

Caius could not answer.

The mother looked at him with curious steadfastness.

"I thought perhaps she was married to you," she said.

Surely the woman had seen what he had seen in the sea; but, question her as he would, Caius could gain nothing more from her—no hint of time or place, or any fact that at all added to his enlightenment. She only grew frightened at his questions, and begged him in moving terms not to tell Day that she had spoken to him—not to tell the people in the village that her daughter had come back, or they would put her again in the asylum. Truly, this last appeared to Cains a not unlikely consequence, but it was not his business to bring it about. It was not for him, who shared her delusion, to condemn her.

After that, Caius knew that either he was mad or what he had seen he had seen, let the explanation be what it might—and he ceased to care much about the explanation. He remembered the look of heart-satisfaction with which Day's wife had told him that her child had returned. The beautiful face looking from out the waves had no doubt wrought happiness in her; and in him also it had wrought happiness, and that which was better. He ceased to wrestle with the difference that the adventure had made in his life, or to try to ignore it; he had learned to love someone far better than himself, and that someone seemed so wholly at one with the nature in which she ranged, and also with the best he could think concerning nature, human or inanimate, that his love extended to all the world for her sake.

CHAPTER 10. TOWED BY THE BEARD

Every morning Caius still took his early way along the shore, but on all these walks he found himself alone in possession of the strand and the vast blue of sea and sky. It was disappointing, yet the place itself exercised a greater and greater charm over him.

He abstained from fooling away his days by the sea. After his one morning walk he refused himself the luxury of being there again, filling his time with work. He felt that the lady of the lovely face would despise him if he spent his time absurdly.

Thus some days passed; and then there came a night when he left a bed on which he had tossed wakefully, and went in the hot August night to the side of the sea when no one knew that he went or came.

The air was exceedingly warm. The harvest moon in the zenith was flooding the world with unclouded light. The tide was ebbing, and therefore there was in the channel that swift, dangerous current sweeping out to sea of which he had once experienced the strength. Caius, who associated his sea-visitant only with the sunlight and an incoming tide, did not expect to see her now; frequent disappointment had bred the absence of hope. He stood on the shore, looking at the current in which he had so nearly perished as a boy. It was glittering with white moon-rays. He thought of himself, of the check and twisting which his motives and ideas had lately received, and as he thought how slight a thing had done it, how mysterious and impossible a thing it was, his mind became stunned, and he faced the breeze, and simply lived in the sweetness of the hour, like an animal, conscious, not of itself, but only of what is external, without past or future.

And now he heard a little crooning song from the waters—no words, no tune that could be called a tune. It reminded him more of a baby's toneless cooing of joy, and yet it had a rhythm to it, too, and both joy and pathos in its cadence. Across the bright path of the moon's reflection he saw her come. Her head and neck were crowned and garlanded with shining weed, as if for a festival, and she stretched out her white arms to him and beckoned to him and laughed. He heard her soft, infant-like laughter.

To-night her beckoning was like a breeze to a leaf that is ready to fall. Caius ceased to think; he only acted. He threw his cap and coat and boots on the shore. The sea-child, gazing in surprise, began to recede quickly. Caius ran into the water; he projected himself toward the mermaid, and swam with all the speed of which he was capable.

The salt in his eyes at first obscured his vision. When he could look about, the sea-child had gone out of the track of the moonlight, and, taking advantage of the current, was moving rapidly out to sea.

He, too, swam with the current. He saw her curly head dark as a dog's in the water; her face was turned from him, and there was evident movement in her body. For the first time he thought he perceived that she was swimming with arms and feet as a woman must swim.

As for Caius, he made all the effort that in him lay, and as she receded past the line of the island right out into the moonlit sea, he swam madly after, reckless of the fact that his swimming power gave him no assurance of being able to return, reckless of everything except the one welcome fact that he was gaining on the sea-child. A fear oppressed him that perhaps this apparent effort of hers and her slow motion were only a ruse to lead him on—that at any moment she might dart from him or sink into her familiar depths. But this fear he did not heed as long as she remained in sight, and—yes, across the surface of the warm moonlit water he was slowly but surely gaining upon her.

On he swam, making strenuous effort at speed. He was growing exhausted with the unaccustomed exercise; he knew that his strength would not hold out much longer. He hardly knew what he hoped or dreamed would come to pass when he overtook the sea-maiden, and yet he swam for dear love, which was more to him than dear life, and, panting, he came close to her.

The sea-maid turned about, and her face flashed suddenly upon him, bright in the moonlight. She put out a glistening arm, perhaps in human feebleness to ward him off, perhaps, in the strength of some unknown means of defence, to warn him that at his peril he approached her.

Caius, reckless of everything, grasped the white wrist, and, stopping his motion, knowing he could not lie mermaid-fashion with head reared in the water, he turned on his back to float, still holding the small hand in his. He held it, and retained his consciousness long enough to know from that time forth that the hand had actually been in his—a living, struggling hand, not cold, but warm. He felt, too, in that wonderful power which we have in extreme moments of noting detail, that the hand had a ring upon it—it was the left hand—and he thought it was a plain gold ring, but it did not occur to him to think of a wedding-ring. Then he knew that this dear hand that he had captured was working him woe, for by it he was drawn beneath the water.

Even then he did not let go, but, still holding the hand, struck out to regain the surface in one of those wild struggles to which inexpert swimmers resort when they feel the deep receiving them into itself.

It would have been better for him if he had let go, for in that vehement struggle he felt the evidence of the sea-maid's power. He remembered—his last thought as he lost consciousness—that with the fishy nature is sometimes given the power to stun an enemy by an electric shock. Some shock came upon him with force, as if some cold metal had struck him on the head. As his brain grew dull he heard the water gurgling over him.

How long he remained stunned he did not know. He felt the water rushing about his head again; he felt that he had been drowned, and he knew, too—in that foolish way in which the half-awakened brain knows the supposed certainties of dreams—that the white hand he had essayed to hold had grasped his beard firmly under his chin, and that thus holding his head above the surface of the water, she was towing him away to unknown regions.

Then he seemed to know nothing again; and again he opened his eyes, to find himself lying on a beach in the moonlight, and the sea-maid's face was bending over his. He saw it distinctly, all tender human solicitude written on the moonlit lineaments. As his eyes opened more her face receded. She was gone, and he gazed vacantly at the sky; then, realizing his consciousness more clearly, he sat up suddenly to see where she had gone.

It seemed to him that, like a kind enchantress, she had transformed herself to break his passion. Yes, he saw her, as he had so often curiously longed to see her, moving over the dry shore—she was going back to her sea. But it was a strange, monstrous thing he saw. From her gleaming neck down to the ground was dank, shapeless form. So a walrus or huge seal might appear, could it totter about erect upon low, fin-like feet. There was no grace of shape, no tapering tail, no shiny scales, only an appearance of horrid quivering on the skin, that here and there seemed glossy in the moonlight.

He saw her make her way toilsomely, awkwardly over the shingle of the beach; and when she reached the shining water, it was at first so shallow that she seemed to wade in it like a land-animal, then, when the water was deep enough to rise up well around her, she turned to him once more a quick glance over her shoulder. Such relief came with the sight of her face, after this monstrous vision, that he saw the face flash on him as a sword might flash out of darkness when light catches its blade. Then she was gone, and he saw the form of her head in the water while she swam swiftly across the silver track of the moonbeams and out into the darkness beyond.

Caius looked around him with senses still drowsy and head aching sorely. He was in no fairy region that might be the home of mermaids, but on the bit of beach from which he had launched himself into the water. His coat and hat lay near him, and just above the spot where he lay was the rude epitaph of baby Day, carved by his own boyish hand so long ago.

Caius put his hand to his head, and found it badly bruised on one side. His heart was bruised, too, partly by the sight of the monstrous body of the lovely sea-child, partly by the fresh experience of his own weakness and incapacity.

It was long before he dragged himself home. It seemed to him to be days before he recovered from the weariness of that secret adventure, and he bore the mark of the bruise on his head for many a day. The mermaid he never saw again.

CHAPTER 11. YEARS OF DISCRETION

Caius Simpson took ship and crossed the sea. The influence of the beautiful face remained with him. That which had come to him was the new birth of mind (not spirit), which by the grace of God comes to many an individual, but is more clearly recognised and recorded when it comes in the life of nations—the opening of the inward eye to the meaning and joy of all things that the outward senses have heretofore perceived as not perceiving them. The art of the Old World claimed him as her own, as beauty on land and sea had already done. The enjoyment of music and pictures became all-important to him, at first because he searched in them for the soul he had seen in the sea-maid's eyes.

Caius was of noble birth, because by inheritance and training he was the slave of right-eousness. For this reason he could not neglect his work, although it had not a first place in his heart. As he was industrious, he did not fail in it; because it was not the thing he loved best, he did not markedly succeed. It was too late to change his profession, and he found in himself no such decided aptitude for anything else as should make him know that this or that would have been preferable; but he knew now that the genius of the physician was not his, that to do his work because it was duty, and to attain the respectable success which circumstance, rather than mental pre-eminence, gives, was all that he could hope. This saddened him; all his ambition revived under the smarting consciousness of inferi-ority to his more talented companions. The pleasures of his life came to him through his receptive faculties, and in the consciousness of having seen the wider vision, and being in consequence a nobler man. But all this, which was so much to him for a year or two, grew to be a less strong sensation than that of disappointment in the fact that he could only so meagrely fulfil his father's ideal and his own. There came a sense of dishonesty, too, in having used the old man's money chiefly in acquiring those mental graces which his father could neither comprehend nor value.

Three years passed. Gradually the memory of his love for the sea-maid had grown indistinct; and, more or less unconscious that this love had been the door to the more wealthy gardens of his mind, he inclined to despise it now as he despised the elegy he had written for the child who was drowned. It was his own passion he was inclined to forget and despise; the sea-maid herself was remembered, and respected, and wondered at, and disbelieved in, and believed in, as of old, but that which remains in the mind, never spoken of, never used as a cause of activity of either thought or action, recedes into the latent rather than the active portion of the memory.

Once, just once, in the first year of his foreign life, he had told to a friend the history of that, his one and only love-story. The result had not been satisfactory. His companion was quite sure that Caius had been the subject of an artful trick, and he did not fail to suggest that the woman had wanted modesty. Nothing, he observed, was more common than for men who were in love to attribute mental and physical charms to women who were in reality vulgar and blatant. Caius, feeling that he could advance no argument, refused to discuss the subject; it was months before he had the same liking for this friend, and it was a sign that what the other called "the sea-myth" was losing its power over him when he returned to this friendship.

Caius did not make many friends. It was not his nature to do so, and though constant to the few that he had, he did not keep up any very lively intercourse. It was partly because of this notable failure in social duty that, when he at last decided that the work of preparation must be considered at an end, and the active work of life begun, no opening immediately revealed itself to his inquiring gaze. Two vacant positions in his native country he heard of and coveted, and before he returned he gathered such testimonials as he could, and sent them in advance, offering himself as a candidate. When he landed in Canada he went at once to his first college to beg in person that the influence of his former teachers might be used on his behalf. The three years that had passed without correspondence had made a difference in the attitude of those who could help him; many of his friends also were dispersed, gone from the place. He waited in Montreal until he heard that he was not the accepted candidate for the better of the two positions, and that the other post would not be filled till the early spring.

Caius went home again. He observed that his parents looked older. The leaves were gone from the trees, the days were short, and the earth was cold. The sea between the little island and the red sandstone cliff was utterly lonely. Caius walked by its side sometimes, but there was no mermaid there.

BOOK II

CHAPTER 1. THE HAND THAT BECKONED

It was evening. Caius was watering his father's horses. Between the barns and the house the space was grass; a log fence divided it, and against this stood a huge wooden pump and a heavy log hollowed out for a trough. House and barns were white; the house was large, but the barns were many times larger. If it had not been that their sloping roofs of various heights and sizes formed a progression of angles not unpleasant to the eye, the buildings would have been very ugly; but they had also a generous and cleanly aspect which was attractive.

Caius brought the horses to the trough in pairs, each with a hempen halter. They were lightly-built, well-conditioned beasts, but their days of labour had wrought in them more of gentleness than of fire. As they drank now, the breeze played with their manes and forelocks, brushing them about their drooping necks and meek faces. Caius pumped the water for them, and watched them meditatively the while. There was a fire low down in the western sky; over the purple of the leafless woods and the bleak acres of bare red earth its light glanced, not warming them, but showing forth their coldness, as firelight glancing through a window-pane glows cold upon the garden snows. The big butter-nut-tree that stood up high and strong over the pump rattled its twigs in the air, as bare bones might rattle.

It was while he was still at the watering that the elder Simpson drove up to the house door in his gig. He had been to the post-office. This was not an event that happened every day, so that the letter which he now handed Caius might as well as not have been retarded a day or two in its delivery. Caius took it, leading the horses to their stalls, and he examined it by the light of the stable lantern.

The writing, the appearance of the envelope and post-mark, were all quite unfamiliar. The writing was the fine Italian hand common to ladies of a former generation, and was, in Caius' mind, connected only with the idea of elderly women. He opened the letter, therefore, with the less curiosity. Inside he found several pages of the same fine writing, and he read it with his arm round the neck of one of the horses. The lantern, which he had hung on a nail in the stall, sent down dim candlelight upon the pair.

When Caius had read the letter, he turned it over and over curiously, and began to read it again, more out of sheer surprise than from any relish for its contents. It was written by one Madame Josephine Le Maître, and came from a place which, although not very far from his own home, was almost as unknown to him as the most remote foreign part. It came from one of the Magdalen Islands, that lie some eighty miles' journey by sea to the north of his native shore. The writer stated that she knew few men upon the main-land—in which she seemed to include the larger island of Prince Edward—that Caius Simpson was the only medical man of whom she had any personal knowledge who was at that time unemployed. She stated, also, that upon the island where she lived there were some hundreds of fisher-folk, and that a very deadly disease, that she supposed to be diphtheria, was among them. The only doctor in the whole group refused to come to them, because he feared to take back the infection to the other islands. Indeed, so great was the dread of this infection, that no helpful person would come to their aid except an English priest, and he was able only to make a short weekly visit. It was some months now since the disease had first appeared, and it was increasing rather than diminishing.

"Come," said the letter, "and do what you can to save the lives of these poor people— their need of you is very great; but do not come if you are not willing to risk your life, for you will risk it. Do not come if you are not willing to be cut off from the world all the months the ice lies in the gulf, for at that time we have no communication with the world. You are a good man; you go to church, and believe in the Divine Christ, who was also a physician. It is because of this that I dare to ask you. There is a schooner that will be lying in the harbour of Souris for two or three weeks after the time that you receive this letter. Then she will come here upon her last winter trip. I have arranged with the captain to bring you to us if you can come."

After that the name of the schooner and its captain was given, a list also of some of the things that he would need to bring with him. It was stated that upon the island he would receive lodging and food, and that there were a few women, not unskilled in nursing, who would carry out his instructions with regard to the sick.

Caius folded the letter after the second reading, finished his work with the horses, and walked with his lantern through the now darkening air to the house. Just for a few seconds he stopped in the cold air, and looked about him at the dark land and the starry sky.

"I have now neither the belief nor the enthusiasm she attributes to me," said Caius.

When he got into the bright room he blinked for a moment at the light by which his father was reading.

The elder man took the letter in his hard, knotted hand, and read it because he was desired to do so. When finished, he cast it upon the table, returning to his newspaper.

"Hoots!" said he; "the woman's mad!" And then meditatively, after he had finished his newspaper paragraph: "What dealings have you ever had with her?"

"I never had any dealings with her."

"When you get a letter from a strange woman"—the father spoke with some heat—" the best thing that you can do with it is to put it in the fire."

Now, Caius knew that his father had, as a usual thing, that kindly and simple way of looking at the actions of his fellow-men which is refinement, so that it was evident that the contents of the letter were hateful. That was to be expected. The point that aroused the son's curiosity was to know how far the father recognised an obligation imposed by the letter. The letter would be hateful just in so far as it was considered worthy of attention.

"I suppose," said the young man dubiously, "that we can easily find out at Souris whether the statements in the letter are true or not?"

The father continued to read his paper.

The lamp upon the unpolished walnut table had no shade or globe upon it, and it glared with all the brilliancy of clean glass, and much wick and oil. The dining-room was orderly as ever. The map of Palestine, the old Bible, and some newly-acquired commentaries, obtruded themselves painfully as ornaments. There was no nook or corner in which anything could hide in shadow; there were no shutters on the windows, for there was no one to pass by, unless it might be some good or evil spirit that floated upon the dark air.

Mr. Simpson continued to read his paper without heeding his son. The mother's voice chiding the maid in the next room was the only sound that broke the silence.

"I'll write to that merchant you used to know at Souris, father," Caius spoke in a business-like voice. "He will be able to find out from all the vessels that come in to what extent there is disease on the Magdalens."

The exciting cause in Caius of this remark was his father's indifference and opposition, and the desire to probe it.

"You'll do nothing of the sort." Simpson's answer was very testy. "What call have you to interfere with the Magdalens?" His anger rose from a cause perhaps more explicable to an onlooker than to himself.

In the course of years there had grown in the mind of Caius much prejudice against the form and measure of his parents' religion. He would have throttled another who dared to criticise them, yet he himself took a certain pleasure in an opportunity that made criticism pertinent rather than impertinent. It was not that he prided himself on knowing or doing better, he was not naturally a theorist, nor didactic; but education had awakened his mind, not only to difficulties in the path of faith, but to a higher standard of altruism than was exacted by old-fashioned orthodoxy.

"I think I'd better write to Souris, sir; the letter is to me, you see, and I should not feel quite justified in taking no steps to investigate the matter."

How easy the hackneyed phrase "taking steps" sounded to Caius! but experience breeds strong instincts. The elder man felt the importance of this first decision, and struck out against it as an omen of ill.

"In my opinion you'll do well to let the matter lie where it is. How will you look making inquiries about sick folk as if you had a great fortune to spend upon philanthropy, when it turns out that you have none? If you'd not spent all my money on your own schooling, perhaps you'd have some to play the fine gentleman with now, and send a hospital and its staff on this same schooner." (This was the first reproach of his son's extravagance which had ever passed his lips; it betokened passion indeed.) "If you write you can't do less than send a case of medicines, and who is to pay for them, I'd like to know? I'm pretty well cleared out. They're a hardened lot of wreckers on those islands—I've heard that told of them many a time. No doubt their own filth and bad living has brought disease upon them, if there's truth in the tale; and as to this strange woman, giving no testimony or certificate of her respectability, it's a queer thing if she's to begin and teach you religion and duty. It's a bold and impudent letter, and I suppose you've enough sense left, with all your new fangles, to see that you can't do all she asks. What do you think you can do? If you think I'm going to pay for charity boxes to be sent to people I've no opinion of, when all the missionary subscriptions will be due come the new year, you think great nonsense, that's all." He brought his large hard hand down on the table, so that the board rang and the lamp quaked; then he settled his rounded shoulders stubbornly, and again unfurled the newspaper.

This strong declaration of wrath, and the reproaches concerning the money, were a relief to Caius. A relief from what? Had he contemplated for a moment taking his life in his hand and obeying the unexpected appeal? Yet he felt no answering anger in return for the rebuke; he only found himself comfortably admitting that if his father put it on the score of expense he certainly had no right to give time or money that did not belong to him. It was due to his parents that all his occupation should henceforth be remunerative.

He put the letter away in his pocket, but, perhaps because he laid it next his heart, the next day its cry awoke within him again, and would not be silenced.

Christianity was identified in his mind with an exclusive way of life, to him no longer good or true; but what of those stirring principles of Socialism that were abroad in the world, flaunting themselves as superior to Christianity? He was a child of the age, and dared not deny its highest precepts. Who would go to these people if he did not go? As to his father, he had coaxed him before for his own advantage; he could coax him now for theirs if he would. He was sufficiently educated to know that it was more glorious to die, even unrenowned, upon such a mission, than to live in the prosperity that belongs to ordinary covetousness, that should it be his duty to obey this call, no other duty remained for him in its neglect.

His personal desire in the matter was neither more nor less noble than are the average feelings of well-meaning people towards such enterprise. He would have been glad to find an excellent excuse to think no more of this mission—very glad indeed to have a more attractive opening for work set before him; but, on the other hand, the thought of movement and of fresh scenes was more attractive than staying where he was. Then, it would be such a virtuous thing to do and to have done; his own conscience and everyone who heard of the action must applaud it. And he did not think so much of the applause of others as of the real worthiness of the deed. Then, again, if he came back safely in the spring, he hoped by that time the offer of some good post would be waiting for him; and it would be more dignified to return from such an excellent work to find it waiting, than to sit at home humbly longing for its advent.

Caius went to Souris and questioned the merchants, talked to the captains of the vessels in the port, saw the schooner upon which Madame Le Maître had engaged his passage. What seemed to him most strange in the working out of this bit of his life's story, was that all that the letter said appeared to be true. The small island called Cloud Island, where the pestilence was, and to which he had been invited, was not one at which larger ships or schooners could land, so that it was only from the harbour of another island that the seamen got their news. On all hands it was known that there was bad disease upon Cloud Island, that no doctor was there, and that there was one lady, a Madame Le Maître, a person of some property, who was devoting herself to nursing the sick. When Caius asked who she was, and where she came from, one person said one thing and one another. Some of the men told him that she was old, some of them affirmed that she was young, and this, not because there was supposed to be any mystery concerning her, but because no one seemed to have taken sufficient interest in her existence to obtain accurate information.

When Caius re-entered the gate of his father's farm he had decided to risk the adventure, and obey the letter in all points precisely.

"Would you let it be said that in all these parts there was no one to act the man but a woman?" he said to his father.

To his mother he described the sufferings that this disease would work, all the details of its pains, and how little children and mothers and wives would be the chief sufferers, dying in helpless pain, or being bereft of those they loved best.

As he talked, the heart of the good woman rose up within her and blessed her son, acknowledging, in spite of her natural desires, that he was in this more truly the great man than she had fancied him in her wildest dreams of opulence and renown. She credited him with far purer motives than he knew himself to possess.

A father's rule over his own money is a very modified thing, the very fact of true fatherhood making him only a partner with his child. Caius was under the impression that his father could have refused him the necessary outfit of medical stores for this expedition, but that was not the way old Simpson looked at it.

"If he must, he must," he said to his wife angrily, gloomily, for his own opinion in the matter had changed little; but to Caius he gave his consent, and all the money he needed, and did not, except at first, express his disapproval, so that Caius took the less pains to argue the matter with him.

It was only at the last, when Caius had fairly set out on his journey, and, having said good-bye, looked back to see his father stand at the gate of his own fields, that the attitude of the stalwart form and gray head gave him his first real insight into the pain the parting had cost—into the strong, sad disapproval which in the father's mind lay behind the nominal consent. Caius saw it then, or, at least, he saw enough of it to feel a sharp pang of regret and self-reproach. He felt himself to be an unworthy son, and to have wronged the best of fathers. Whether he was doing right or wrong in proceeding upon his mission he did not know. So in this mind he set sail.

CHAPTER 2. THE ISLES OF ST. MAGDALEN

The schooner went out into the night and sailed for the north star. The wind was strong that filled her sails; the ocean turbulent, black and cold, with the glittering white of moonlight on the upper sides of the waves. The little cabin in the forecastle was so hot and dirty that to Caius, for the first half of the night, it seemed preferable almost to perish of cold upon the deck rather than rock in a narrow bunk below. The deck was a steep inclined plane, steady, but swept constantly with waves, as an incoming tide sweeps a beach. Caius was compelled to crouch by what support he could find, and, lying thus, he was glad to cover himself up to the chin with an unused sail, peeping forth at the gale and the moonlight as a child peeps from the coverings of its cot.

With the small hours of the night came a cold so intense that he was driven to sleep in the cabin where reigned the small iron stove that brewed the skipper's odorous pot. After he had slept a good way into the next day, he came up again to find the gale still strong and the prospect coloured now with green of wave and snow of foam, blue of sky and snow of winged cloud. The favourable force was still pushing them onward toward the invisible north star.

It was on the evening of that day that they saw the islands; five or six hilly isles lay in a half-circle. The schooner entered this bay from the east. Before they came near the purple hills they had sighted a fleet of island fishing boats, and now, as night approached, all these made also for the same harbour. The wind bore them all in, they cutting the water before them, gliding round the point of the sand-bar, making their way up the channel of the bay in the lessening light, a chain of gigantic sea-birds with white or ruddy wings.

All around the bay the islands lay, their hills a soft red purple in the light of a clear November evening. In the blue sky above there were layers of vapour like thin gray gossamers, on which the rosy light shone. The waters of the bay were calmer than the sea outside, yet they were still broken by foam; across the foam the boats went sweeping, until in the shadow of the isles and the fast-descending night they each furled their sails and stopped their journey. It was in the western side of the bay that the vessels lay, for the gale was from the west, and here they found shelter; but night had descended suddenly, and Caius could only see the black form of the nearest island, and the twinkling lights that showed where houses were collected on its shore. They waited there till the moon rose large and white, touching the island hills again into visible existence. It was over one small rocky island that she rose; this was the one that stood sentry at the entrance of the bay, and on either side of it there were moon-lit paths that stretched far out into the gulf. On the nearer island could be seen long sand reaches, and dark rounded hills, and in a hollow of the hills the clustered lights. When the moonlight was bright the master of the schooner lowered a boat and set Caius and his traps ashore, telling him that some day when the gale was over he could make his way to the island of Cloud. The skipper said that the gale might blow one day, or two, or three, or more, but it could not blow always, and in the meantime there was entertainment to be had for those who could pay for it on the nearer isle.

When Caius stood upon the beach with his portmanteaus beside him, some half a dozen men clustered round; in their thick garments and mufflers they looked outlandish enough. They spoke English, and after much talking they bore his things to a small house on the hillside. He heard the wind clamour against the wooden walls of this domicile as he stood in its porch before the door was opened. The wind shouted and laughed and shook the house, and whistled and sighed as it rushed away. Below him, nearer the shore, lay the village, its white house-walls lit by the moonlight, and beyond he could see the ships in the glittering bay.

When the door opened such a feast of warmth and comfort appeared to his eyes that he did not soon forget it, for he had expected nothing but the necessaries of life. Bright decoration of home-made rugs and ornaments was on all sides, and a table was laid.

They were four spinsters of Irish descent who kept this small inn, and all that good housewifery could do to make it comfortable was done. The table was heaped with such dainties as could be concocted from the homely products of the island; large red cranberries cooked in syrup gave colour to the repast. Soon a broiled chicken was set before Caius, and steaming coffee rich with cream.

To these old maids Caius was obliged to relate wherefore he had come and whither he was bound. He told his story with a feeling of self-conscious awkwardness, because, put it in as cursory a manner as he would, he felt the heroism of his errand must appear; nor was he with this present audience mistaken. The wrinkled maidens, with their warm Irish hearts, were overcome with the thought that so much youth and beauty and masculine charm, in the person of the young man before them, should be sacrificed, and, as it seemed to them, foolishly.

The inhabitants of Cloud Island, said these ladies, were a worthless set; and in proof of it they related to him how the girls of The Cloud were not too nice in their notions to marry with the shipwrecked sailors from foreign boats, a thing they assured him that was never done on their own island. Italian, or German, or Norwegian, or whoever the man might be, if he had good looks, a girl at The Cloud would take him!

And would not they themselves, Caius asked, in such a case, take pity on a stranger who had need of a wife?

Whereat they assured him that it was safer to marry a native islander, and that no self-respecting woman could marry with a man who was not English, or Irish, or Scotch, or French. It was of these four latter nationalities that the native population of the islands was composed.

But the ladies told him worse tales than these, for they said the devil was a frequent visitor at Cloud Island, and at times he went out with the fishers in their boats, choosing now one, now another, for a companion; and whenever he went, there was a wonderful catch of fish; but the devil must have his full share, which he ate raw and without cleaning —a thing which no Christian could do. He lived in the round valleys of the sand-dune that led to The Cloud. It was a convenient hiding-place, because when you were in one valley you could not see into the next, and the devil always leaped into the one that you were not in. As to the pestilence, it was sent as a judgment because the people had these impious dealings with the Evil One; but the devil could put an end to it if he would.

It was strange to see the four gray-haired sisters as they sat in a row against the wall and told him in chiming sentences these tales with full belief.

"And what sort of a disease is it?" asked Caius, curious to hear more.

"It's the sore throat and the choke, sir," said the eldest sister, "and a very bad disease it is, for if it doesn't stop at the throat, it flies direct to the stomach, sir, and then you can't breathe."

Caius pondered this description for a few moments, and then he formed a question which was to the point.

"And where," said he, "is the stomach?"

At which she tapped her chest, and told him it was there.

He had eaten somewhat greedily, and when he found that the linen of his bed was snow-white and the bed itself of the softest feathers, he lay down with great contentment. Not even the jar and rush of the wind as it constantly assaulted the house, nor the bright moonlight against the curtainless window, kept him awake for a moment. He slept a dreamless sleep.

CHAPTER 3. BETWEEN THE SURF AND THE SAND

Next day the wind had grown stronger; the same clear skies prevailed, with the keen western gale, for the west wind in these quarters is seldom humid, and at that season it was frosty and very dry, coming as it did over the already snow-covered plains of Gaspé and Quebec. It seemed strange to Caius to look out at the glorious sunshine and be told that not a boat would stir abroad that day, and that it would be impossible for even a cart to drive to the Cloud Island.

He knew so little of the place to which he had come that when the spinsters spoke of driving to another island it seemed to him that they spoke as wildly as when they told of the pranks of the Evil One. He learned soon that these islands were connected by long sand ridges, and that when the tide was down it was possible to drive upon the damp beach from one to another; but this was not possible, they told him, in a western gale, for the wind beat up the tide so that one could not tell how far it would descend or how soon it would return. There was risk of being caught by the waves under the hills of the dune, which a horse could not climb, and, they added, he had already been told who it was who lived in the sand hollows.

In the face of the sunny morning, Caius could not forbear expressing his incredulity of the diabolical legend, and his hostesses did not take the trouble to argue the point, for it is to be noted that people seldom argue on behalf of the items of faith they hold most firmly. The spinsters merely remarked that there were a strange number of wrecks on the sand-bar that led to The Cloud, and that, go where he would in the village, he would get no sand-pilot to take him across while the tide was beaten up by the wind, and a pilot he must have, or he would sink in the quicksands and never be seen again.

Caius walked, with the merry wind for a playfellow, down through long rows of fish-sheds, and heard what the men had to say with regard to his journey. He heard exactly what the women had told him, for no one would venture upon the dune that day.

Then, still in company with the madcap wind, he walked up on the nearer hills, and saw that this island was narrow, lying between blue fields of sea, both bay and ocean filled with wave crests, ever moving. The outer sea beat upon the sandy beach with a roar and volume of surf such as he had never seen before, for under the water the sand-bank stretched out a mile but a little below the sea's level, and the breakers, rolling in, retarded by it and labouring to make their accustomed course, came on like wild beasts that were chafed into greater anger at each bound, so that with ever-increasing fury they roared and plunged until they touched the verge.

From the hills he saw that the fish-sheds which stood along the village street could only be a camping place for the fishers at the season of work, for all along the inner sides of the hills there were small farm-houses, large enough and fine enough to make good dwellings. The island was less savage than he had supposed. Indignation rose within him that people apparently so well-to-do should let their neighbours die without extending a helping hand. He would have been glad to go and bully some owner of a horse and cart into taking him the last stage of his journey without further delay; but he did not do this, he only roamed upon the hills enjoying the fair prospect of the sea and the sister isles, and went back to his inn about two o'clock. There he feasted again upon the luxurious provision that the spinsters had been making for the appetite that the new air had given him. He ate roast duck, stuffed with a paste of large island mushrooms, preserved since their season, and tarts of bake-apple berries, and cranberries, and the small dark mokok berry —three kinds of tart he ate, with fresh cream upon them, and the spinster innkeepers applauded his feat. They stood around and rejoiced at his eating, and again they told him in chorus that he must not go to the other island where the people were sick.

It was just then that a great knock came at the front door; the loudness of the wind had silenced the approaching footsteps. A square-built, smooth-faced man, well wrapped in a coat of ox fur, came into the house, asking for Caius Simpson by name. His face was one which it was impossible to see without remarking the lines of subtle intelligence displayed in its leathery wrinkles. The eyes were light blue, very quick, almost merry—and yet not quite, for if there was humour in them, it was of the kind that takes its pleasures quietly; there was no proneness to laughter in the hard-set face.

When Caius heard his own name spoken, he knew that something unexpected had happened, for no one upon the island had asked his name, and he had not given it.

The stranger, who, from his accent, appeared to be a Canadian of Irish parentage, said, in a few curt words, that he had a cart outside, and was going to drive at once to Cloud Island, that he wished to take the young doctor with him; for death, he observed, was not sitting idle eating his dinner at The Cloud, and if anyone was coming to do battle with him it would be as well to come quickly.

The sarcasm nettled Caius, first, because he felt himself to be caught napping; secondly, because he knew he was innocent.

The elder of the spinsters had got behind the stranger, and she intimated by signs and movements of the lips that the stranger was unknown, and therefore mysterious, and not to be trusted; and so quickly was this pantomime performed that it was done before Caius had time to speak, although he was under the impression that he rose with alacrity to explain to the newcomer that he would go with him at once.

The warning that the old maid gave resulted at least in some cautious questioning. Caius asked the stranger who he was, and if he had come from The Cloud that day.

As to who he was, the man replied that his name was John O'Shea, and he was the man who worked the land of Madame Le Maître. "One does not go and come from Cloud Island in one day at this season," said he. "'Tis three days ago since I came. I've been waiting up at the parson's for the schooner. To-day we're going back together, ye and me."

He was sparing of language. He shut his mouth over the short sentences he had said, and that influence which always makes it more or less difficult for one man to oppose the will of another caused Caius to make his questions as few as possible.

Was it safe, he asked, to drive to Cloud Island that day?

The other looked at him from head to foot. "Not safe," he said, "for women and childer; but for men"—the word was lingered upon for a moment—"yes, safe enough."

The innkeepers were too mindful of their manners as yet to disturb the colloquy with open interruption; but with every other sort of interruption they did disturb it, explaining by despairing gestures and direful shakings of the head that, should Caius go with this gentleman, he would be driving into the very jaws of death.

Nevertheless, after O'Shea's last words Caius had assented to the expedition, although he was uncertain whether the assent was wise or not. He had the dissatisfaction of feeling that he had been ruled, dared, like a vain schoolboy, into the hasty consent.

"Now, if you are servant to Madame Le Maître at The Cloud, how is it that you've never been seen on this island?" It was the liveliest of the sisters who could no longer keep silence.

While Caius was packing his traps he was under the impression that O'Shea had replied that, in the first place, he had not lived long at The Cloud, and, in the second, visitors from The Cloud had not been so particularly welcome at the other islands. His remarks on the last subject were delivered with brief sarcasm. After he had started on the journey Caius wondered that he had not remembered more particularly the gist of an answer which it concerned him to hear.

At the time, however, he hastened to strap together those of his bundles which had been opened, and, under the direction of O'Shea, to clothe himself in as many garments as possible, O'Shea arguing haste for the sake of the tide, which, he said, had already begun to ebb, and there was not an hour to be lost.

The women broke forth once more, this time into open expostulation and warning. To them O'Shea vouchsafed no further word, but with an annoying assumption that the doctor's courage would quail under their warnings, he encouraged him.

"There's a mere boy, a slim lad, on my cart now," he said, "that's going with us; he's no more froightened than a gull is froightened of the sea."

Caius showed his valour by marching out of the door, a bag in either hand.

No snow had as yet fallen on the islands. The grass that was before the inn door was long and of that dry green hue that did not suggest verdure, for all the juices had gone back into the ground. It was swept into silver sheens by the wind, and as they crossed it to reach the road where the cart stood, the wind came against them all with staggering force. The four ladies came out in spite of the icy blast, and attended them to the cart, and stood to watch them as they wended their way up the rugged road that led over a hill.

The cart was a small-sized wooden one—a shallow box on wheels; no springs, no paint, had been used in its making. Some straw had been spread on the bottom, and on this Caius was directed to recline. His bags also were placed beside him. O'Shea himself sat on the front of the cart, his legs dangling, and the boy, who was "no more froightened of the journey than a sea-gull is of the sea," perched himself upon one corner of the back and looked out backwards, so that his face was turned from Caius, who only knew that he was a slim lad because he had been told so; a long gray blanket-coat with capuchin drawn over the head and far over the face covered him completely.

Caius opposed his will to the reclining attitude which had been suggested to him, and preferred to sit upon the flat bottom with the desire to keep erect; and he did sit thus for awhile, like a porcelain mandarin with nodding head, for, although the hardy pony went slowly, the jolting of the cart on the rough, frozen road was greater than it is easy for one accustomed to ordinary vehicles to imagine.

Up the hill they went, past woods of stunted birch and fir, past upland fields, from which the crops had long been gathered. They were making direct for the southern side of the island. While they ascended there was still some shelter between them and the fiercest blast of the gale, and they could still look down at the homely inn below, at the village of fishers' sheds and the dancing waters of the bay. He had only passed one night there, and yet Caius looked at this prospect almost fondly. It seemed familiar in comparison with the strange region into which he was going.

When the ridge was gained and the descent began, the wind broke upon them with all its force. He looked below and saw the road winding for a mile or more among the farms and groves of the slope, and then out across a flat bit of shrub-covered land; beyond that was the sand, stretching here, it seemed, in a tract of some square miles. The surf was dimly seen like a cloud at its edge.

It was not long that he sat up to see the view. The pony began to run down the hill; the very straw in the bottom of the cart danced. Caius cast his arms about his possessions, fearing that, heavy though they were, they would be thrown out upon the roadside, and he lay holding them. The wind swept over; he could hear it whistling against the speed of the cart; he felt it like a knife against his cheeks as he lay. He saw the boy brace himself, the lithe, strong muscles of his back, apparent only by the result of their action, swayed balancing against the jolting, while, with thickly-gloved hands, he grasped the wooden ledge on which he sat. In front O'Shea was like an image carved of the same wood as the cart, so firmly he held to it. Well, such hours pass. After a while they came out upon the soft, dry sand beyond the scrubby flat, and the horse, with impeded footsteps, trudged slowly.

The sand was so dry, driven by the wind, that the horse and cart sank in it as in driven snow. The motion, though slow, was luxurious compared to what had been. O'Shea and the boy had sprung off the cart, and were marching beside it. Caius clambered out, too, to walk beside them.

"Ye moight have stayed in, Mr. Doctor," said O'Shea. "The pony is more than equal to carrying ye."

Again Caius felt that O'Shea derided him. He hardly knew why the man's words always gave him this impression, for his manner was civil enough, and there was no particular reason for derision apparent; for, although O'Shea's figure had broadened out under the weight of years, he was not a taller man than Caius, and the latter was probably the stronger of the two. When Caius glanced later at the other's face, it appeared to him that he derived his impression from the deep, ray-like wrinkles that were like star-fish round the man's eyes; but if so, it must have been that something in the quality of the voice reflected the expression of the face, for they were not in such plight as would enable them to observe one another's faces much. The icy wind bore with it a burden of sparkling sand, so that they were often forced to muffle their faces, walking with heads bowed.

Since Caius would walk, O'Shea ordered the boy back into the cart, and the two men ploughed on through the sand beside the horse, whose every hair was turned by the wind, which now struck them sideways, and whose rugged mane and forelock were streaming horizontally, besprinkled with sand. The novelty of the situation, the beauty of the sand-wreaths, the intoxication of the air, the vivid brilliancy of the sun and the sky, delighted Caius. The blue of heaven rounded the sandscape to their present sight, a dome of blue flame over a plain whose colour was like that of an autumn leaf become sear. Caius, in his exhilaration, remarked upon the strangeness of the place, but either the prospect was too common to O'Shea to excite his interest, or the enterprise he meditated burdened his mind; he gave few words in answer, and soon they, too, relapsed into the silence that the boy and the pony had all the time observed.

An hour's walk, and another sound rang in their ears beside the whistling of the wind, low at first and fitful, louder and louder, till the roar of the surf was deafening. Then they came to the brink and heard all the notes of which the chords of its more distant music had been composed, the gasping sob of the under tow, the rush of the lifting wave as it upreared itself high, the silken break of its foam, the crash of drums with which it fell, the dash of wave against wave, and the cry of the foremost waves that bemoaned themselves prostrate upon the beach.

The cart, with its little company, turned into the narrow strip of dark damp sand that the tide had already left bare. Here the footing was much firmer, and the wind struck them obliquely. The hardy pony broke into its natural pace, a moderate trot. In spite of this pace, the progress they made was not very swift, and it was already four by the clock.

O'Shea climbed to his place on the front of the cart; the boy sprang down and ran to warm himself, clapping his gloved hands as he ran. It was not long before Caius clambered into his straw seat again, and, sitting, watched the wonder of the waves. So level was the beach, so high was the surf, that from the low cart it seemed that gigantic monsters were constantly arising from the sea; and just as the fear of them overshadowed the fascinated mind, they melted away again into nothingness. As he looked at the waves he saw that their water, mixed with sand, was a yellowish brown, and dark almost to black when the curling top yawned before the downfall; but so fast did each wave break one upon the other that glossy water was only seen in glimpses, and boiling fields of foam and high crests of foam were the main substance of all that was to be seen for a hundred yards from the shore.

Proceeding thus, they soon came to what was actually the end of the island, and were on the narrow ridge of sand-dunes which extended a distance of some twenty miles to the next island. The sand-hills rising sheer from the shore, fifty, sixty, or a hundred feet in height, bordered their road on the right. To avoid the soft dry sand of their base the pony often trotted in the shallow flow of the foam, which even yet now and then crept over all the damp beach to the high-water mark. The wind was like spur and lash; the horse fled before it. Eyes and ears grew accustomed even to the threatening of the sea-monsters. The sun of the November afternoon sank nearer and nearer the level of sand and foam; they could not see the ocean beyond the foam. When it grew large and ruddy in the level atmosphere, and some flakes of red, red gold appeared round it, lying where the edge of the sea must be, like the Islands of the Blessed, when the crests of the breakers near and far began to be touched with a fiery glow, when the soft dun brown of the sand-hills turned to gold, Caius, overcome with having walked and eaten much, and drunk deeply of the wine of the wild salt wind, fell into a heavy dreamless slumber, lying outstretched upon his bed of straw.

CHAPTER 4. WHERE THE DEVIL LIVED

Caius did not know how long he slept. He woke with a sudden start and a presentiment of evil. It was quite dark, as black as starlight night could be; for the foam of the waves hardly glimmered to sight, except here and there where some phosphorescent jelly was tossed among them like a blue death-light. What had wakened Caius was the sound of voices talking ahead of the cart, and the jerk of the cart as it was evidently being driven off the smooth beach on to a very rough and steep incline.

He sat up and strove to pierce the darkness by sight. They had come to no end of their journey. The long beach, with its walls of foam and of dune, stretched on without change. But upon this beach they were no longer travelling; the horse was headed, as it were, to the dune, and now began to climb its almost upright side.

With an imprecation he threw himself out of the cart at a bound into sand so soft that he sank up to the knees and stumbled against the upright side of the hill. The lower voice he had heard was silent instantly. O'Shea stopped the pony with a sharp word of interrogation.

"Where are you going?" shouted Caius. "What are you going to do?"

He need not have shouted, for the wind was swift to carry all sounds from his lips to

O'Shea; but the latter's voice, as it came back to him, seemed to stagger against the force of the wind and almost to fail.

"Where are we going? Well, we're going roight up towards the sky at present, but in a minute we'll be going roight down towards the other place. If ye just keep on at that side of the cart ye'll get into a place where we'll have a bit of shelter and rest till the moon rises."

"What is the matter? What are you turning off the road for?" Caius shouted again, half dazed by his sleep and sudden awakening, and wholly angry at the disagreeable situation. He was cold, his limbs almost numb, and to his sleepy brain came the sudden remembrance of the round valleys in the dune of which he had heard, and the person who lived in them.

His voice was inadequately loud. The ebullition of his rage evidently amused O'Shea, for he laughed; and while Caius listened to his laughter and succeeding words, it seemed to him that some spirit, not diabolic, hovered near them in the air, for among the sounds of the rushing of the wind and of the sea came the soft sound of another sort of laughter, suppressed, but breaking forth, as if in spite of itself, with irresistible amusement; and although Caius felt that it was indulged at his own expense, yet he loved it, and would fain have joined in its persuasive merriment. While the poetical part of him listened, trying to catch this illusive sound, his more commonplace faculties were engaged by the answer of O'Shea:

"It's just as ye loike, Mr. Doctor. You can go on towards The Cloud by the beach if you've got cat's eyes, or if you can feel with your toes where the quicksands loy; but the pony and me are going to take shelter till the moon's up."

"Well, where are you going?" asked Caius. "Can't you tell me plainly? I never heard of a horse that could climb a wall."

"And if the little beast is good-natured enough to do it for ye, it's as shabby a trick as I know to keep him half-way up with the cart at his back. He's a cliver little pony, but he's not a floy; and I never knew that even a floy could stand on a wall with a cart and doctor's medicine bags a-hanging on to it. G'tup!"

This last sound was addressed to the pony, which in the darkness began once more its astonishing progress up the sand-hill.

The plea for mercy to the horse entered Caius' reason. The spirit-like laughter had in some mysterious way soothed his heart. He stood still, detaining O'Shea no longer, and dimly saw the horse and cart climb up above him. O'Shea climbed first, for his tones were heard caressing and coaxing the pony, which he led. Caius saw the cart, a black mass, disappear over the top of the hill, which was here not more than twenty feet high. When it was gone he could dimly descry a dark figure, which he supposed to be the boy, standing on the top, as if waiting to see what he would do; so, after holding short counsel with himself, he, too, began to stagger upward, marvelling more and more at the feat of the pony as he went, for though the precipice was not perpendicular, it had this added difficulty, that all its particles shifted as they were touched. There was, however, some solid substance underneath, for, catching at the sand grasses, clambering rather than walking, he soon found himself at the top, and would have fallen headlong if he had not perceived that there was no level space by seeing the boy already half-way down a descent, which, if it was unexpected, was less precipitous, and composed of firmer ground. He heard O'Shea and the cart a good way further on, and fancied he saw them moving. The boy, at least, just kept within his sight; and so he followed down into a hollow, where he felt crisp, low-growing herbage beneath his feet, and by looking up at the stars he could observe that its sandy walls rose all around him like a cup. On the side farthest from the sea the walls of the hollow rose so high that in the darkness they looked like a mountainous region.

They had gone down out of the reach of the gale; and although light airs still blew about them, here the lull was so great that it seemed like going out of winter into a softer clime.

When Caius came up with the cart he found that the traces had already been unfastened and the pony set loose to graze.

"Is there anything for him to eat?" asked Caius curiously, glad also to establish some friendly interchange of thought.

"One doesn't travel on these sands," said O'Shea, "with a horse that can't feed itself on the things that grow in the sand. It's the first necessary quality for a horse in these parts."

"What sort of things grow here?" asked Caius, pawing the ground with his foot.

He could not quite get over the inward impression that the mountainous-looking region of the dune over against them was towered with infernal palaces, so weird was the place.

O'Shea's voice came out of the darkness; his form was hardly to be seen.

"Sit yourself down, Mr. Doctor, and have some bread and cheese—that is, if ye've sufficiently forgotten the poies of the old maids. The things that grow here are good enough to sit on, and that's all we want of them, not being ponies."

The answer was once more an insult in its allusion to the pies (Caius was again hungry), and in its refusal of simple information; but the tone was more cheerful, and O'Shea had relaxed from his extreme brevity. Caius sat down, and felt almost convivial when he found that a parcel of bread and cheese and a huge bottle of cold tea were to be shared between them. Either the food was perfect of its kind or his appetite good sauce, for never had anything tasted sweeter than the meal. They all three squatted in the darkness round the contents of the ample parcel, and if they said little it was because they ate much.

Caius found by the light of a match that his watch told it was the hour of seven; they had been at hard travel for more than four hours, and had come to a bit of the beach which could not be traversed without more light. In another hour the moon would be up and the horse rested.

When the meal was finished, each rested in his own way. O'Shea laid himself flat upon his back, with a blanket over his feet. The boy slipped away, and was not seen until the waving grass on the tops of the highest dunes became a fringe of silver. Until then Caius paced the valley, coming occasionally in contact with the browsing pony; but neither his walk nor meditation was interrupted by more formidable presence.

"Ay—ee—ho—ee—ho!" It was a rallying call, a shrill cry, from O'Shea. It broke the silence the instant that the moon's first ray had touched the dune. The man must have been lying looking at the highest head, for when Caius heard the unexpected sound he looked round more than once before he discovered its cause, and then knew that while he had been walking the whole heaven and earth had become lighter by imperceptible degrees. As he watched now, the momentary brightening was very perceptible. The heights and shadows of the sand-hills stood out to sight; he could see the line where the low herbage stopped and the waving bent began. In the sky the stars faded in a pallid gulf of violet light. The mystery of the place was less, its beauty a thousandfold greater: and the beauty was still of the dream-exciting kind that made him long to climb all its hills and seek in all its hollows, for there are some scenes that, by their very contour, suggest more than they display, and in which the human mind cannot rid itself of the notion that the physical aspect is not all that there is to be seen. But whatever the charm of the place, now that light had revealed it Caius must leave it.

The party put themselves in line of march once more. The boy had gone on up where the wall of the dell was lowest, and Caius tramped beside O'Shea, who led the pony.

Once up from the hollow, their eyes were dazzled at first with the flash of the moonlight upon the water. From the top of the sand ridge they could see the sea out beyond the surf—a measureless purple waste on which far breakers rose and blossomed for a moment like a hedge of whitethorn in May, and sank again with a glint of black in the shadow of the next uprising.

They went down once more where they could see nothing but the surf and the sand-hills. The boy had walked far on; they saw his coated and cowled figure swaying with the motion of his walk on the shining beach in front. The tide was at its lowest. What the fishermen had said of it was true: with the wind beating it up it had gone down but a third of its rightful distance; and now the strip that it had to traverse to be full again seemed alarmingly narrow, for a great part of their journey was still to be made. The two men got up on the cart; the boy leaped up when they reached him, before O'Shea could bring it to full stop for him, and on they went. Even the pony seemed to realize that there was need of haste.

They had travelled about two miles more when, in front of them, a cape of rock was seen jutting across the beach, its rocky headland stretching far into the sea. Caius believed that the end of their journey was near; he looked eagerly at the new land, and saw that there were houses upon the top of the cliff. It seemed unnecessary even to ask if this was their destination. Secure in his belief, he willingly got off the cart at the base of the cliff, and trudged behind it, while O'Shea drove up a track in the sand which had the similitude of a road; rough, soft, precipitous as it was, it still bore tracks of wheels and feet, where too far inland to be washed by the waves. The sight of them was like the sight of shore to one who has been long at sea. They went up to the back of the cliff, and came upon its high grassy top; the road led through where small houses were thickly clustered on either side. Caius looked for candle, or fire, or human being, and saw none, and they had not travelled far along the street of this lifeless village when he saw that the road led on down the other side of the headland, and that the beach and the dune stretched ahead of them exactly as they stretched behind.

"Is this a village of the dead?" he asked O'Shea.

The man O'Shea seemed to have in him some freak of perverseness which made it hard for him to answer the simplest question. It was almost by force that Caius got from him the explanation that the village was only used during certain fishing seasons, and abandoned during the winter—unless, indeed, its houses were broken into by shipwrecked sailors, whose lives depended upon finding means of warmth.

The cart descended from the cliff by the same sandy road, and the pony again trotted upon the beach; its trot was deceptive, for it had the appearance of making more way than it did. On they went—on, on, over this wonderful burnished highroad which the sea and the moonlight had laid for their travel. Behind and before, look as they would, they could see only the weird white hills of sand, treeless, almost shadowless now, the seahorses foaming and plunging in endless line, and between them the road, whose apparent narrowing in the far perspective was but an emblem of the truth that the waves were encroaching upon it inch by inch.

CHAPTER 5. DEVILRY

When the cart and its little company had travelled for almost another hour, a dark object in the midst of the line of foam caught their sight. It was the boy who first saw it, and he suddenly leaned forward, clutching O'Shea's arm as if in fear.

The man looked steadily.

"She's come in since we passed here before."

The boy apparently said something, although Caius could not catch the voice.

"No," said O'Shea; "there's cargo aboard of her yit, but the men are off of her."

It was a black ship that, sailless and with masts pitifully aslant, was fixed on the sand among the surf, and the movement of the water made her appear to labour forward as if in dying throes making effort to reach the shore.

The boy seemed to scan the prospect before him now far more eagerly than before; but the wreck, which was, as O'Shea said, deserted, seemed to be the only external object in all that gleaming waste. They passed on, drawing up for a minute near her at the boy's instigation, and scanning her decks narrowly as they were washed by the waves, but there was no sign of life. Before they had gone further Caius caught sight of the dark outline of another wreck; but this one was evidently of some weeks' standing, for the masts were gone and the hulk half broken through. There was still another further out. The mere repetition of the sad story had effect to make the scene seem more desolate. It seemed as if the sands on which they trod must be strewed with the bleached skeletons of sailors, and as if they embedded newly-buried corpses in their breast. The sandhills here were higher than they had been before, and there were openings between them as if passages led into the interior valleys, so that Caius supposed that here in storms or in flood-tides the waves might enter into the heart of the dune.

They had not travelled far beyond the first and nearest wreck, when the monotony of their journey was broken by a sudden strange excitement which seized on them all, and which Caius, although he felt it, did not at once understand.

The pony was jerked back by the reins which O'Shea held, then turned staggering inland, and lashed forward by the whip, used for the first time that day. Caius, jerked against the side of the cart, lifted up a bruised head, gazing in wonder to see nothing in the path; but he saw that the boy had sprung lightly from the cart, and was standing higher up on the sand, his whole attitude betraying alarm as he gazed searchingly at the ground.

In a moment the pony reared and plunged, and then uttered a cry almost human in its fear. Then came the sensation of sinking, sinking with the very earth itself. O'Shea had jumped from the cart and cut the traces. Caius was springing out, and felt his spring guided by a hand upon his arm. He could not have believed that the boy had so much strength, yet, with a motion too quick for explaining words, he was guided to a certain part of the sand, pushed aside like a child to be safe, while the boy with his next agile

48

movement tugged at the portmanteaus that contained the medical stores, and flung them at Caius' feet.

It was a quicksand. The pony cried again—cried to them for help. Caius next found himself with O'Shea holding the creature's head, and aiding its mad plunging, even while his own feet sank deeper and deeper. There was a moment when they all three plunged forward together, and then the pony threw itself upon its side, by some wild effort extricating its feet, and Caius, prone upon the quivering head, rolled himself and dragged it forward. Then he felt strong hands lifting him and the horse together.

What seemed strangest to Caius, when he could look about and think, was that he had now four companions—the boy, O'Shea, and two other men, coated and muffled—and that the four were all talking together eagerly in a language of which he did not understand a word.

He shook the wet sand from his clothes; his legs and arms were wet. The pony stood in an entrance to a gap in the sand-hills, quivering and gasping, but safe, albeit with one leg hurt. The cart had sunk down till its flat bottom lay on the top of the quicksand, and there appeared to float, for it sunk no further. A white cloud that had winged its way up from the south-west now drifted over the moon, and became black except at its edges. The world grew much darker, and it seemed colder, if that were possible.

It soon occurred to Caius that the two men now added to their party had either met O'Shea by appointment, or had been lying in wait for the cart, knowing that the quicksand was also waiting to engulf it. It appeared to him that their motives must be evil, and he was not slow to suspect O'Shea of being in some plot with them. He had, of course, money upon him, enough certainly to attract the cupidity of men who could seldom handle money, and the medical stores were also convertible into money. It struck him now how rash he had been to come upon this lonely drive without any assurance of O'Shea's respectability.

These thoughts came to him because he almost immediately perceived that he was the subject of conversation. It seemed odd to stand so near them and not understand a word they said. He heard enough now to know the language they were speaking was the patois that, in those parts, is the descendant of the Jersey French. These men, then, were Acadians—the boy also, for he gabbled freely to them. Either they had sinister designs on him, or he was an obstruction to some purpose that they wished to accomplish. This was evident now from their tones and gestures. They were talking most vehemently about him, especially the boy and O'Shea, and it was evident that these two disagreed, or at least could not for some time agree, as to what was to be his fate.

Caius was defenceless, for so peaceful was the country to which he was accustomed that he carried no weapon. He took his present danger little to heart. There was a strange buoyancy—born, no doubt, of the bracing wind—in his spirit. If they were going to kill him—well, he would die hard; and a man can but die once. A laugh arose from the men; it sounded to him as strange a sound, for the time and place, as the almost human cry of the horse a few minutes before. Then O'Shea came towards him with menacing gestures. The two men went back into the gap of the sand-hills from whence they must have come.

"Look here," said O'Shea roughly, "do ye value your life?"

"Certainly."

Caius folded his arms, and made this answer with well-bred contempt.

"And ye shall have your life, but on one condition. Take out of your bags what's needed for dealing with the sick this noight, for there's a dying man ye must visit before ye sleep, and the condition is that ye walk on to The Cloud by yourself on this beach without once looking behoind ye. Moind what I say! Ye shall go free—yerself, yer money, and yer midicines—if ye walk from here to the second house that is a loighthouse without once turning yer head or looking behoind ye." He pointed to the bags with a gesture of rude authority. "Take out what ye need, and begone!"

"I shall do nothing of the sort," replied Caius, his arms still folded.

The boy had come near enough to hear what was said, but he did not interfere.

"And why not?" asked O'Shea, a jeer in his tones.

"Because I would not trust one of you not to kill me as soon as my back was turned."

"And if your back isn't turned, and that pretty quick, too, ye'll not live many hours."

"I prefer to die looking death in the face; but it'll be hard for the man who attempts to touch me."

"Oh! ye think ye'll foight for it, do ye?" asked O'Shea lightly; "but ye're mistaken there —the death ye shall doie will admit of no foighting on your part."

"There is something more in all this business than I understand." Apart from the question whether he should die or live, Caius was puzzled to understand why his enemies had themselves fallen foul of the quicksand, or what connection the accident could have with the attack upon his life. "There is more in this than I understand," he repeated loudly.

"Just so," replied O'Shea, imperturbable; "there is more than ye can understand, and I offer ye a free passage to a safe place. Haven't ye wits enough about ye to take it and be thankful?"

"I will not turn my back." Caius reiterated his defiance.

"And ye'll stroike out with yer fist at whatever comes to harm ye? Will ye hit in the face of the frost and the wind if ye're left here to perish by cold, with your clothes wet as they are? or perhaps ye'll come to blows with the quicksand if half a dozen of us should throw ye in there."

"There are not half a dozen of you," he replied scornfully.

"Come and see." O'Shea did not offer to touch him, but he began to walk towards the opening in the dune, and dragged Caius after him by mere force of words. "Come and see for yourself. What are ye afraid of, man? Come! if ye want to look death in the face, come and see what it is ye've got to look at."

Caius followed reluctantly, keeping his own distance. O'Shea passed the shivering pony, and went into the opening of the dune, which was now all in shadow because of the black cloud in the sky. Inside was a small valley. Its sand-banks might have been made of bleached bones, they looked so gray and dead. Just within the opening was an unexpected sight—a row of hooded and muffled figures stood upright in the sand. There was something appalling in the sight to Caius. Each man was placed at exactly the same distance from his fellow; they seemed to stand with heads bowed, and hands clasped in front of their breasts; faces and hands, like their forms, were hooded and muffled. Caius did not think, or analyze his emotion. No doubt the regular file of the men, suggesting discipline which has such terrible force for weal or woe, and their attitudes, suggesting motives and thoughts of which he could form not the faintest explanation, were the two elements which made the scene fearful to him.

O'Shea stopped a few paces from the nearest figure, and Caius stopped a few paces nearer the opening of the dune.

"Ye see these men?" said O'Shea.

Caius did not answer.

O'Shea raised his voice:

"I say before them what I have said, that if ye'll swear here before heaven, as a man of honour, that ye'll walk from here to the loighthouse on The Cloud—which ye shall find in the straight loine of the beach—without once turning yer head or looking behoind ye, neither man nor beast nor devil shall do ye any hurt, and yer properties shall be returned to ye when a cart can be got to take them. Will ye swear?"

Caius made no answer. He was looking intently. As soon as the tones of O'Shea's voice were carried away by the bluster of the wind, as far as the human beings there were concerned there was perfect stillness; the surf and the wind might have been sweeping the dunes alone.

"And if I will not swear?" asked Caius, in a voice that was loud enough to reach to the last man in the long single rank.

O'Shea stepped nearer him, and, as if in pretence of wiping his face with his gloved hand, he sent him a hissing whisper that gave a sudden change of friendliness and confidence to his voice, "Don't be a fool! swear it."

"Are these men, or are they corpses?" asked Caius.

The stillness of the forms before him became an almost unendurable spectacle.

He had no sooner spoken than O'Shea appealed to the men, shouting words in the queer guttural French. And Caius saw the first man slowly raise his hand as if in an attitude of oath-taking, and the second man did likewise. O'Shea turned round and faced him, speaking hastily. The shadow of the cloud was sending dark shudderings of lighter and darker shades across the sand hollow, and these seemed almost like a visible body of the wind that with searching blast drifted loose sand upon them all. With the sweep of the shadow and the wind, Caius saw the movement of the lifted hand go down the line.

"I lay my loife upon it," said O'Shea, "that if ye'll say on yer honour as a man, and as a gintleman, that ye'll not look behoind ye, ye shall go scot-free. It's a simple thing enough; what harm's there in it?"

The boy had come near behind Caius. He said one soft word, "Promise!" or else Caius imagined he said it. Caius knew at least what the boy wished him to do.

The pony moved nearer, shivering with cold, and Caius realized that the condition of wet and cold in which they were need not be prolonged.

"I promise," he shouted angrily, "and I'll keep the promise, whatever infernal reason there may be for it; but if I'm attacked from behind——" He added threats loud and violent, for he was very angry.

Before he had finished speaking—the thought might have been brought by some movement in the shadow of the cloud, and by the sound of the wind, or by his heated brain—but the thought came to him that O'Shea, under his big fur-coat, had indulged in strange, harsh laughter.

Caius cared nothing. He had made his decision; he had given his word; he had no thought now but to take what of his traps he could carry and be gone on his journey.

CHAPTER 6. THE SEA-MAID

Caius understood that he had still three miles of the level beach to tread. At first he hardly felt the sand under his feet, they were so dead with cold. The spray from the roaring tide struck his face sideways. He had time now to watch each variation, each in and out of the dune, and he looked at them eagerly, as the only change that was afforded to the monotony. Then for the first time he learned how completely a man is shut out from all one half of the world by the simple command not to look behind him, and all the unseen half of his world became rife, in his thought, with mysterious creatures and their works. At first he felt that he was courting certain death by keeping the word he had given; in the clap of the waves he seemed to hear the pistol-shot that was to be his doom, or the knife-like breath of the wind seemed the dagger in the hand of a following murderer. But as he went on and no evil fate befell, his fear died, and only curiosity remained—a curiosity so lively that it fixed eagerly upon the stretch of the surf behind him, upon his own footsteps left on the soft sand, upon the sand-hills that he had passed, although they were almost the same as the sand-hills that were before. It would have been a positive joy to him to turn and look at any of these things. While his mind dwelt upon it, he almost grudged each advancing step, because it put more of the interesting world into the region from which he was shut out as wholly as if a wall of separation sprang up between the behind and before.

By an effort of will he turned his thought from this desire, or from considering what the mysterious something could be that it was all-important for him not to see, or who it was that in this desolate place would spy upon him if he broke his vow.

When his activity had set the blood again coursing warmly in his veins, all that was paltry and depressing passed from his mind and heart, as a mist is rolled away by the wind. The sweet, wild air, that in those regions is an elixir of life to the stranger, making him young if he be old, and if he be young making him feel as demigods felt in days of yore, for a day and a night had been doing its work upon him. Mere life and motion became to him a delight such as he had never felt before; and when the moon came out again from the other side of the cloud, the sight of her beams upon surf and sand was like a rare wild joy. He was glad that no one interfered with his pleasure, that he was, as far as he knew, alone with the clouds that were winging their way among moonbeams in the violet sky, and with the waves and the wind with which he held companionship.

He had gone a mile, it might be more; he heard a step behind him. In vain he tried to convince himself that some noise natural to the lonely beach deceived him. In the high tide of life that the bracing air had brought him, his senses were acute and true. He knew that he heard this step: it was light, like a child's; it was nimble, like a fawn's; sometimes it was very near him. He was not in the least afraid; but do what he would, his mind could form no idea of what creature it might be who thus attended him. No dark or fearful picture crossed his mind just then; all its images were good.

The fleet of white clouds that were sailing in the sky rang glad changes upon the beauty of the moonlit scene. Half a mile or more Caius walked listening to the footstep; then he came on a wrecked boat buried in the sand, its rim laid bare by the tide. Caius struck his foot and fell upon it.

Striking his head, stunned for a moment, then springing up again, in the motion of falling or rising, he knew not how, he saw the beach behind him—the waves that were now nearing the foot of the dune, the track between with his footsteps upon it, and, standing in this track, alert to fly if need be, the figure of a girl. Her dress was all blown by the wind, her curling hair was like a twining garland round her face, and her face—ah! that face: he knew it as well as, far better than he knew his own; its oval curves, its dimpled sweetness, its laughing eyes. Just for such brief seconds of time as were necessary for perfect recognition he saw it; and then, impelled by his former purpose—no time now for a new volition—he got himself up and walked on, with his eyes in front as before.

He thought the sea-maid did not know that he had seen her, for her footsteps came on after his own. Or, if she knew, she trusted him not to turn. That was well; she might trust him. Never in his life had Caius felt less temptation to do the thing that he held to be false. He knew now, for he had seen the whole line of the beach, that there was nothing there for him to fear, nothing that could give any adequate reason to any man to compel him to walk as he now walked. That did not matter; he had given his word. In the physical exaltation of the hour the best of him was uppermost. Like the angels, who walk in heavenly paths, he had no desire to be a thing that could stoop from moral rectitude. The knowledge that his old love of the sea was his companion only enhanced the strength of his vow, only made all that the strength of vows mean more dear to him; and the moonlit shore was more beautiful, and life, each moment that he was then living, more absolutely good.

So they went on, and he did not try to think where the sea-maid had come from, or whether the gray flapping dress and the girlish step were but the phantom guise that she could don for the hour, or whether, if he should turn and pursue her, she would drop from her upright height into the scaly folds that he had once seen, and plunge into the waves, or whether *that* had been the masquerade, and she a true woman of the land. He did not know or care. Come what come might, his spirit walked the beach that night with the beautiful spirit that the face of the sea-maid interpreted to him.

CHAPTER 7. THE GRAVE LADY

The hills of Cloud Island were a fair sight to see in the moonlight. When the traveller came close to them, the beach ended obviously in a sandy road which led up on the island. There was a small white wooden house near the beach; there was candlelight within, but Caius took no notice of it. The next building was a lighthouse, which stood three hundred yards farther on. The light looking seaward was not visible. He passed the distance swiftly, and no sooner were his feet level with the wall of the square wooden tower, than he turned about on the soft sandy road and faced the wind that had been racing with him, and looked. The scene was all as he might have expected to see it; but there was no living creature in sight. He stood in the gale, bare-headed, looking, looking; he had no desire to enter the house. The sea-maid was not in sight, truly; but as long as he stood alone in the moonlight scene, he felt that her presence was with him. Then he remembered the dying man of whom he had been told, who lay in such need of his ministrations. The thought came with no binding sense of duty such as he had felt concerning the keeping of his vow. He would have scorned to do a dishonourable thing in the face of the uplifting charm of the nature around him, and, more especially, in the presence of his love; but what had nature and this, her beautiful child, to do with the tending of disease and death? Better let the man die; better remain himself in the wholesome outside. He felt that he would put himself at variance with the companions of the last glorious hour if he attended to the dictates of this dolorous duty. Yet, because of a dull habit of duty he had, he turned in a minute, and went into the house where he had been told he would receive guidance for the rest of his journey.

He had no sooner knocked at the substantial door on the ground-floor of the light-house than it was opened by a sallow-faced, kindly-looking old woman. She admitted him, as if he were an expected comer, into a large square room, in which a lamp and a fire were burning. The room was exquisitely neat and clean, as if the inspector of lighthouses might be looked for at any moment. The woman, who was French, spoke a little English, and her French was of a sort which Caius could understand and answer. She placed a chair for him by the heated stove, asked where Mr. O'Shea and the cart had tarried, listened with great interest to a brief account of the accident in the quicksand, and, without more delay, poured out hot strong coffee, which Caius drank out of a large bowl.

"Are you alone in the house?" asked Caius. The impression was strong upon him that he was in a place where the people bore a dangerous or mysterious character. A woman to be alone, with open doors, must either be in league with those from whom danger might be feared, or must possess mysterious powers of self-defence.

The woman assured him that she was alone, and perfectly safe. She gave a kindly and careful glance at the traveller's boots, which had been wet, and brought him another pair. It was evident she knew who Caius was, and wherefore he had come to the island, and that her careful entertainment of him was prearranged. It was arranged, too, that she should pass him on to the patient for whom his skill was chiefly desired that night as quickly as possible. She gave him only reasonable time to be warmed and fed, telling him the while what a good man this was who had lately been taken so very ill, what an excellent husband and father, how important his life was to the welfare of the community.

"For," said she, "he is truly rather rich and very intelligent; so much so that some would even say that he was the friend of Madame Le Maître." Her voice had a crescendo of vehemence up to this last name.

Caius had his marching orders once more. His hostess went out with him to the moonlit road to point his way. She showed him where the road divided, and which path to take, and said that he must then pass three houses and enter the fourth. She begged him, with courteous authority, to hasten.

The houses were a good way apart. After half an hour's fast walking, Caius came to the appointed place. The house was large, of light-coloured wood, shingled all over roof and sides, and the light and shades in the lapping of the shingles gave the soft effect almost as of feathers in the lesser light of night. It stood in a large compound of undulating grassy ground.

The whole lower floor of this house was one room. In the middle of it, on a small pallet bedstead, lay the sick man. Beside him was a woman dressed in gray homespun, apparently his wife, and another woman who wore a dress not unlike that of a nun, a white cap being bandaged closely round her forehead, cheeks and chin. The nun-like dress gave her great dignity. She seemed to Caius a strong-featured woman of large stature, apparently in early middle age. He was a good deal surprised when he found that this was Madame Le Maître. He had had no definite notion of her, but this certainly did not fulfil his idea.

It was but the work of a short time to do all that could be done that night for the sick man, to leave the remedies that were to be used. It was now midnight. The hot stove in the room, causing reaction from the strongly-stimulating air, made him again feel heavy with sleep. The nun-like lady, who had as yet said almost nothing to him, now touched him on the shoulder and beckoned him to follow her. She led him out into the night again, round the house and into a barn, in either side of which were tremendous bins of hay.

"Your house," she said, "is a long way from here, and you are very tired. In the house here there is the infection." Here she pointed him to the hay, and, giving him a warm blanket, bade him good-night.

Caius shut the door, and found that the place was lit by dusky rays of moonlight that came through chinks in its walls. He climbed the ladder that reached to the top of the hay, and rolled himself and his blanket warmly in it. The barn was not cold. The airiness of the walls was a relief to him after the infected room. Never had couch felt more luxurious.

CHAPTER 8. HOW THEY LIVED ON THE CLOUD

When the chinks of moonlight had been replaced by brighter chinks of sunlight, the new doctor who had come so gallantly to the aid of the sufferers on Cloud Island opened his eyes upon his first day there.

He heard some slight sounds, and looked over the edge of his bed to see a little table set forth in the broad passage between the two stores of hay. A slip of a girl, of about fourteen years of age, was arranging dishes upon it. When Caius scrambled down, she informed him, with childish timidity of mien, that Madame Le Maître had said that he was to have his breakfast there before he went in to see "father." The child spoke French, but Caius spoke English because it relieved his mind to do so.

"Upon my word!" he said, "Madame Le Maître keeps everything running in very good order, and takes prodigious care of us all."

"Oh, oui, monsieur," replied the child sagely, judging from his look of amusement and the name he had repeated that this was the proper answer.

The breakfast, which was already there, consisted of fish, delicately baked, and coffee. The young doctor felt exceedingly odd, sitting in the cart-track of a barn and devouring these viands from a breakfast-table that was tolerably well set out with the usual number of dishes and condiments. The big double door was closed to keep out the cold wind, but plenty of air and numerous sunbeams managed to come in. The sunbeams were golden bars of dust, crossing and interlacing in the twilight of the windowless walls. The slip of a girl in her short frock remained, perhaps from curiosity, perhaps because she had been bidden to do so, but she made herself as little obvious as possible, standing up against one corner near the door and shyly twisting some bits of hay in her hands. Caius, who was enjoying himself, discovered a new source of amusement in pretending to forget her presence and then looking at her quickly, for he always found the glance of her big gray eyes was being withdrawn from his own face, and child-like confusion ensued.

When he had eaten enough, he set to his proper work with haste and diligence. He made the girl tell him how many children there were, and find them all for him, so that in a trice he had them standing in a row in the sunlight outside the barn, with their little tongues all out, that the state of their health might be properly inspected. Then he went in to his patient of the night before.

The disease was diphtheria. It was a severe case; but the man had been healthy, and Caius approved the arrangements that Madame Le Maître had made to give him plenty of air and nourishment.

The wife was alone with her husband this morning, and when Caius had done all that was necessary, and given her directions for the proper protection of herself and the children, she told him that her eldest girl would go with him to the house of Madame Le Maître. That lady, said she simply, would tell him where he was to go next, and all he was to do upon the island.

"Upon my word!" said Caius again to himself, "it seems I am to be taken care of and instructed, truly."

He had a sense of being patronized; but his spirits were high—nothing depressed him; and, remembering the alarming incident of the night before, he felt that the lady's protection might not be unnecessary.

When he got to the front of the house, for the first time in the morning light, he saw that the establishment was of ample size, but kept with no care for a tasteful appearance. There was no path of any sort leading from the gate in the light paling to the door; all was a thick carpet of grass, covering the unlevelled ground. The grass was waving madly in the wind, which coursed freely over undulating fields that here displayed no shrubs or trees of any sort. Caius wondered if the wind always blew on these islands; it was blowing now with the same zest as the day before; the sun poured down with brilliancy upon everything, and the sea, seen in glimpses, was blue and tempestuous. Truly, it seemed a land which the sun and the moon and the wind had elected to bless with lavish self-giving.

When Caius opened the gate of the whitewashed paling, the girl who was to be his guide came round from the back of the house after him, and on her track came a sudden rush of all the other children, who, with curls and garments flying in the wind and delightful bursts of sudden laughter, came to stand in a row again with their tongues outstretched at Caius' retreating form.

The girl could only talk French, and she talked very little of that, giving him "yes" or "no" demurely, as they went up the road which ran inland through the island hills, keeping about midway between sea and sea. Caius saw that the houses and small farms on either side resembled those which he had seen on the other island. Small and rough many of them were; but their whitewashed walls, the strong sunshine, and the large space of grass or pine shrubs that was about each, gave them an appearance of cleanliness. There was no sign of the want or squalor that he had expected; indeed, so prosperous did many of the houses look, that he himself began to have an injured feeling, thinking that he had been brought to befriend people who might very well have befriended themselves.

It was when they came out at a dip in the hills near the outer sea again that the girl stopped, and pointing Caius to a house within sight, went back. This house in the main resembled the other larger houses of the island; but pine and birch trees were beginning to grow high about it, and on entering its enclosure Caius trod upon a gravel path, and noticed banks of earth that in the summer time had held flowers. In front of the white veranda two powerful mastiffs were lying in the sun. These lions were not chained; they were looking for him before he appeared, but did not take the trouble to rise at the sight of him; only a low and ominous rumble, as of thunder beneath the earth, greeted his approach, and gave Caius the strong impression that, if need was, they would arise to some purpose.

A young girl opened the door. She was fresh and pretty-looking, but of plebeian figure and countenance. Her dress was again gray homespun, hanging full and short about her ankles. Her manner was different from that of those people he had been lately meeting, for it had that gentle reserve and formality that bespeaks training. She ushered him into a good-sized room, where three other girls like herself were engaged in sewing. Sitting at a table with a book, from which she had apparently been reading to them, was the woman in the nun-like dress whom he had met before. The walls of the room were of unpainted pinewood, planed to a satin finish, and adorned with festoons of gray moss such as hangs from forest boughs. This was tied with knots of red bitter-sweet berries; the feathers of sea-birds were also displayed on the walls, and chains of their delicate-coloured eggs were hanging there. Caius had not stepped across the threshold before he began to suspect that he had passed from the region of the real into the ideal.

"She is a romantic-minded woman," he said to himself. "I wonder if she has much sense, after all?"

Then the woman whom he was thus inwardly criticising rose and came across the room to meet him. Her perfect gravity, her dignity of bearing, and her gracious greeting, impressed him in spite of himself. Pictures that one finds in history and fiction of lady abbesses rose before his mind; it was thus that he classified her. His opinion as to the conscious romance of her life altered, for the woman before him was very real, and he knew in a moment that she had seen and suffered much. Her eyes were full of suffering and of solicitude; but it did not seem to him that the suffering and solicitude were in any way connected with a personal need, for there was also peace upon her face.

The room did not contain much furniture. When Caius sat down, and the lady had resumed her seat, he found, as is apt to be the way in empty rooms, that the chairs were near the wall, and that he, sitting facing her, had left nearly the room's width between them. The sewing maidens looked at them with large eyes, and listened to everything that was said; and although they were silent, except for the sound of their stitching, it was so evident that their thoughts must form a running commentary that it gave Caius an odd feeling of acting in company with a dramatic chorus. The lady in front of him had no such feeling; there was nothing more evident about her than that she did not think of how she appeared or how she was observed.

"You are very good to have come." She spoke with a slight French accent, whether natural or acquired he could not tell. Then she left that subject, and began at once to tell the story of the plague upon the island—when it began, what efforts she and a few others had made to arrest it, the carelessness and obstinacy with which the greater part of the people had fostered it, its progress. This was the substance of what she said; but she did not speak of the best efforts as being her own, nor did she call the people stupid and obsti-nate. She only said:

"They would not have their houses properly cleaned out; they would not wash or burn garments that were infected; they would not use disinfectants, even when we could procure them; they will not yet. You may say that in this wind-swept country there can be nothing in nature to foster such a disease, nothing in the way the houses are built; but the disease came here on a ship, and it is in the houses of the people that it lingers. They will not isolate the sick; they will not——"

She stopped as if at a loss for a word. She had been speaking in a voice whose music was the strain of compassion.

"In fact," said Caius, with some impatience, "they are a set of fools, and worse, for they won't take a telling. Your duty is surely done. They do not deserve that you should risk your life nursing them; they simply deserve to be left to suffer."

She looked at him for a minute, as if earnestly trying to master a view of the case new to her.

"Yes," speaking slowly. He saw that her hands, which were clasped in her lap, pressed themselves more closely together—"yes, that is what they deserve; but, you see, they are very ignorant. They do not see the importance of these precautions; they have not believed me; they will not believe you. They think quite honestly and truly that they will get on well enough in doing their own way."

"Pig-headed!" commented Caius. Then, perceiving that he had not quite carried her judgment along with his: "You yourself, madam, have admitted that they do not deserve that either you or I should sacrifice our lives to them."

"Ah, no," she replied, trouble of thought again in her eyes; "they do not deserve that. But what do we deserve—you and I?"

There was no studied effect in the question. She was like one trying to think more clearly by expressing her thought aloud.

"Madam," replied he, the smile of gallantry upon his lips, "I have no doubt that you deserve the richest blessings of earth and heaven. For myself——" He shrugged his shoulders, just about to say conventionally, flippantly, that he was a sad, worthless fellow, but in some way her sincerity made him sincere, and he finished: "I do not know that I have done anything to forfeit them."

He supposed, as soon as he had said the words, that she would have a theological objection to this view, and oppose it by rote; but there was nothing of disapproval in her mien; there was even a gleam of greater kindliness for him in her eye, and she said, not in answer, but as making a remark by the way:

"That is just as I supposed when I asked you to come. You are like the young ruler, who could not have been conceited because our Lord felt greatly attracted to him."

Before this Caius had had a pleasing consciousness, regarding himself as an interesting stranger talking to a handsome and interested woman. Now he had wit enough to perceive that her interest in him never dipped to the level of ordinary social relationships. He felt a sense of remoteness, and did not even blush, though knowing certainly that satire, although it was not in her mind, was sneering at him from behind the circumstance.

The lady went right on, almost without pause, taking up the thread of her argument: "But when the angels whisper to us that the best blessings of earth and heaven are humility and faith and the sort of love that does not seek its own, do we get up at once and spend our time learning these things? or do we just go on as before, and think our own way good enough? 'We are fools and worse, and will not take a telling.'" A smile broke upon her lip now for the first time as she looked at him. "'Pig-headed!'" she said.

Caius had seen that smile before. It passed instantly, and she sat before him with grave, unruffled demeanour; but all his thoughts and feelings seemed a-whirl. He could not collect his mind; he could not remember what she had said exactly; he could not think what to answer; indeed, he could not think at all. There had been a likeness to his phantastic lady-love of the sea; then it was gone again; but it left him with all his thoughts confounded. At length—because he felt that he must look like a fool indeed—he spoke, stammering the first thing that occurred to him:

"The patient that I have seen did not appear to be in a house that was ill-ventilated or —or—that is, he was isolated from the rest of the family."

He perceived that the lady had not the slightest knowledge of what it was that had really confused him. He knew that in her eyes, in the eyes of the maidens, it must appear that her home-thrust had gone to his heart, that he had changed the subject because too weak to be able to answer her. He was mortified at this, but he could not retrace his steps in the conversation, for she had already answered him.

The household he had already visited, she said, with a few others, had helped her by following sanitary rules; and then she went on talking about what those rules were, what could and could not be done in the circumstances of the families affected.

As she talked on, Caius knew that the thing he had thought must be false and foolish. This woman and that other maiden were not the same in thought, or character, or deed, or aspect. Furthermore, what experience he had made him feel certain that the woman who had known him in that relationship could not be so indifferent to his recognition, so indifferent to all that was in him to which her beauty appealed, as this woman was, and of this woman's indifference he felt convinced.

The provision made for the board and lodging of the new doctor was explained to him. It was not considered safe for him to live with any of the families of the island. A very small wooden building, originally built as a stable, but never used, had been hastily remodelled into a house for him. It was some way further down the winding road, within sight of the house of Madame Le Maître.

Caius was taken to this new abode, and found that it contained two rooms, furnished with the necessities and many of the comforts of life. The stove was good; abundance of fuel was stacked near the house; simple cooking utensils hung in the outer room; adjoining it, or rather, in a bit of the same building set apart, was a small stable, in which a very good horse was standing. The horse was for his use. If he could be his own bed-maker, cook, and groom, it was evident that he would lack for nothing. A man whom Madame Le Maître sent showed Caius his quarters, and delivered to him the key; he also said that Madame Le Maître would be ready in an hour to ride over the island with him and introduce him to all the houses in which there was illness.

Caius was left for the hour to look over his establishment and make friends with his horse. It was all very surprising.

CHAPTER 9. THE SICK AND THE DEAD

The bit of road that lay between Madame Le Maître's house and the house allotted to Caius led, winding down a hill, through a stunted fir-wood. The small firs held out gnarled and knotty branches towards the road; their needles were a dark rich green.

Down this road Caius saw the lady come riding. Her horse was a beautiful beast, hardly more than a colt, of light make and chestnut colour. She herself was not becomingly attired; she wore just the same loose black dress that she had worn in the house, and over the white cap a black hood and cloak were muffled. No doubt in ancient times, before carriages were in use, ladies rode in such feminine wrappings; but the taste of Caius had been formed upon other models. He mounted his own horse and joined her on the road without remark. He had found no saddle, only a blanket with girths, and upon this he supposed he looked quite as awkward as she did. The lady led, and they rode on across the island.

Caius knew that now it was the right time to tell Madame Le Maître what had occurred the night before, and the ill-usage he had suffered. As she appeared to be the most important person on the island, it was right that she should know of the mysterious band of bandits upon the beach—if, indeed, she did not already know; perhaps it was by power of these she reigned. He found himself able to conjecture almost anything.

When he had quickened his horse and come beside her for the purpose of relating his adventure, she began to speak to him at once. She told him what number of cases of illness were then on her list—six in all. She told him the number who had already died; and then they came past the cemetery upon the hillside, and she pointed out the new-made graves. It appeared that, although at that time there was an abatement in the number of cases, diphtheria had already made sad ravages among the little population; and as the winter would cause the people to shut up their houses more and more closely, it was certain to increase rather than to diminish. Then Madame Le Maître told him of one case, and of another, in which the family bereavement seemed particularly sad. The stories she told had great detail, but they were not tedious. Caius listened, and forgot that her voice was musical or that her hood and cloak were ugly; he only thought of the actors in the short sad idylls of the island that she put before him.

When they entered the first house, he discovered that she herself had been in the habit of visiting each of the sick every day as nurse, and, as far as her simple skill could go, as doctor too. In this house it was a little child that lay ill, and as soon as Caius saw it he ceased to hope for its recovery. They used the new remedies that he had brought with him, and when he looked round for someone who could continue to apply them, he found that the mother was already dead, and the father took no charge of the child—he was not there. A half-grown boy of about fifteen was its only nurse, and he was not deft or wise, although love, or a rude sense of conscience, had kept him from deserting his post.

"When we have visited the others, I will come back and remain," said Madame Le Maître.

So they rode on down the hill and along the shingled beach that edged a lagoon. Here the sea lapped softly and they were sheltered from the wind. Here, too, they saw the other islands lying in the crescent they composed, and they saw the waves of the bay break on the sand-bank that was the other arm of the lagoon. Still Caius did not tell about his adventure of the night before. The lady looked preoccupied, as if she was thinking about the Angel of Death that was hovering over the cottage they had left.

The next house was a large one, and here two children were ill. They were well cared for, for two of the young girls whom he had seen in Madame Le Maître's house were there for the time to nurse them.

They took one of these damsels with them when they went on. She was willing to walk, but Caius set her upon his horse and led it; in this way they made quicker progress. Up a hill they went, and over fields, and in a small house upon a windy slope they found the mother of a family lying very ill. Here, after Caius had said all that there was to say, and Madame Le Maître, with skilful hands, had done all that she could do in a short time, they left the young girl.

At the next and last house of their round, where the day before one child had been ill, they now found three tossing and crying with pain and fever. When it was time for them to go, Caius saw his companion silently wring her hands at the thought of leaving them, for the mother, worn out and very ignorant, was the only nurse. It did not seem that it could be helped. Caius went out to his horse, and Madame Le Maître to hers, but he saw her stand beside it as if too absent in mind to spring to its back; her face was looking up into the blue above.

"You are greatly troubled," said Caius.

"Oh yes," her voice was low, but it came like the sound of a cry. "I do not know what to do. All these months I have begged and entreated the people to keep away from those houses where there was illness. It was their only hope. And now that they begin to understand that, I cannot bring the healthy to nurse the sick, even if they were willing to come. They will take no precautions as we do. It is not safe; I have tried it."

She did not look at Caius, she was looking at the blue that hung over the sea which lay beneath them, but the weariness of a long long effort was in her tone.

"Could we not manage to bring them all to one house that would serve as a hospital?"

"Now that you have come, perhaps we can," she said, "but at present——" She looked helplessly at the door of the house they had left.

"At present I will nurse these children," Caius said. "I do not need to see the others again until evening."

He tied his horse in a shed, and nursed the children until the moon was bright. Then, when he had left them as well as might be for the night, he set out to return on his former track by memory. The island was very peaceful; on field or hill or shore he met no one, except here and there a plodding fisherman, who gave him "Good-evening" without apparently knowing or caring who he was. The horse they knew, no doubt, that was enough.

He made the same round as before, beginning at the other end. At the house where the woman was ill the girl who was nursing her remained. At the next house the young girl, who was dressed for the road, ingenuously claimed his protection for her homeward way.

"I will go with you, monsieur, it will be more safe for me."

So he put her on his horse, but they did not talk to one another.

At the third house they found Madame Le Maître weeping passionately over a dead baby, and the lout of a boy weeping with her. It surprised Caius to feel suddenly that he could almost have wept, too, and yet he believed that the child was better dead.

Someone had been out into the winter fields and gathered the small white everlasting flowers that were still waving there, and twined them in the curls of the baby's hair, and strewed them upon the meagre gray sheet that covered it.

When they rode down to the village they were all quite silent. Caius felt as if he had lived a long time upon this island. His brain was full of plans for a hospital and for disinfecting the furniture of the houses.

He visited the good man in whose barn he had slept the preceding night. He went to his little house and fed himself and his horse. He discovered his portmanteaus that O'Shea had promised to deliver, and found that their contents had not been tampered with; but even this did not bring his mind back with great interest to the events of the former night. He was thinking of other things, and yet he hardly knew of what he was thinking.

CHAPTER 10. A LIGHT-GIVING WORD

The next morning, before Caius went out, he wrote a short statement of all that had occurred beside the quicksand. The motive that prompted him to do this was the feeling that it would be difficult for him to make the statement to Madame Le Maître verbally. He began to realize that it was not easy for him to choose the topics of conversation when they were together.

She did not ride with him next day, as now he knew the road, but in the course of the morning he saw her at the house where the three children were ill, and she came out into the keen air with him to ask some questions, and no doubt for the necessary refreshment of leaving the close house, for she walked a little way on the dry, frozen grass.

Heavy as was the material of her cloak and hood, the strong wind toyed with its outer parts as with muslin, but it could not lift the closely-tied folds that surrounded her face and heavily draped her figure. Caius stood with her on the frozen slope. Beneath them they could see the whole stretch of the shining sand-dune that led to the next island, the calm lagoon and the rough water in the bay beyond. It did not seem a likely place for outlaws to hide in; the sun poured down on every hill and hollow of the sand.

Caius explained then that his portmanteaus, with the stores, had arrived safely; but that he had reason to think that the man O'Shea was not trusty, that, either out of malice or fear of the companions among whom he found himself, he had threatened his, Dr. Simpson's, life in the most unwarrantable manner. He then presented the statement which he had drawn up, and commended it to her attention.

Madame Le Maître had listened to his words without obvious interest; in fact, he doubted if she had got her mind off the sick children before she opened the paper. He would have liked to go away now, leaving the paper with her, but she did not give him that opportunity.

"Ah! this is——" Then, more understandingly, "This is an account you have written of your journey hither?"

Caius intimated that it was merely a complaint against O'Shea. Yet he felt sure, while she was reading it, that, if she had any liveliness of fancy, she must be interested in its contents, and if she had proper appreciation, she must know that he had expressed himself well. When she had finished, however, instead of coveting the possession of the document, she gently gave it back to him.

"I am sorry," she said sincerely, "that you were put to inconvenience. It was so kind of you to come, that I had hoped to make your journey as comfortable as possible; but the sands are very treacherous, not because the quicksands are large or deep, but because they shift in stormy weather, sometimes appearing in one place, and sometimes in another. It has been explained"—she was looking at him now, quite interested in what she was saying—"by men who have visited these islands, that this is to be accounted for by the beds of gypsum that lie under the sand, for under some conditions the gypsum will dissolve."

The explanation concerning the gypsum was certainly interesting, but the nature of the quicksand was not the point which Caius had brought forward.

"It is this fact, that one cannot tell where the sand will be soft, that makes it necessary to have a guide in travelling over the beach. The people here become accustomed to the appearance of the soft places, but it seems that O'Shea must have been deceived by the moonlight."

"I do not blame him for the accident," said Caius, "but for what happened afterwards."

Her slight French accent gave to each of her words a quaint, distinct form of its own. "O'Shea is—he is what you might call *funny* in his way of looking at things." She paused a moment, as if entirely conscious of the inadequacy of the explanation. "I do not think," she continued, as if in perplexity, "that I can explain this matter any more; but if you will talk to O'Shea——"

"Madam," burst out Caius, "can it be that there is a large band of lawless men who have their haunts so near this island, and you do not know of it? That," he added, with emphatic reproach, "is impossible."

"I never heard of any such band of men."

Madame Le Maître spoke gently, and the dignity of her gentleness was such that Caius was ashamed of his vehemence and his reproach. What he wondered at, what he chafed at, was, that she showed no wonder concerning an incident which her last statement made all the more remarkable. She began to turn to go towards the house, and the mind of Caius hit upon the one weak point in her own acknowledged view of the matter.

"You have said that it is not safe for a stranger to walk upon the sands without a guide; if you doubt my statement that these men threatened my life, it yet remains that I was left to finish my journey alone. I do not believe that there was danger myself. I do not believe that a man would sink over his head in these holes; but according to their belief and yours, madam——"

He stopped, for she had turned round with a distinct flash of disapproval in her eyes.

"I do not doubt your statement." She paused, and he knew that his accusation had been rude. "It would not occur to me"—there was still the slight quaintness of one unaccustomed to English—"that you could do anything unworthy of a gentleman." Another pause, and Caius knew that he was bound over to keep the peace. "I think O'Shea got himself into trouble, and that he did the best he could for you; but O'Shea lives not far from your own house. He is not my servant, except that he rents my husband's land." She paused again.

Caius would have urged that he had understood otherwise, or that hitherto he had not found O'Shea either civil or communicative; but it appeared that the lady had something more to say after her emphasis of pause, and when she said it Caius bid her good-day without making further excuse or justification. She said:

"I did not understand from O'Shea that he allowed you to walk on the sands without some one who would have warned you if there had been danger."

When Caius was riding on his way, he experienced something of that feeling of exaltation that he had felt in the presence of his inexplicable lady-love. Had he not proof at least now that she was no dream or phantasy, and more than that, that she inhabited the same small land with him? These people knew her; nay (his mind worked quickly), was it not evident that she had been the link of connection between them and himself? She knew him, then—his home, his circumstances, his address. (His horse was going now where and how it would; the man's mind was confounded by the questions that came upon it pell-mell, none waiting for an answer.) In that other time when she had lived in the sea, and he had seen her from the desolate bit of coast, who was she? Where had she really lived? In what way could she have gained her information concerning him? What could have tempted her to play the part of a fishy thing? He remembered the monstrous skin that had covered her; he remembered her motion in the water. Then he thought of her in the gray homespun dress, such as a maid might trip her garden in, as he had seen her travelling between the surf and the dune in the winter blast. Well, he lived in an enchanted land; he had to deal with men and women of no ordinary stuff and make, but they acknowledged their connection with her. He was sure that she must be near him. The explanation must come—of that, burning with curiosity as he was, he recked little. A meeting must come; all his pulses tingled with the thought. It was a thought of such a high sort of bliss to him that it seemed to wrap and enfold his other thoughts; and when he remembered again to guide his horse—all that day as he went about his work—he lived in it and worked in it.

He went that evening to visit O'Shea, who lived in a good-sized house half a mile or so from his own. From this interview, and from the clue which Madame Le Maître had given, he began strongly to suspect that, for some reason unknown, O'Shea's threatenings were to be remembered more in the light of a practical joke than as serious. As to where the men had come from who had played their part, as to where the boy had gone to, or whether the boy and the lady were one—on these heads he got no light. The farmer affected stupidity—affected not to understand his questions, or answered them with such whimsical information on the wrong point that little was revealed. Yet Caius did not quarrel with O'Shea. Was it not possible that he, rude, whimsical man that he was, might have influence with the sea-maid of the laughing face?

Next morning Caius received a formal message—the compliments of Madame Le Maître, and she would be glad if he would call upon her before he went elsewhere. He passed again between the growling mastiffs, and found the lady with her maidens engaged in the simple household tasks that were necessary before they went to their work of mercy. Madame Le Maître stood as she spoke to him:

"When I wrote to you I said that if you came to us you would have no chance of returning until the spring. I find that that is not true. Our winter has held off so long that another vessel from the mainland has called—you can see her lying in the bay. She will be returning to Picton to-morrow. I think it right to tell you this; not that we do not need you now as much as we did at first; not but that my hope and courage would falter if you went; but now that you have seen the need for yourself, how great or how little it is, just as you may think, you ought to reconsider, and decide whether you will stay or not."

Caius spoke hastily:

"I will stay."

"Think! it is for four months of snow and ice, and you will receive no letters, see no one that you could call a friend."

"I will stay."

"You have already taught me much; with the skill that you have imparted and the stores that you have brought, which I will pay for, we should be much better off than if you had not come. We should still feel only gratitude to you."

"I have no thought of leaving."

"Remember, you think now that you have come that it is only a handful of people that you can benefit, and they will not comprehend the sacrifice that you have made, or be very grateful."

"Yes, I think that," replied Caius, admitting her insight. "At the same time, I will remain."

She sighed, and her sigh was explained by her next words:

"Yet you do not remain for love of the work or the people."

Caius felt that his steady assertion that he would remain had perhaps appeared to vaunt a heroism that was not true. He supposed that she had seen his selfishness of motive, and that it was her time now to let him see that she had not much admiration for him, so that he might make his choice without bias.

"It is true that I do not love the people, but I will pass the winter here."

If the lady had had the hard thought of him that he attributed to her, there was no further sign of it, for she thanked him now with a gratitude so great that silent tears trembled in her eyes.

CHAPTER 11. THE LADY'S HUSBAND

It was impossible but that Caius should take a keen interest in his medical work. It was the first time that he had stood alone to fight disease, and the weight of the responsibility added zest to his care of each particular case. It was, however, natural to him to be more interested in the general weal than in the individual, more interested in a theoretical problem than in its practical working. His mind was concerned now as to where and how the contagion hid itself, reappearing as it had done, again and again in unlikely places; for there could be assuredly no home for it in air, or sea, or land. Nor could drains be at fault, for there were none. Next to this, the subject most constantly in his mind was the plan of the hospital.

Madame Le Maître had said to him: "I have tried to persuade the people to bring their sick to beds in my house, where we would nurse them, but they will not. It is because they are angry to think that the sick from different families would be put together and treated alike. They have great notions of the differences between themselves, and they cannot realize the danger, or believe that this plan would avert it; but now that you have come, no doubt you will be able to explain to them more clearly. Perhaps they will listen to you, because you are a man and a doctor. Also, what I have said will have had time to work. You may reap where I have sown."

She had looked upon him encouragingly, and Caius had felt encouraged; but when he began to talk to the people, both courage and patience quickly ebbed. He could not countenance the plan of bringing the sick into the house where Madame Le Maître and the young girls lived. He wanted the men who were idle in the winter time to build a temporary shed of pine-wood, which would have been easy enough, but the men laughed at him. The only reason that Caius did not give them back scorn for scorn and anger for their lazy indifference was the reason that formed his third and greatest interest in his work; this was his desire to please Madame Le Maître.

If he had never known and loved the lady of the sea, he thought that his desire to please Madame Le Maître would have been almost the same. She exercised over him an inexplicable influence, and he would have felt almost superstitious at being under this spell if he had not observed that everyone who came much in contact with her, and who was able to appreciate her, was ruled also, and that, not by any claim of authority she put forth, but just because it seemed to happen so. She was more unconscious of this influence than anyone. Those under her rule comprised one or two of the better men of the island, many of the poor women, the girls in her house, and O'Shea. With regard to himself, Caius knew that her influence, if not augmented, was supplemented, by his belief that in pleasing her he was making his best appeal to the favour of the woman he loved.

He never from the first day forgot his love in his work. His business was to do all that he could to serve Madame Le Maître, whose heart was in the healing of the people, but his business also was to find out the answer to the riddle in which his own heart was bound up. The first step in this, obviously, was to know more about Madame Le Maître and O'Shea. The lady he dared not question; the man he questioned with persistency and with what art he could command.

It was one night, not a week after his advent, that he had so far come to terms with O'Shea that he sat by the stove in the latter's house, and did what he could to keep up conversation with little aid from his host.

O'Shea sat on one wooden chair, with his stockinged feet crossed upon another, and his legs forming a bridge between. He was smoking, and in the lamplight his smooth, queer face looked like a brown apple that had begun to shrivel—just begun, for O'Shea was not old, and only a little wrinkled.

His wife came often into the room, and stood looking with interest at Caius. She was a fair woman, with a broad tranquil face and much light hair that was brushed smoothly.

Caius talked of the weather, for the snow was falling. Then, after awhile:

"By the way, O'Shea, *who* is Madame Le Maître?"

The other had not spoken for a long time; now he took his clay pipe out of his mouth, and answered promptly:

"An angel from heaven."

"Ah, yes; that, of course."

Caius stroked his moustache with the action habitual to drawing-room gallantry; then, instead of persisting, he formed his question a little differently:

"Who is Mr. Le Maître?"

"Sea-captain," said O'Shea.

"Oh! then *where* is he?"

"Don't know."

"Isn't that rather strange, that his wife should be here, and that you should not know where the husband is?"

"I can't see the ships on the other side of the world."

"Where did he go to?"

"Well, when he last sailed"—deliberately—"he went to Newcastle. His ship is what they call a tramp; it don't belong to any loine. So at Newcastle she was hired to go to Africy. Like enough, there she got cargo for some place else."

"Oh! a very long voyage."

"She carries steam; the longest voyage comes to an end quick enough in these days."

"Has Madame Le Maître always lived on this island? Was she married here?"

"She came here a year this October past. She came from a place near the Pierced Rock, south of Gaspé Basin. I lived there myself. I came here because the skipper had good land here that she said I could farm."

Caius meditated on this.

"Then, you have known her ever since she was a child?"

"Saw her married."

"What does her husband look like?"

"Well"—a long pause of consideration—"like a man."

"What sort of a man?"

"Neither like you nor me."

"I never noticed that we were alike."

"You trim your beard, I haven't any; the skipper, he's hairy."

Caius conceived a great disgust for the captain. He felt pretty well convinced also that he was no favourite with O'Shea. He would have liked much to ask if Madame Le Maître liked her husband, but if his own refinement had not forbidden, he had a wholesome idea that O'Shea, if roused, would be a dangerous enemy.

"I don't understand why, if she is married, she wears the dress of a religious order."

"Never saw a nun dressed jist like her. Guess if you went about kissing and embracing these women ye would find it an advantage to be pretty well covered up; but"—here a long time of puffing at the pipe—"it's an advantage for more than women not to see too much of an angel."

"Has she any relations, anyone of her own family? Where do they live?"

There was no answer.

"I suppose you knew her people?"

O'Shea sprang up and opened the house door, and the snow drove in as he held it.

"I thought," he said, "I heard a body knocking."

"No one knocked," said Caius impatiently.

"I heard someone." He stood looking very suspiciously out, and so good was his acting, if it was acting, that Caius, who came and looked over his shoulder, had a superstitious feeling when he saw the blank, untrodden snow stretching wide and white into the glimmering night. He remembered that the one relative he believed the lady to have had appeared to him in strange places and vanished strangely.

"You didn't hear a knock; you were dreaming." Caius began to button on his coat.

"I wasn't even asleep." O'Shea gave a last suspicious look to the outside.

"O'Shea," said Caius, "has—has Madame Le Maître a daughter?"

The farmer turned round to him in astonishment. "Bless my heart alive, no!"

The snow was only two or three inches deep when Caius walked home; it was light as plucked swan's-down about his feet. Everywhere it was falling slowly in small dry flakes. There was little wind to make eddies in it. The waning moon had not yet risen, but the landscape, by reason of its whiteness, glimmered just visible to the sight.

CHAPTER 12. THE MAIDEN INVENTED

The fishing-boats and small schooners were dragged high up on the beach. The ice formed upon the bay that lay in the midst of the islands. The carpet of snow grew more and more thick upon field and hill, and where the dwarf firwoods grew so close that it could not pass between their branches, it draped them, fold above fold, until one only saw the green here and there standing out from the white garment.

In these days a small wooden sleigh was given to Caius, to which he might harness his horse, and in which he might sit snug among oxskins if he preferred that sort of travelling to riding. Madame Le Maître still rode, and Caius discarded his sleigh and rode also.

Missing the warmth of the skins, he was soon compelled by the cold to copy Robinson Crusoe and make himself breeches and leggings of the hides.

In these first weeks one hope was always before his eyes. In every new house which he entered, at every turn of the roads, which began to be familiar to him, he hoped to see the maiden who had followed him upon the beach. He dreamed of her by night; he not only hoped, he expected to see her each day. It was of course conceivable that she might have returned to some other island of the group; but Caius did not believe this, because he felt convinced she must be under the protection of his friends; and also, since he had arrived the weather had been such that it would have been an event known to all the fishermen if another party had made a journey along the sands. When the snow came the sands were impassable. As soon as the ice on the bay would bear, there would be coming and going, no doubt; but until then Caius had the restful security that she was near him, and that it could not be many days before he saw her. The only flaw in his conclusion was that the fact did not bear it out; he did not see her.

At length it became clear that the maiden was hiding herself. Caius ceased to hope that he would meet her by chance, because he knew he would already have done so if it were not willed otherwise. Then his mind grew restless again, and impatient; he could not even imagine where she could lie hidden, or what possible reason there could be for a life of uncomfortable concealment.

Caius had not allowed either O'Shea or Madame Le Maître to suspect that in his stumble he had involuntarily seen his companion on the midnight journey. He did not think that the sea-maid herself knew that he had seen her there. He might have been tempted now to believe that the vision was some bright illusion, if its reality had not been proved by the fact that Madame Le Maître knew that he had a companion, and that O'Shea had staked much that he should not take that long moonlight walk by her side.

Since the day on which he had become sure that the sea-maid had such close and real connection with human beings that he met every day, he had ceased to have those strange and uncomfortable ideas about her, which, in half his moods, relegated her into the region of freaks practised upon mortals by the denizens of the unseen, or, still farther, into the region of dreams that have no reality. However, now that she had retired again into hiding, this assurance of his was small comfort.

He would have resolutely inquired of Madame Le Maître who it was who had been sent to warn him of danger if need be upon the beach, but that the lady was not one to allow herself willingly to be questioned, and in exciting her displeasure he might lose the only chance of gaining what he sought. Then, too, with the thought of accosting the lady upon this subject there always arose in his mind the remembrance of the brief minute in which, to his own confounding, he had seen the face of the sea-maid in the lady's own face, and a phantom doubt came to him as to whether she were not herself the sea-maid, disfigured and made aged by the wrappings she wore. He did not, however, believe this. He had every reason to refuse the belief; and if he had had no other, this woman's character was enough, it appeared to him, to give the lie to the thought. A more intelligent view concerning that fleeting likeness was that the two women were nearly related to one another, the younger in charge of the elder; and that the younger, who had for some purpose or prank played about in the waters near his home, must have lived in some house there, must have means of communication with the place, and must have acquainted Madame Le Maître with his position when the need of a physician arose. What was so dissatisfying to him was that all this was the merest conjecture, that the lady whom he loved was a person whom he had been obliged to invent in order to explain the appearances that had so charmed him. He had not a shadow of proof of her existence.

The ice became strong, and bridged over the bay that lay within the crescent of islands. All the islands, with their dunes, were covered with snow; the gales which had beaten up the surf lessened in force; and on the long snow-covered beaches there was only a fringe of white breakers upon the edge of a sea that was almost calm.

The first visitor of any importance who came across the bay was the English clergyman. Nearly all the people on Cloud Island were Protestants, in so far as they had any religion. They were not a pious people, but it seemed that this priest had been exceedingly faithful to them in their trouble, and when he had been obliged to close the church for fear of the contagion, had visited them regularly, except in those few weeks between the seasons when the road by the beach had been almost impassable.

Caius was first aware of the advent of this welcome visitor by a great thumping at his door one morning before he had started on his daily round. On opening it, he saw a hardy little man in a fur coat, who held out his hand to him in enthusiastic greeting.

"Well, now, this is what I call being a good boy—a very good boy—to come here to look after these poor folk."

Caius disclaimed the virtue which he did not feel.

"Motives! I don't care anything about motives. The point is to do the right thing. I'm a good boy to come and visit them; you're a good boy to come and cure them. They are not a very grateful lot, I'm sorry to say, but we have nothing to do with that; we're put here to look after them, and what we feel about it, or what they feel about it, is not the question."

He had come into Caius' room, stamping the snow off his big boots. He was a spare, elderly man, with gray hair and bright eyes. His horse and sleigh stood without the door, and the horse jingled its bells continually.

Here was a friend! Caius decided at once to question this man concerning Madame Le Maître, and—that other lady in whose existence he believed.

"The main thing that you want on these islands is nerve," said the clergyman. "It would be no good at all now"—argumentatively—"for the Bishop to send a man here who hadn't nerve. You never know where you'll meet a quicksand, or a hole in the ice. Chubby and I nearly went under this morning and never were seen again. Some of these fellows had been cutting a hole, and—well, we just saw it in time. It would have been the end of us, I can tell you; but then, you see, if you are being a good boy and doing what you're told, that does not matter so much."

It appeared that Chubby was the clergyman's pony. In a short time Caius had heard of various other adventures which she and her master had shared together. He was interested to know if any of them would throw any light upon the remarkable conduct of O'Shea and his friends; but they did not.

"The men about here," he said—"I can't make anything out of them—are they lawless?"

"You see"—in explanatory tone—"if you take a man and expose him to the sea and the wind for half his life, you'll find that he is pretty much asleep the other half. He may walk about with his eyes open, but his brain's pretty much asleep; he's just equal to lounging and smoking. There are just two things these men can do—fish, and gather the stuff from wrecks. They'll make from eight dollars a day at the fishing, and from sixteen to twenty when a wreck's in. They can afford to be idle the rest of the time, and they are gloriously idle."

"Do they ever gather in bands to rob wrecked ships, or for other unlawful purposes?"

"Oh no, not in the least! Oh no, nothing of the kind! They'll steal from a wreck, of course, if they get the chance; but on the sly, not by violence. Their worst sin is independence and self-righteousness. You can't teach the children anything in the schools, for instance, for the parents won't have them punished; they are quite sure that their children never do anything wrong. That comes of living so far out of the world, and getting their living so easily. I can tell you, Utopia has a bad effect on character."

Caius let the matter go for that time; he had the prospect of seeing the clergyman often.

Another week, when the clergyman had come to the island and Caius met him by chance, they had the opportunity of walking up a long snowy hill together, leading their horses. Caius asked him then about Madame Le Maître and O'Shea, and heard a plain consecutive tale of their lives and of their coming to the island, which denuded the subject of all unknown elements and appeared to rob it of special interest.

Captain Le Maître, it appeared, had a life-long lease of the property on Cloud Island, and also some property on the mainland south of Gaspé Basin; but the land was worth little except by tillage, and, being a seaman, he neglected it. His father had had the land before him. Pembroke, the clergyman, had seen his father. He had never happened to see the son, who would now be between forty and fifty years of age; but when Madame Le Maître had come to look after the farm on Cloud Island, she had made herself known to him as in charge of her husband's affairs. She found that she could not get the land worked by the islanders, and had induced O'Shea, who it seemed was an old farm hand of her own father's, to settle upon this farm, which was a richer one than the one he had had upon the mainland. The soil of the islands, Pembroke said, was in reality exceedingly rich, but in no case had it ever been properly worked, and he was in hopes that now Madame Le Maître might produce a model farm, which would be of vast good in showing the islanders how much they lost by their indifferent manner of treating their land.

"Why did she come to the islands?"

"Conscientiousness, I think. The land here was neglected; the people here certainly present a field white to harvest to anyone who has the missionary spirit."

"Is she—is she very devout?" asked Caius.

"Well, yes, in her own way she is—mind, I say in her own way. I couldn't tell you, now, whether she is Protestant or Papist; I don't believe she knows herself."

"He that sitteth between two stools——" suggested Caius, chiefly for want of something to say.

"Well, no, I wouldn't say that. Bless you! the truest hearts on God's earth don't trouble about religious opinions; they have got the essential oil expressed out of them, and that's all they want."

To Caius this subject of the lady's religion appeared a matter in which he had no need to take interest, but the other went on:

"She was brought up in a convent, you know—a country convent somewhere on the Gaspé coast, and, from what she tells me, the nuns had the good policy to make her happy. She tells me that where the convent gardens abutted on the sea, she and her fellows used to be allowed to fish and row about. You see, her mother had been a Catholic, and the father, being an old miser, had money, so I suppose the sisters thought they could make a nun of her; and very likely they would have done, for she is just that sort, but the father stopped that little game by making her marry before he died."

"I always had an idea that the people on the coast up there were all poor and quite uneducated."

"Well, yes, for the most part they are pretty much what you would see on these islands; but our Bishop tells me that, here and there, there are excellent private houses, and the priests' houses and the convents are tolerably well off. But, to tell you the truth, I think this lady's father had some education, and his going to that part of the country may be accounted for by what she told me once about her mother. Her mother was a dancer, a ballet-dancer, a very estimable and pious woman, her daughter says, and I have no doubt it is true; but an educated man who makes that sort of marriage, you know, may prefer to live out of the world."

Caius was becoming interested.

"If she has inherited her mother's strength and lightness, that explains how she gets on her horse. By Jove! I never saw a woman jump on a horse without help as she does."

"Just so; she has marvellous strength and endurance, and the best proof of that, is the work she is doing nowadays. Why, with the exception of three days that she came to see my wife, and would have died if she hadn't, she has worked night and day among these sick people for the last six months. She came to see my wife pretty much half dead, but the drive on the sand and a short rest pretty well set her up again."

Pembroke drifted off here into discourse about the affairs of his parish, which comprised all the Protestant inhabitants of the island. His voice went on in the cheerful, jerky, matter-of-fact tone in which he always talked. Caius did not pay much heed, except that admiration for the sweet spirit of the man and for the pluck and hardihood with which he carried on his work, grew in him in spite of his heedlessness, for there was nothing that Pembroke suspected less than that he himself was a hero.

"Pretty tough work you have of it," said Caius at last; "if it was only christening and marrying and burying them all, you would have more than enough to do, with the distances so great."

"Oh, bless you! my boy, yes; it's the distance and the weather; but what are we here for but to do our work? Life isn't long, any way, but I'll tell you what it is—a man needs to know the place to know what he can do and what he can't. Now, the Bishop comes over for a week in summer—I don't know a finer man than our Bishop anywhere; he doesn't give himself much rest, and that's a fact; but they've sent him out from England, and what does he know about these islands? He said to me that he wanted me to have morning service every Sunday, as I have it at Harbour Island, and service every Sunday afternoon here on The Cloud."

"He might as well have suggested that you had morning service on the Magdalens, afternoon service in Newfoundland, and evening service in Labrador."

"Exactly, just as possible, my boy; but they had the diphtheria here, so I couldn't bring him over, even in fair weather, to see how he liked the journey."

All this time Caius was cudgelling his brains to know how to bring the talk back to Madame Le Maître, and he ended by breaking in with an abrupt inquiry as to how old she was.

A slight change came over Pembroke's demeanour. It seemed to Caius that his confidential tone lapsed into one of suspicious reserve.

"Not very old"—dryly.

Caius perceived that he was being suspected of taking an undue interest in the bene-factress of the island. The idea, when it came from another, surprised him.

"Look here! I don't take much interest in Madame Le Maître, except that she seems a saint and I'd like to please her; but what I want to know is this—there is a girl who is a sister, or niece, or daughter, or some other relation of hers, who is on these islands. Who is she, and where is she?"

"Do you mean any of the girls she has in her house? She took them from families upon the island only for the sake of training them."

"I don't mean any of those girls!"—this with emphasis.

"I don't know who you mean."

Caius turned and faced him. Do what he would, he could not hide his excited interest.

"You surely must know. It is impossible that there should be a girl, young, beautiful and refined, living somewhere about here, and you not know."

"I should say so—quite impossible."

"Then, be kind enough to tell me who she is. I have an important reason for asking."

"My dear boy, I would tell you with all the pleasure in the world if I knew."

"I have seen her." Caius spoke in a solemn voice.

The priest looked at him with evident interest and curiosity. "Well, where was she, and who was she?"

"You must know: you are in Madame Le Maître's confidence; you travel from door to door, day in and day out; you know everybody and everything upon these islands."

"I assure you," said the priest, "that I never heard of such a person."

CHAPTER 13. WHITE BIRDS; WHITE SNOW; WHITE THOUGHTS

By degrees Caius was obliged to give up his last lingering belief in the existence of the lady he loved. It was a curious position to be in, for he loved her none the less. Two months of work and thought for the diseased people had slipped away, and by the mere lapse of time, as well as by every other proof, he had come to know that there was no maiden in any way connected with Madame Le Maître who answered to the visions he had seen, or who might be wooed by the man who had ceased to care for all other women for her sweet sake.

After Caius had arrived the epidemic had become worse, as it had been prophesied it would, when the people began to exclude the winter air from their houses. In almost every family upon the little isle there was a victim, and Caius, under the compelling force of the orders which Madame Le Maître never gave and the wishes she never expressed, became nurse as well as doctor, using what skill he had in every possible office for the sick, working early and late, and many a time the night through. It was not a time to prattle of the sea-maid to either Madame Le Maître or O'Shea, who both of them worked at his side in the battle against death, and were, Caius verily believed, more heroic and successful combatants than himself. Some solution concerning his lady-love there must be, and Caius neither forgot nor gave up his intention of probing the lives of these two to discover what he wished; but the foreboding that the discovery would work him no weal made it the easier to lay the matter aside and wait. They were all bound in the same icy prison; he could afford patience.

The question of the hospital had been solved in this way. Madame Le Maître had taken O'Shea and his wife and children to live with her, and such patients as could be persuaded or forced into hospital were taken to his house and nursed there. Then, also, as the disease became more prevalent, people who had thus far refused all sanitary measures, in dire fear opened their doors, and allowed Caius and O'Shea to enter with whitewash brushes and other means of disinfection.

Caius was successful in this, that, in proportion to the number of people who were taken ill, the death-rate was only one third of what it had been before he came. He and his fellow-workers were successful also in a more radical way, for about the end of January it was suddenly observed among them that there were no new cases of illness. The ill and the weak gradually recovered. In a few more weeks the Angels of Death and Disease retired from the field, and the island was not depopulated. Whether another outbreak might or might not occur they could not tell; but knowing the thoroughness of the work which they had done, they were ready to hope that the victory was complete. Gradually their work ceased, for there was no one in all the happy island who needed nursing or medical attendance. Caius found then how wonderfully free the place was from all those ailments which ordinarily beset humanity.

This was in the middle of February, when the days were growing long, and even the evening was bright and light upon the islands of snow and the sea of ice.

It appeared to Caius that Madame Le Maître had grown years older during the pestilence. Deep lines of weariness had come in her face, and her eyes were heavy with want of sleep and sympathetic tears. Again and again he had feared that the disease would attack her, and, indeed, he knew that it had only been the constant riding about the island hills in the wonderful air that had kept the little band of workers in health. As it was, O'Shea had lost a child, and three of the girls in the house of Madame Le Maître had been ill. Now that the strain was over, Caius feared prostration that would be worse than the disease itself for the lady who had kept up so bravely through it all; but, ever feeling an impossibility in her presence of speaking freely of anything that concerned herself, he had hardly been able to express the solicitude he felt before it was relieved by the welcome news that she had travelled across the bay to pay a visit to Pembroke's wife.

She had gone without either telling Caius of her intention or bidding him good-bye, and, glad as he was, he felt that he had not deserved this discourtesy at her hands. Indeed, looking back now, he felt disposed to resent the indifference with which she had treated him from first to last. Not as the people's doctor. In that capacity she had been eager for his services, and grateful to him with a speechless, reverent gratitude that he felt to be much more than his due; but as a man, as a companion, as a friend, she had been simply unconscious of his existence. When she had said to him at the beginning, "You will be lonely; there is no one on the island to whom you can speak as a friend," he perceived now that she had excluded herself as well as the absent world from his companionship. It seemed to him that it had never once occurred to her that it was in her power to alter this.

Truly, if it had not been for Pembroke, the clergyman, Caius would never have had a companionable word; and he had found that there were limits to the interest he could take in Pembroke, that the stock of likings and disliking that they had in common was not great. Then, too, since the day on which he had questioned him so vehemently about the relatives of Madame Le Maître, he fancied that the clergyman had treated him with apprehensive reserve.

At the time when he had little or nothing to do, and when Madame Le Maître had left Cloud Island, Caius would have been glad enough to go and explore the other islands, or to luxuriate again in the cookery of the old maids at the inn at which he had first been housed. Two considerations kept him from this holiday-taking. In the first place, in fear of a case of illness he did not like to leave the island while its benefactress was away; and, secondly, it was reported that all visitors from The Cloud were ruthlessly shut out from the houses upon the other islands, because of the unreasoning terror which had grown concerning the disease. Whether he, who carried money in his pocket, would be shut out from these neighbouring islands also, he did not care to inquire. He felt too angry with the way the inhabitants behaved to have any dealings with them.

The only means of amusement that remained to Caius in these days were his horse and a gun that O'Shea lent him. With his lunch in his pocket, he rode upon the ice as far as he might go and return the same day. He followed the roads that led by the shores of the other islands; or, where the wind had swept all depth of snow from the ice, he took a path according to his own fancy on the untrodden whiteness.

Colonies of Arctic gulls harboured on the island, and the herring gulls remained through the winter; these, where he could get near their rocks upon the ice, he at first took delight in shooting; but he soon lost the zest for this sport, for the birds gave themselves to his gun too easily. He was capable of deriving pleasure from them other than in their slaughter, and often he rode under their rocky homes, noting how dark their white plumage looked against their white resting-places, where groups of them huddled together upon the icy battlements and snowdrift towers of the castles that the frost had built them. He would ride by slowly, and shoot his gun in the air to see them rise and wheel upward, appearing snow-white against the blue firmament; and watched them sink again, growing dark as they alighted among the snow and ice. His warning that he himself must be nearing home was to see the return of such members of the bird-colony as had been out for the deep-sea fishing. When he saw them come from afar, flying high, often with their wings dyed pink in the sunset rays, he knew that his horse must gallop homeward, or darkness might come and hide such cracks and fissures in the ice as were dangerous.

The haunts of the birds which he chiefly loved were on the side of the islands turned to the open sea, for at this time ice had formed on all sides, and stretched without a break for a mile or so into the open. There was a joy in riding upon this that made riding upon the bay tame and uninteresting; for not only was the seaward shore of island and dune wilder, but the ice here might at any time break from the shore or divide itself up into large islands, and when the wind blew he fancied he heard the waves heaving beneath it, and the excitement which comes with danger, which, by some law of mysterious nature, is one of the keenest forms of pleasure, would animate his horse and himself as they flew over it.

His horse was not one of the native ponies; it was a well-bred, delicately-shaped beast, accustomed to be made a friend of by its rider, and giving sympathetic response to all his moods. The horse belonged to Madame Le Maître, and was similar to the one she rode. This, together with many other things, proved to Caius that the lady who lived so frugally had command of a certain supply of money, for it could not be an easy or cheap thing to transport good horses to these islands.

Whatever he did, however his thoughts might be occupied, it was never long before they veered round to the subject that was rapidly becoming the one subject of absorbing interest to him. Before he realized what he did, his mind was confirmed in its habit; at morn, and at noontime, and at night, he found himself thinking of Madame Le Maître. The lady he was in love with was the youthful, adventurous maiden who, it seemed, did not exist; the lady that he was always thinking of was the grave, subdued, self-sacrificing woman who in some way, he knew not how, carried the mystery of the other's existence within herself. His mind was full of almost nothing but questions concerning her, for, admire and respect her as he might, he thought there was nothing in him that responded with anything like love to her grave demeanour and burdened spirit.

CHAPTER 14. THE MARRIAGE SCENE

By riding across the small lagoon that lay beside Cloud Island to the inward side of the bay, and then eastward some twelve miles toward an island that was little frequented, the last of the chain on this horn of the crescent, one came under the highest and boldest façade of cliffs that was to be found in all that group. It was here that Caius chanced to wander one calm mild day in early March, mild because the thermometer stood at less than 30° below the freezing point, and a light vault of pearly cloud shut in the earth from the heaven, and seemed, by way of contrast with other days, to keep it warm. He had ridden far, following out of aimless curiosity the track that had been beaten on the side of the bay to this farthest island. It was a new road for him; he had never attempted it before; and no sooner had he got within good sight of the land, than his interest was wholly attracted by the cliffs, which, shelving somewhat outward at the top, and having all their sides very steep and smooth, were, except for a few crevices of ice, or an outward hanging icicle, or here and there a fringe of icicles, entirely free from snow and ice. He rode up under them wonderingly, pleased to feast his eyes upon the natural colour of rock and earth, and eager, with what knowledge of geology he had, to read the story they told.

This story, as far as the history of the earth was concerned, was soon told; the cliffs were of gray carboniferous limestone. Caius became interested in the beauty of their colouring. Blue and red clay had washed down upon them in streaks and patches; where certain faults in the rock occurred, and bars of iron-yielding stone were seen, the rust had washed down also, so that upon flat facets and concave and convex surfaces a great variety of colour and tint, and light and shade, was produced.

He could not proceed immediately at the base of the cliffs, for in their shelter the snow had drifted deep. He was soon obliged to keep to the beaten track, which here ran about a quarter of a mile distant from the rock. Walking his horse, and looking up as he went, his attention was arrested by perceiving that a whitish stain on a smooth dark facet of the rock assumed the appearance of a white angel in the act of alighting from aërial flight. The picture grew so distinct that he could not take his eyes from it, even after he had gone past, until he was quite weary of looking back or of trying to keep his restive horse from dancing forward. When, at last, however, he turned his eyes from the majestic figure with the white wings, his fancy caught at certain lines and patches of rust which portrayed a horse of gigantic size galloping upon a forward part of the cliff. The second picture brought him to a standstill, and he examined the whole face of the hill, realizing that he was in the presence of a picture-gallery which Nature, it seemed, had painted all for her own delight. He thought himself the discoverer; he felt at once both a loneliness and elation at finding himself in that frozen solitude, gazing with fascinated eyes at one portion of the rock after another where he saw, or fancied he saw, sketches of this and that which ravished his sense of beauty both in colour and form.

In his excitement to see what would come next, he did not check the stepping of his horse, but only kept it to a gentle pace. Thus he came where the road turned round with the rounding cliff, and here for a bit he saw no picture upon the rock; but still he looked intently, hoping that the panorama was not ended, and only just noticed that there was another horse beside his own within the lonely scene. In some places here the snow was drifted high near the track; in others, both the road and the adjoining tracts of ice were swept by the wind almost bare of snow. He soon became aware that the horse he had espied was not upon the road. Then, aroused to curiosity, he turned out of his path and rode through shallow snow till he came close to it.

The horse was standing quite still, and its rider was standing beside it, one arm embracing its neck, and with head leaning back against the creature's glossy shoulder. The person thus standing was Madame Le Maître, and she was looking up steadfastly at the cliffs, of which this point in the road displayed a new expanse.

So silently had the horse of Caius moved in the muffling snow that, coming up on the other side, he was able to look at the lady for one full moment before she saw him, and in that moment and the next he saw that the sight of him robbed her face of the peace which had been written there. She was wrapped as usual in her fur-lined cloak and hood. She looked to him inquiringly, with perhaps just a touch of indignant displeasure in her expression, waiting for him to explain, as if he had come on purpose to interrupt her.

"I am sorry. I had no idea you were here, or I would not have come."

The next moment he marvelled at himself as to how he had known that this was the right thing to say; for it did not sound polite.

Her displeasure was appeased.

"You have found my pictures, then," she said simply.

"Only this hour, and by chance."

By this time he was wondering by what road she had got there. If she had ridden alone across the bay from Harbour Island, where the Pembrokes lived, she had done a bold thing for a woman, and one, moreover, which, in the state of health in which he had seen her last, would have been impossible to her.

Madame Le Maître had begun to move slowly, as one who wakes from a happy dream. He perceived that she was making preparations to mount.

"I cannot understand it," he cried; "how can these pictures come just by chance? I have heard of the Picture Rocks on Lake Superior, for instance, but I never conceived of anything so distinct, so lovely, as these that I have seen."

"The angels make them," said Madame Le Maître. She paused again (though her bridle had been gathered in her hand ready for the mount), and looked up again at the rock.

Caius was not unheedful of the force of that soft but absolute assertion, but he must needs speak, if he spoke at all, from his own point of view, not hers.

"I suppose," he said, "that the truth is there is something upon the rock that strikes us as a resemblance, and our imagination furnishes the detail that perfects the picture."

"In that case would you not see one thing and I another?"

Now for the first time his eyes followed hers, and on the gray rock immediately opposite he suddenly perceived a picture, without definite edge it is true, but in composition more complete than anything he had seen before. What had formerly deligh[...] been, as it were, mere sketches of one thing or another scattered in different p[...] here there was a large group of figures, painted for the most part in varied tints[...] and blue, and pink.

In the foreground of this picture a young man and young woman, radiant both in[...] and apparel, stood before a figure draped in priestly garments of sober gray. Behind the[...] in a vista, which seemed to be filled with an atmosphere of light and joy, a band of figures[...] were dancing in gay procession, every line of the limbs and of the light draperies suggesting motion and glee. How did he know that some of these were men, and some were women? He had never seen such dresses as they wore, which seemed to be composed of tunics and gossamer veils of blue and red. Yet he did know quite distinctly which were men and which were women, and he knew that it was a marriage scene. The bride wore a wreath of flowers; the bridegroom carried a sheaf or garland of fruit or grain, which seemed to be a part of the ceremony. Caius thought he was about to offer it to the priest.

For some minutes the two looked up at the rock quite silently. Now the lady answered his last remark:

"What is it you see?"

"You know it best; tell me what it is."

"It is a wedding. Don't you see the wedding dance?"

He had not got down from his horse; he had a feeling that if he had alighted she would have mounted. He tried now, leaning forward, to tell her how clearly he had seen the meaning, if so it might be called, of the natural fresco, and to find some words adequately to express his appreciation of its beauty. He knew that he had not expressed himself well, but she did not seem dissatisfied at the tribute he paid to a thing which she evidently regarded with personal love.

"Do you think," she said, "that it will alter soon, or become defaced? It has been just the same for a year. It might, you know, become defaced any day, and then no one would have seen it but ourselves. The islanders, you know, do not notice it."

"Ah, yes," said Caius; "beauty is made up of two parts—the objects seen and the understanding eye. We only know how much we are indebted to training and education when we find out to what extent the natural eye is blind."

This remark did not seem to interest her. He felt that it jarred somehow, and that she was wishing him away.

"But why," he asked, "should angels paint a marriage? They neither marry——" He stopped, feeling that she might think him flippant if he quoted the text.

"Because it is the best thing to paint," she said.

"How the best?"

"Well, just the best human thing: everyone knows that."

"Has her marriage been so gloriously happy?" said Caius to himself as the soft assurance of her tones reached his ears, and for some reason or other he felt desolate, as a soul might upon whom the door of paradise swung shut. Then irritably he said: "*I* don't know it. Most marriages seem to me——" He stopped, but she had understood.

"But if this picture crumbles to pieces, that does not alter the fact that the angels made it lovely." (Her slight accent, because it made the pronunciation of each word more careful, gave her speech a quaint suggestion of instruction that perhaps she did not intend.)

ırts in just the same way; it is the best thing we can think of,

t is the best from our point of view, you will allow that it
institution. The angels should try to teach us to look at

...it. I don't believe there is anything higher for us. I don't
...rried in heaven."

...ireason she set aside authority when it clashed with her opinion. To
...had never been so attractive as now, when, for the first time to him, she was
...ving herself of kin to ordinary folk; and yet, so curiously false are our notions of saint-
hood that she seemed to him the less devout because she proved to be more loving.

"You see"—she spoke and paused—"you see, when I was at school in a convent I had
a friend. I was perfectly happy when I was with her and she with me; it was a marriage.
When we went in the garden or on the sea, we were only happy when we were with each
other. That is how I learned early that it is only perfect to be two. Ah, when one knows
what it is to be lonely, one learns that that is true; but many people are not given grace to
be lonely—they are sufficient to themselves. They say it is enough to worship God; it is a
lie. He cannot be pleased; it is selfish even to be content to worship God alone."

"The kind of marriage you think of, that perhaps may be made in heaven." Caius was
feeling again that she was remote from him, and yet the hint of passionate loneliness in
tone and words remained a new revelation of her life. "Is not religion enough?" He asked
this only out of curiosity.

"It is not true religion if we are content to be alone with God; it is not the religion of the
holy Christ; it is a fancy, a delusion, a mistake. Have you not read about St. John? Ah, I do
not say that it is not often right to live alone, just as it may be right to be ill or starving.
That is because the world has gone wrong; and to be content, it is to blaspheme; it is like
saying that what is wrong is God's ideal for us, and will last for ever."

Caius was realizing that as she talked she was thinking only of the theme, not at all of
him; he had enough refinement in him to perceive this quite clearly. It was the first time
that she had spoken of her religion to him, and her little sermon, which he felt to be too
wholly unreasonable to appeal to his mind, was yet too wholly womanly to repel his
heart.

Some dreamy consciousness seemed to come to her now that she had tarried longer
than she wished, and perhaps that her subject had not been one that she cared to discuss
with him. She turned and put her hand on the pommel, and sprang into the saddle. He
had often seen her make that light, wonderful spring that seated her as if by magic on her
horse's back, but in her last weeks of nursing the sick folk she had not been strong enough
to do it. He saw now how much stronger she looked. The weeks of rest had made her a
different woman; there was a fresh colour in her cheek, and the tired lines were all gone.
She looked younger by years than when he saw her last—younger, too, than when he had
first seen her, for even then she was weary. If he could only have seen the line of her chin,
or the height of her brow, or the way her hair turned back from her temples, he thought
that he might not have reckoned the time when he had first seen her in the sick-room at
Cloud Island as their first meeting.

"You are going on?" said Madame Le Maître.

"Unless I can be of service to you by turning with you."

He knew by the time of day that he must turn shortly; but he had no hope that she wanted him to go with her.

"You can do me more service," she said, and she gave him a little smile that was like the ghost of the sea-maid's smile, "by letting me go home alone."

He rode on, and when he looked back he saw that her horse was galloping and casting up a little cloud of light snow behind it, so that, riding as it were upon a small white cloud, she disappeared round the turn of the cliffs.

Caius found no more pictures that day that he felt to be worthy of much attention. He went back to the festive scene of the marriage, and moving his horse nearer and further from it, he found that only from the point where the lady had taken her stand was it to be distinctly seen. Twenty yards from the right line of vision, he might have passed it, and never known the beauty that the streaks and stains could assume.

When he went home he amused himself by seeking on the road for the track of the other horse, and when he found that it turned to Cloud Island he was happier. The place, at least, would not be so lonely when the lady was at home.

BOOK III

CHAPTER I. HOW HE HUNTED THE SEALS

At this time on the top of the hills the fishermen were to be seen loitering most of the day, looking to see if the seals were coming, for at this season the seals, unwary creatures, come near the islands upon the ice, and in the white world their dark forms can be descried a long distance off. There was promise of an easy beginning to seal-fishing this year, for the ice had not yet broken from the shore on the seaward side of the island, and there would not at first be need of boats.

Caius, who had only seen the fishermen hanging about their doors in lazy idleness, was quite unprepared for the excitement and vigour that they displayed when this first prey of the year was seen to approach.

It was the morning after Madame Le Maître had returned to her home that Caius, standing near his own door, was wondering within himself if he might treat her like an ordinary lady and give her a formal call of welcome. He had not decided the point when he heard sounds as of a mob rushing, and, looking up the road that came curving down the hill through the pine thicket, he saw the rout appear—men, women and children, capped and coated in rough furs, their cheeks scarlet with the frost and exercise, their eyes sparkling with delight. Singly down the hill, and in groups, they came, hand-in-hand or arm-in-arm, some driving in wooden sleighs, some of them beating such implements of tinware as might be used for drums, some of them shouting words in that queer Acadian French he could not understand, and all of them laughing.

He could not conceive what had happened; the place that was usually so lonely, the people that had been so lazy and dull—everything within sight seemed transformed into some mad scene of carnival. The crowd swept past him, greeting him only with shouts and smiles and grimaces. He knew from the number that all the people from that end of the island were upon the road to the other end, and running after with hasty curiosity, he went far enough to see that the news of their advent had preceded them, and that from every side road or wayside house the people came out to join in the riotous march.

Getting further forward upon the road, Caius now saw what he could not see from his own door, a great beacon fire lit upon the hill where the men had been watching. Its flame and smoke leaped up from the white hill into the blue heaven. It was the seal-hunting, then, to which all the island was going forth. Caius, now that he understood the tumult, experienced almost the same excitement. He ran back, donned clothes suitable for the hunt across the ice, and, mounting his horse, rode after the people. They were all bound for the end of the island on which the lighthouse stood, for a number of fish-sheds, used for cooking and sleeping in the fishing season, were built on the western shore not far from the light; and from the direction in which the seals had appeared, these were the sheds most convenient for the present purpose.

By the time Caius reached the sheds, the greater number of the fishermen were already far out upon the ice. In boots and caps of the coarse gray seal-skin, with guns or clubs and knives in their hands, they had a wild and murderous aspect as they marched forward in little bands. The gait, the very figure, of each man seemed changed; the slouch of idleness had given place to the keen manner of the hunter. On shore the sheds, which all winter had been empty and lonely, surrounded only by curling drifts, had become the scene of most vigorous work. The women, with snow-shovels and brooms, were clearing away the snow around them, opening the doors, lighting fires in the small stoves inside, opening bags and hampers which contained provision of food and implements for skinning the seals. The task that these women were performing was one for the strength of men; but as they worked now their merriment was loud. All their children stood about them, shouting at play or at such work as was allotted to them. Some four or five of the women, with Amazonian strength, were hauling from one shed a huge kettle, in which it was evidently meant to try the fat from certain portions of the seal.

Caius held his horse still upon the edge of the ice, too well diverted with the activity on the shore to leave it at once. Behind the animated scene and the row of gray snow-thatched sheds, the shore rose white and lonely. Except for the foot-tracks on the road by which they had come, and the peak of the lighthouse within sight, it would have seemed that a colony had suddenly sprung to life in an uninhabited Arctic region.

It was from this slope above the sheds that Caius now heard himself hailed by loud shouting, and, looking up, he saw that O'Shea had come there to overlook the scene below. Some women stood around him. Caius supposed that Madame Le Maître was there.

O'Shea made a trumpet of his hands and shouted that Caius must not take his horse upon the ice that day, for the beast would be frightened and do himself harm.

Caius was affronted. The horse was not his, truly, but he believed he knew how to take care of it, yet, as it belonged to a woman, he could not risk disobeying this uncivil prohibition. Although he was accustomed to the rude authority which O'Shea assumed whenever he wished to be disagreeable, Caius had only learned to take it with an outward appearance of indifference—his mind within him always chafed; this time the affront to his vanity was worse because he believed that Madame Le Maître had prompted, or certainly permitted, the insult. It did not soothe him to think that, with a woman's nervousness, she might have more regard for his safety than that of the horse. The brightness died out of the beautiful day, and in a lofty mood of ill-used indifference he assured himself that a gentleman could take little interest in such barbarous sport as seal-hunting. At any rate, it would go on for many a day. He certainly had not the slightest intention of dismounting at O'Shea's command in order to go to the hunt.

Caius held his horse as quiet as he could for some ten minutes, feigning an immense interest in the occupation of the women; then leisurely curvetted about, and set his horse at a light trot along the ice close by the shore.

He rode hastily past the only place where he could have ascended the bank, and after that he had no means of going home until he had rounded the island and returned by the lagoon. The distance up to the end was seven miles. Caius rode on under the lonely cliffs where the gulls wintered, and threading his way upon smooth places on the ice, came, in the course of not much more than an hour, up to the end of the cliffs, crossed the neck of the sand-bar, and followed the inward shore till he got back to the first road.

Now, on this end of the island very few families lived. Caius had only been upon the road he was about to traverse once or twice. The reason it was so little built upon was that the land here belonged entirely to the farm of Madame Le Maître, which stretched in a narrow strip for a couple of miles from O'Shea's dwelling to the end of the island. The only point of interest which this district had for Caius was a cottage which had been built in a very sheltered nook for the accommodation of two women, whose business it was to care for the poultry which was kept here. Caius had been told that he might always stop at this lodge for a drink of milk or beer or such a lunch as it could afford, and being thirsty by reason of hard riding and ill-temper, he now tried to find the path that led to it.

CHAPTER 2. ONCE MORE THE VISION

When Caius turned up the farm road, which was entirely sheltered between gentle slopes, the bright March sun felt almost hot upon his cheek. The snow road under his horse's hoofs was full of moisture, and the snowy slopes glistened with a coating of wet. He felt for the first time that the spring of the year had come.

He was not quite certain where lay the cottage of which he was in quest; and, by turning up a wrong path, he came to the back of its hen-houses. At first he only saw the blank wall of a cowshed and two wooden structures like old-fashioned dovecotes, connected by a high fence in which there was no gate. Up to this fence he rode to look over it, hoping to speak to the people he heard within; but it was too high for him to see over. Passing on, he brought his head level with a small window that was let into the wall of one of the hen-houses. The window had glass in it which was not at all clean, but a fragment of it was broken, and through this Caius looked, intending to see if there was any gate into the yard which he could reach from the path he was on.

Through the small room of deserted hen-roosts, through the door which was wide open on the other side, he saw the sunny space of the yard beyond. All the fowls were gathered in an open place that had been shovelled between heaps of hard-packed snow. There were the bright tufts of cocks' tails and the glossy backs of hens brown and yellow; there were white ducks, and ducks that were green and black, and great gray geese of slender make that were evidently descended from the wild goose of the region. On the snow-heaps pigeons were standing—flitting and constantly alighting—with all the soft dove-colours in their dress. In front of the large feathered party was a young woman who stood, basin in hand, scattering corn, now on one side, now on another, with fitful caprice.

She made game of the work of feeding them, coquettishly pretending to throw the boon where she did not throw it, laughing the while and talking to the birds, as if she and they led the same life and talked the same language. Caius could not hear what she said, but he felt assured that the birds could understand.

For some few minutes Caius looked at this scene; he did not know how long he looked; his heart within him was face to face with a pain that was quite new in his life, and was so great that he could not at first understand it, but only felt that in comparison all smaller issues of life faded and became as nothing.

Beyond the youthful figure of the corn-giver Caius saw another woman. It was the wife of O'Shea, and in a moment her steadfast, quiet face looked up into his, and he knew that she saw him and did not tell of his presence; but, as her eyes looked long and mutely into his, it seemed to him that this silent woman understood something of the pain he felt. Then, very quietly, he turned his horse and rode back by the path that he had come.

The woman he had seen was the wife of the sea-captain Le Maître. He said it to himself as if to be assured that the self within him had not in some way died, but could still speak and understand. He knew that he had seen the wife of this man, because the old cloak and hood, which he knew so well, had only been cast off, and were still hanging to the skirts below the girlish waist, and the white cap, too, had been thrown aside upon the snow—he had seen it. As for the girl herself, he had loved her so long that it seemed strange to him that he had never known until now how much he loved her. Her face had been his one thought, his one standard of womanly beauty, for so many years that he was amazed to find that he had never known before how beautiful she was. A moment since and he had seen the March sunshine upon all the light, soft rings of curling hair that covered her head, and he had seen her laughter, and the oval turn of the dimpled chin, and within the face he had seen what he knew now he had always seen, but never before so clearly—the soul that was strong to suffer as well as strong to enjoy.

By the narrow farm-path which his horse was treading Caius came to the road he had left, and, turning homeward, could not help coming in front of the little cottage whose back wall he had so lately visited. He had no thought but of passing as quickly as might be, but he saw O'Shea's wife standing before the door, looking for him with her quiet, eager eyes. She came out a few steps, and Caius, hardly stopping, stooped his head to hear what she had to say.

"I won't tell her," said the woman; then she pleaded: "Let her be, poor thing! Let her be happy while she can."

She had slipped back into the house; Caius had gone on; and then he knew that he had this new word to puzzle over. For why should he be supposed to molest the happy hours of the woman he loved, and what could be the sorrow that dogged her life, if her happy hours were supposed to be rare and precious? O'Shea's wife he had observed before this to be a faithful and trusted friend of her mistress; no doubt she spoke then with the authority of knowledge and love.

Caius went home, and put away his horse, and entered his small house. Everything was changed to him; a knowledge that he had vaguely dreaded had come, but with a grief that he had never dreamed of. For he had fancied that if it should turn out that his lady-love and Madame Le Maître were one, his would only be the disappointment of having loved a shadow, a character of his own creating, and that the woman herself he would not love; but now that was not what had befallen him.

All the place was deserted; not a house had shown a sign of life as he passed. All the world had gone after the seals. This, no doubt, was the reason why the two women who had not cared for the hunting had taken that day for a holiday. Caius stood at his window and looked out on the sea of ice for a little while. He was alone in the whole locality, but he would not be less alone when the people returned. They had their interests, their hopes and fears; he had nothing in common with any of them; he was alone with his pain, and his pain was just this, that he was alone. Then he looked out further and further into the world from which he had come, into the world to which he must go back, and there also he saw himself to be alone. He could not endure the thought of sharing the motions of his heart and brain with anyone but the one woman from whom he was wholly separated. Time might make a difference; he was forced to remember that it is commonly said that time and absence abate all such attachments. He did not judge that time would make much difference to him, but in this he might be mistaken.

A man who has depth in him seldom broods over real trouble—not at first, at least. By this test may often be known the real from the fanciful woe. Caius, knew, or his instincts knew, that his only chance of breasting the current was, not to think of its strength, but to keep on swimming. He took his horse's bits and the harness that had been given him for his little sleigh, cleaning and burnishing everything with the utmost care, and at the same time with despatch. He had some chemical work that had been lying aside for weeks waiting to be done, and this afternoon he did it. He had it on his mind to utilize some of his leisure by writing long letters that he might post when it was possible for him to go home; to-night he wrote two of them.

While he was writing he heard the people coming in twos and threes along the road back to their houses for the night. He supposed that O'Shea had got home with the girls he had been escorting, and that his wife had come home, and that Madame Le Maître had come back to her house and taken up again her regular routine of life.

CHAPTER 3. "LOVE, I SPEAK TO THEY FACE"

Caius thought a good deal about the words that O'Shea's wife had said to him. He did not know exactly what she meant, nor could he guess at all from what point of view concerning himself she had spoken; but the general drift of her meaning appeared to be that he ought not to let Madame Le Maître know where and how he had seen her the day before. In spite of this, he knew that he could neither be true to himself, nor to the woman he was forced to meet daily, if he made any disguise of the recognition which had occurred. He was in no hurry to meet her; he hoped little or nothing from the interview, but dreaded it. Next day he went without his horse out to where the men were killing the seals upon the edge of the ice.

The warm March sun, and the March winds that agitated the open sea, were doing their work. To-day there was water appearing in places upon the ice where it joined the shore, and when Caius was out with a large band of men upon the extreme edge of the solid ice, a large fragment broke loose. There were some hundred seals upon this bit of ice, which were being butchered one by one in barbarous fashion, and so busy were the men with their work that they merely looked at the widening passage of gray water and continued to kill the beasts that they had hedged round in a murderous ring. It was the duty of those on the shore to bring boats if they were needed. The fragment on which they were could not float far because the sea outside was full of loose ice, and, as it happened, when the dusk fell the chasm of water between them and the shore was not too broad to be jumped easily, for the ice, having first moved seaward, now moved landward with the tide.

For two or three days Caius lent a hand at killing and skinning the gentle-eyed animals. It was not that he did not feel some disgust at the work; but it meant bread to the men he was with, and he might as well help them. It was an experience, and, above all, it was distraction. When the women had seen him at work they welcomed him with demonstrative joy to the hot meals which they prepared twice a day for the hunters. Caius was not quite sure what composed the soups and stews of which he partook, but they tasted good enough.

When he had had enough of the seal-hunt it took him all the next day to cleanse the clothes he had worn from the smell of the fat, and he felt himself to be effeminate in the fastidiousness that made him do it.

During all these days the houses and roads of the island were almost completely deserted, except that Caius supposed that, after the first holiday, the maids who lived with Madame Le Maître were kept to their usual household tasks, and that their mistress worked with them.

At last, one day when Caius was coming from a house on one of the hills which he had visited because there was in it a little mortal very new to this world, he saw Madame Le Maître riding up the snowy road that he was descending. He felt glad, at the first sight of her, that he was no longer a youth but had fully come to man's estate, and had attained to that command of nerve and conquest over a beating heart that is the normal heritage of manhood. This thought came to him because he was so vividly reminded of the hour in which he had once before sought an interview with this lady—even holding her hand in his—and of his ignominious repulse. In spite of the sadness of his heart, a smile crossed his face, but it was gone before he met her. He had quite given up wondering now about that seafaring episode, and accepted it only as a fact. It did not matter to him why or how she had played her part; it was enough that she had done it, and all that she did was right in his eyes.

The lady's horse was walking slowly up the heavy hill; the reins she hardly held, letting them loose upon its neck. It was evident that with her there was no difference since the time she had last seen Caius; it appeared that she did not even purpose stopping her horse. Caius stopped it gently, laying his hand upon its neck.

"What is it?" she asked, with evident curiosity, for the face that he turned to her made her aware that there was something new in her quiet life.

It was not easy to find his words; he did not care much to do so quickly. "I could not go on," he said, "without letting you know——" He stopped.

She did not answer him with any quick impatient question. She looked at the snowy hill in front of her. "Well?" she said.

"The other day, you know," he said, "I rode by the back of your poultry farm, and—I saw you when you were feeding the birds."

"Yes?" she said; she was still looking gravely enough at the snow. The communication so far did not affect her much.

"Then, when I saw you, I knew that I had seen you before—in the sea—at home."

A red flush had mantled her face. There was perhaps an air of offence, for he saw that she held her head higher, and knew what the turn of the neck would be in spite of the clumsy hood; but what surprised him most was that she did not express any surprise or dismay.

"I did not suppose," she said, in her own gentle, distant way, "that if you had a good memory for that—foolish play, you would not know me again." Her manner added: "I have attempted no concealment."

"I did not know you in that dress you wear"—there was hatred for the dress in his tone as he mentioned it—"so I supposed that you did not expect me to know who you were."

She did not reply, leaving the burden of finding the next words upon him. It would seem that she did not think there was more to say; and this, her supreme indifference to his recognition or non-recognition, half maddened him. He suddenly saw his case in a new aspect—she was a cruel woman, and he had much with which to reproach her.

"'That foolish play,' as you call it——" he had begun angrily, but a certain sympathy for her, new-born out of his own trouble, stopped him, and he went on, only reproach in his tone: "It was a sad play for me, because my heart has never been my own since. I could not find out who you were then, or where you hid yourself; I do not know now, but ——" He stopped; he did not wish to offend her; he looked at the glossy neck of the horse he was holding. "I was young and very foolish, but I loved you."

The sound of his own low sad tones was still in his ears when he also heard the low music of irrepressible laughter, and, looking up, he saw that the recollection which a few minutes before had made him smile had now entirely overcome the lady's gravity. She was blushing, she was trying not to laugh; but in spite of herself she did laugh more and more heartily, and although her merriment was inopportune, he could not help joining in it to some extent. It was so cheerful to see the laughter-loving self appear within the grave face, to be beside her, and to have partnership in her mirth. So they looked in each other's eyes, and they both laughed, and after that they felt better.

"And yet," said he, "it was a frolic that has worked sorrow for me."

"Come," said she, lifting her reins, "you will regret if you go on talking this way."

She would have gone on quite lightly and contentedly, and left him there as if he had said nothing of love, as if their words had been the mere reminiscence of a past that had no result in the present, as if his heart was not breaking; but a fierce sense of this injustice made him keep his hold of her bridle. She could weep over the pains of the poor and the death of their children. She should not go unmindful that his happiness was wrecked.

"Do you still take me for the young muff that I used to be, that you pay no heed to what I say? I would scorn to meet you every day while I must remain here and conceal from you the fact which, such is my weakness, is the only fact in life for me just now. My heart is breaking because I have found that the woman I love is wholly out of my reach. Can you not give that a passing thought of pity? I have told you now; when we meet, you will know that it is not as indifferent acquaintances, but as—enemies if you will, for you, a happy married woman—will count me your enemy! Yet I have not harmed you, and the truth is better at all costs."

She was giving him her full attention now, her lips a little parted as if with surprise, question plainly written upon her face. He could not understand how the cap and hood had ever concealed her from him. Her chief beauty lay, perhaps, in the brow, in the shape of the face, and in its wreath of hair—or at least in the charm that these gave to the strong character of the features; but now that he knew her, he knew her face wholly, and his mind filled in what was lacking; he could perceive no lack. He looked at her, his eyes full of admiration, puzzled the while at her evident surprise.

"But surely," she said, "you cannot be so foolish—you, a man now—to think that the fancy you took to a pretty face, for it could have been nothing more, was of any importance."

"Such fancies make or mar the lives of men."

"Of unprincipled fools, yes—of men who care for appearance more than sympathy. But you are not such a man! It is not as if we had been friends; it is not as if we had ever spoken. It is wicked to call such a foolish fancy by the name of love; it is desecration."

While she was speaking, her words revealed to Caius, with swift analysis, a distinction that he had not made before. He knew now that before he came to this island, before he had gone through the three months of toil and suffering with Josephine Le Maître, it would truly have been foolish to think of his sentiment concerning her as more than a tender ideal. Now, that which had surprised him into a strength of love almost too great to be in keeping with his character, was the unity of two beings whom he had believed to be distinct—the playmate and the saint.

"Whether the liking we take to a beautiful face be base or noble depends, madame, upon the face; and no man could see yours without being a better man for the sight. But think: when I saw the face that had been enshrined for years in my memory yesterday, was it the face of a woman whom I did not know—with whom I had never spoken?" He was not looking at her as he spoke. He added, and his heart was revealed in the tone: "*You* do not know what it is to be shut out from all that is good on earth."

There came no answer; in a moment he lifted his eyes to see what response she gave, and he was astonished to detect a look upon her face that would have become an angel who had received some fresh beatitude. It was plain that now she saw and believed the truth of his love; it appeared, too, that she felt it to be a blessing. He could not understand this, but she wasted no words in explanation. When her eyes met his, the joy in her face passed into pity for a minute; she looked at him quietly and frankly; then she said:

"Love is good in itself, and suffering is good, and God is good. I think," she added very simply, as a child might have done, "that you are good, too. Do not fear or be discouraged."

Then, with her own hand, she gently disengaged his from the bridle and rode up the hill on her errand of mercy.

CHAPTER 4. HOPE BORN OF SPRING

"Love is good; suffering is good; God is good"—that was what she had answered him when he had said that for her sake he was shut out from all that was good on earth. His heart did not rebel so bitterly against this answer as it would have done if he had not felt assured that she spoke of what she had experienced, and that his present experience was in some sort a comradeship with her. Then, again, there was the inexplicable fact that the knowledge of the way in which he regarded her had given her pleasure; that was a great consolation to him, although he did not gather from it any hope for the future. Her whole manner indicated that she was, as he supposed her to be, entirely out of his reach, not only by the barrier of circumstance, but by her own deliberate preference; and yet he was certain that she was glad that he loved her. What did that mean? He had so seen her life that he knew she was incapable of vanity or selfish satisfaction; when she was glad it was because it was right to be glad. Caius could not unravel this, and yet, deep within him, he knew that there was consistency in it. Had she not said that love in itself was good? it must be good, then, both to the giver and receiver. He felt a certain awe at finding his own poor love embraced in such a doctrine; he felt for the first time how gross and selfish, how unworthy, it was.

It was now the end of March; the snow was melting; the ice was breaking; it might be three or four weeks before ships could sail in the gulf, but it would not be longer. There was no sign of further outbreak of diphtheria upon the island. Caius felt the time of his going home to be near; he was not glad to think of leaving his prison of ice. Two distinct efforts were made at this time to entertain him.

O'Shea made an expedition to the island of the picture rocks, and, in rough kindliness, insisted upon taking Caius with him, not to see the rocks—O'Shea thought little of them. They had an exciting journey, rowing between the ice-floes in the bay, carrying their boat over one ice fragment and then another, launching it each time into a sea of dangers. They spent a couple of days entertained by the chief man of this island, and came back again at the same delightful jeopardy of their lives.

After this Mr. Pembroke took Caius home with him, driving again over the sand-dune, upon which, now that the drifts had almost melted, a road could be made. All winter the dunes had been absolutely deserted, impassable by reason of the depth of snow. It would seem that even the devil himself must have left their valleys at this time, or have hibernated. The chief interest to Caius in this expedition was to seek the hollow where he had seen, or thought he had seen, the band of mysterious men to which O'Shea introduced him; but so changed was the appearance of the sand by reason of the streams and rivulets of melting snow, and so monotonous was the dune, that he grew confused, and could not in the least tell where the place had been. He paid a visit to Pembroke's house, and to the inn kept by the old maids, and then went back to his own little wooden domicile with renewed contentment in its quaint appointments, in its solitude, but above all in its nearness to that other house in which the five women lived guarded by the mastiffs.

Caius knew well enough that these plans for his amusement had been instigated by Madame Le Maître. She was keeping out of his way, except that now and then he met her upon the roads and exchanged with her a friendly greeting.

The only satisfaction that Caius sought for himself at this time was an occasional visit to O'Shea's house. All winter there had been growing upon him a liking for the man's wife, although the words that he exchanged with her were at all times few. Now the feeling that he and she were friends had received a distinct increase. It was a long time since Caius had put to anyone the questions which his mind was constantly asking concerning Madame Le Maître. Apart from any thought of talking about the object of their mutual regard, it was a comfort to him to be in the presence of O'Shea's wife. He felt sure that she understood her mistress better than anyone else did, and he also suspected her of a lively sympathy with himself, although it was not probable that she knew more concerning his relation to Josephine Le Maître than merely the fact that it would be hard for any man to see so much grace and beauty and remain insensible. Caius sat by this woman's hearth, and whittled tops and boats for her children on the sunny doorstep when the days grew warm at noon, and did not expect any guerdon for doing it except the rest that he found in the proximity and occupation. Reward came to him, however. The woman eyed him with more and more kindliness, and at length she spoke.

It was one day towards the end of the month, when the last film of snow had evaporated from many a field and slope, and the vivid green of grass appeared for the first time to gladden the eyes, although many an ice-wreath and snowy hollow still lay between. On such a day the sight of a folded head of saxifrage from which the pearls are just breaking makes the heart of man bound with a pleasure that has certainly no rational cause which is adequate.

Caius came up from the western shore, where he had been watching a distant ship that passed on the other side of the nearer ice-floes, and which said, by no other signal than that of her white sails, that winter was gone. The sea, whose rivers and lakes among the ice had of late looked so turbid by reason of frozen particles in the water, was clear now to reflect once more the blue above it, and the ice-cakes were very white in the sunshine. Caius turned his back upon this, and came up a stony path where large patches of the hill were green; and by chance he came upon O'Shea's wife, who was laying out linen to bleach at some distance from her own house. Close to her Caius saw the ledge of rock on which the first flowers of the year were budding, and straightway fell in love with them. Knowing that their plants would flourish indoors as well as out, he stooped to lift the large cakes of moss in which their roots were set. The woman, who wore a small pink shawl tied over her head and shoulders, came near to where he was stooping, and made no preface, but said:

"He's dead, sir; or if he isn't, and if he should come back, O'Shea will kill him!"

Caius did not need to ask of whom she spoke.

"Why?" he asked. "Why should O'Shea want to kill him?"

"It would kill her, sir, if he came back to her. She couldn't abide him no ways, and O'Shea says it's as good one murder should be done as another, and if he was hung for it he wouldn't mind. O'Shea's the sort of man that would keep his word. He'd just feel it was a kind of interesting thing to do, and he worships her to that extent. But I feel sure, sir, that Le Maître is dead. God would not be so unkind as to have me and the children bereft in that way."

Her simple belief in her husband's power to settle the matter was shocking to Caius, because he felt that she probably knew her husband perfectly.

"But why," said he again, "would it kill her if he came back?"

"Well, what sort of a decent man is it that would have stayed away from her all these years, poor lamb? Why, sir, she wasn't but a child at the convent when her father had them married, and she back to school, and he away to his ship, and never come to see her since."

Caius turned as he knelt upon the grass, and, holding the emerald moss and saxifrage plants in his hand, looked up at her. "He went away two years ago," he said, repeating defiantly what he believed he had heard.

"He went away six year ago," corrected she; "but it's two years now since aught was heard of him, and his ship went down, sir, coming back from Afriky—that we know; but word came that the crew were saved, but never a word from him, nor a word of him, since."

"Did she"—his throat would hardly frame the words—a nervous spasm impeded them; yet he could not but ask—"did she care for him?"

"Oh well, sir, as to that, he was a beautiful-looking man, and she but a child; but when she came to herself she wrote and asked him never to come back; she told me so; and he never did."

"Well, that at least was civil of him." Caius spoke in full earnest.

"No, sir; he's not civil; he's a beast of a man. There's no sort of low trick that he hasn't done, only it can't be proved against him; for he's the sort of beast that is a snake; he only married madame for the money he'll get with her. It was when *she* learned that that she wrote to him not to come back; but he never sent an honest word to say whether he'd stay away or not. She knows what he is, sir, for folks that he'd cheated and lied to come to her to complain. Young as she is, there's white threads in her hair, just to think that he might come back at any time. It's making an old woman of her since she's come of an age to think; and she the merriest, blithest creature that ever was. When she first came out of the convent, to see her dance and sing was a sight to make old eyes young."

"Yes," said Caius eagerly, "I know it was—I am sure it was."

"Oh, but you never saw her, sir, till the shadow had come on her."

"Do you know when it was I first saw her?" said Caius, looking down at the grass.

"She told me 'twas when she went to Prince Edward's Land, the time she went to see the wife of her father's brother. 'Twas the one time that O'Shea let her out of his sight; but no one knew where she was, so if the Captain had come at that time he couldn't have found her without coming to O'Shea first. And the other time that O'Shea let her go was the first winter she came here, for he knew no one could come at the islands for the snow, and we followed by the first ship in spring."

"Couldn't she get a separation?"

"O'Shea says the law is that way made that she couldn't."

"If she changed her name and went away somewhere——" Caius spoke thoughtfully.

"And that's what O'Shea has been at her to do, for at least it would give her peace; but she says, no, she'll do what's open and honest, and God will take care of her. And I'm sure I hope He will. But it's hard, sir, to see a young thing, so happy by nature as her, taking comfort in nothing but prayers and hymns and good works, so young as she is; it's enough to make the angels themselves have tears in their eyes to see it."

At this the woman was wiping her own eyes; and, making soft sniffing sounds of uncultivated grief, she went back to her work of strewing wet garments upon the grass.

Caius felt that O'Shea's wife had read the mind of the angels aright.

CHAPTER 5. TO THE HIGHER COURT

If Caius, as he went his way carrying the moss and budding flowers, could have felt convinced with O'Shea's wife that Le Maître was dead, he would have been a much happier man. He could not admit the woman's logic. Still, he was far happier than he had been an hour before. Le Maître might be dead. Josephine did not love Le Maître. He felt that now, at least, he understood her life.

Having the flowers, the very first darlings of the spring, in his hand, he went, in the impulse of the new sympathy, and knocked at her house door. He carried his burden of moss, earth, moisture, and little gray scaly insects that, having been disturbed, crawled in and out of it, boldly into the room, whose walls were still decorated with the faded garlands of the previous autumn.

"Let me talk to you," said Caius.

The lady and the one young girl who happened to be with her had bestirred themselves to receive his gift. Making a platter serve as the rock-ledge from which the living things had been disturbed, they set them in the window to grow and unfold the more quickly. They had brought him a bowl also in which to wash his hands, and then it was that he looked at the lady of the house and made his request.

He hardly thought she would grant it; he felt almost breathless with his own hardihood when he saw her dismiss the girl and sit before him to hear what he might have to say. He knew then that had he asked her to talk to him he would have translated the desire of his heart far better.

"O'Shea's wife has been talking to me," he said.

"About me?"

"I hope you will forgive us. I think she could not help speaking, and I could not help listening."

"What did she say?"

It was the absolutely childlike directness of her thoughts and words that always seemed to Caius to be the thing that put the greatest distance between them.

"I could not tell you what she said; I would not dare to repeat it to you, and perhaps she would not wish you to know; but you know she is loyal to you, and what I can tell you is, that I understand better now what your life is—what it has been."

Then he held out his hands with an impulsive gesture towards her. The large table was between them; it was only a gesture, and he let his hands lie on the table. "Let me be your friend; you may trust me," he said. "I am only a very ordinary man; but still, the best friendship I have I offer. You need not be afraid of me."

"I am not afraid of you." She said it with perfect tranquillity.

He did not like her answer.

"Are we friends, then?" he asked, and tried to smile, though he felt that some unruly nerve was painting the heaviness of his heart in his face.

"How do you mean it? O'Shea and his wife are my friends, each of them in a very different way——" She was going on, but he interrupted:

"They are your friends because they would die to serve you; but have you never had friends who were your equals in education and intelligence?" He was speaking hastily, using random words to suggest that more could be had out of such a relation than faithful service.

"Are you my equal in intelligence and education?" she asked appositely, laughter in her eyes.

He had time just for a momentary flash of self-wonder that he should so love a woman who, when she did not keep him at some far distance, laughed at him openly. He stammered a moment, then smiled, for he could not help it.

"I would not care to claim that for myself," he said.

"Rather," she suggested, "let us frankly admit that you are the superior in both."

He was sitting at the table, his elbows upon it, and now he covered his face with his hands, half in real, half in mock, despair:

"What can I do or say?" he groaned. "What have I done that you will not answer the honest meaning you can understand in spite of my clumsy words?"

Then he had to look at her because she did not answer, and when he saw that she was still ready to laugh, he laughed, too.

"Have you never ceased to despise me because I could not swim? I can swim now, I assure you. I have studied the art. I could even show you a prize that I took in a race, if that would win your respect."

"I am glad you took the prize."

"I have not yet learned the magic with which mermaids move."

"No, and you have not heard any excuse for the boldness of that play yet. And I was almost the cause of your death. Ah! how frightened I was that night—of you and for you! And again when I went to see Mr. Pembroke before the snow came, and the storm came on and I was obliged to travel with you in O'Shea's great-coat—that again cannot seem nice to you when you think of it. Why do you like what appears so strange? You came here to do a noble work, and you have done it nobly. Why not go home now, and be rid of such a suspicious character as I have shown myself to be? Wherever you go, our prayers and our blessings will follow you."

Caius looked down at the common deal board. There were dents and marks upon it that spoke of constant household work. At length he said:

"There is one reason for going that would seem to me enough: if you will tell me that you neither want nor need my companionship or help in any way; but if you cannot tell me that——"

"Want," she said very sadly. "Ah, do you think I have no heart, no mind that likes to talk its thoughts, no sympathies? I think that if *anyone*—man, woman, or child—were to come to me from out the big world, where people have such thoughts and feelings as I have, and offer to talk to me, I could not do anything else than desire their companionship. Do you think that I am hard-hearted? I am so lonely that the affection even of a dog or a bird would be a temptation to me, if it was a thing that I dared not accept, because it would make me weaker to live the life that is right. That is the way we must tell what is right or wrong."

In spite of himself, he gathered comfort from the fact that, pausing here, without adequate reason that was apparent, she took for granted that the friendship he offered would be a source of weakness to her.

She never stooped to try to appear reasonable. As she had been speaking, a new look had been coming out of the habitual calmness of her face, and now, in the pause, the calm went suddenly, and there was a flash of fire in her eyes that he had never seen there before:

"If I were starving, would you come and offer me bread that you knew I ought not to eat? It would be cruel." She rose up suddenly, and he stood before her. "It is cruel of you to tantalize me with thoughts of happiness because you know I must want it so much. I could not live and not want it. Go! you are doing a cowardly thing. You are doing what the devil did when our Lord was in the wilderness. But He did not need the bread He was asked to take, and I do not need your friendship. Go!"

She held out the hand—the hand that had so often beckoned to him in play—and pointed him to the door. He knew that he was standing before a woman who had been irritated by inward pain into a sudden gust of anger, and now, for the first time, he was not afraid of her. In losing her self-control she had lost her control of him.

"Josephine," he cried, "tell me about this man, Le Maître! He has no right over you. Why do you think he is not dead? At least, tell me what you know."

It seemed that, in the confusion of conflicting emotions, she hardly wondered why he had not obeyed her.

"Oh, he is not dead!" She spoke with bitterness. "I have no reason to suppose so. He only leaves me in suspense that he may make me the more miserable." And then, as if realizing what she had said, she lifted her head again proudly. "But remember it is nothing to you whether he is alive or dead."

"Nothing to me to know that you would be freed from this horrible slavery! It is not of my own gain, but of yours, I am thinking."

He knew that what he had said was not wholly true, yet, in the heat of the moment, he knew that to embody in words the best that might be was to give himself the best chance of realizing it; and he did not believe now that her fierce assertion of indifference for him was true either, but his best self applauded her for it. For a minute he could not tell what Josephine would do next. She stood looking at him helplessly; it seemed as though her subsiding anger had left a fear of herself in its place. But what he dreaded most was that her composure should return.

"Do not be angry with me," he said; "I ask because it is right that I should know. Can you not get rid of this bond of marriage?"

"Do you think," she asked, "that the good God and the Holy Virgin would desire me to put myself—my life—all that is sacred—into courts and newspapers? Do you think the holy Mother of God—looking down upon me, her child—wants me to get out of trouble in *that* way?" Josephine had asked the question first in distress; then, with a face of peerless scorn, she seemed to put some horrid scene from before her with her hand. "The dear God would rather I would drown myself," she said; "it would at least be"—she hesitated for a word, as if at a loss in her English—"at least be cleaner."

She had no sooner finished that speech than the scorn died out of her face:

"Ah, no," she cried repentant; "the men and women who are driven to seek such redress—I—I truly pity them—but for me—it would not be any use even if it were right. O'Shea says it would be no use, and he knows. I don't think I would do it if I could; but I could not if I would."

"Surely he is dead," pleaded Caius. "How can you live if you do not believe that?"

She came a little nearer to him, making the explanation with child-like earnestness:

"You see, I have talked to God and to the holy Mother about this. I know they have heard my prayers and seen my tears, and will do what is good for me. I ask God always that Le Maître may not come back to me, so now I know that if" (a gasping sigh retarded for a moment the breath that came and went in her gentle bosom) "if he does come back it will be God's will. Who am I that I should know best? Shall I choose to be what you call a 'missionary' to the poor and sick—and refuse God's will? God can put an end to my marriage if He will; until He does, I will do my duty to my husband: I will till the land that he left idle; I will honour the name he gave me. I dare not do anything except what is very, very right, because I have appealed to the Court of Heaven. You asked me just now if I did not want and need friendship; it does not matter at all what I want, and whatever God does not give me you may be sure I do not need."

He knew that the peace he dreaded had come back to her. She had gone back to the memory of her strength. Now he obeyed the command she had given before, and went out.

CHAPTER 6. "THE NIGHT IS DARK"

Caius went home to his house. Inconsistency is the hall-mark of real in distinction from unreal life. A note of happy music was sounding in his heart. The bright spring evening seemed all full of joy. He saw a flock of gannets stringing out in long line against the red evening sky, and knew that all the feathered population of the rocks was returning to its summer home. Something more than the mere joy of the season was making him glad; he hardly knew what it was, for it appeared to him that circumstances were untoward.

It was in vain that he reasoned that there was no cause for joy in the belief that Josephine took delight in his society; that delight would only make her lot the harder, and make for him the greater grievance. He might as well have reasoned with himself that there was no cause for joy in the fact of the spring; he was so created that such things made up the bliss of life to him.

Caius did not himself think that Josephine owed any duty to La Maître; he could only hope, and try to believe, that the man was dead. Reason, common-sense, appeared to him to do away with what slight moral or religious obligation was involved in such a marriage; yet he was quite sure of one thing—that this young wife, left without friend or protector, would have been upon a very much lower level if she had thought in the manner as he did. He knew now that from the first day he had seen her the charm of her face had been that he read in it a character that was not only wholly different to, but nobler than, his own. He reflected now that he should not love her at all if she took a stand less high in its sweet unreasonableness, and his reason for this was simply that, had she done otherwise, she would not have been Josephine.

The thought that Josephine was what she was intoxicated him; all the next day time and eternity seemed glorious to him. The islands were still ringed with the pearly ring of ice-floes, and for one brief spring day, for this lover, it was enough to be yet imprisoned in the same bit of green earth with his lady, to think of all the noble things she had said and done, and, by her influence, to see new vistas opening into eternity in which they two walked together. There was even some self-gratulation that he had attained to faith in Heaven. He was one of those people who always suppose that they would be glad to have faith if they could. It was not faith, however, that had come to him, only a refining and quickening of his imagination.

Quick upon the heels of these high dreams came their test, for life is not a dream.

Between the Magdalen Islands and the mainland, besides the many stray schooners that came and went, there were two lines of regular communication—one was by a sailing vessel which carried freight regularly to and from the port of Gaspé; the other was by a small packet steamer that once a week came from Nova Scotia and Prince Edward's Island, and returned by the same route. It was by this steamer, on her first appearance, that Caius ought reasonably to return to his home. She would come as soon as the ice diminished; she would bring him news, withheld for four months, of how his parents had fared in his absence. Caius had not yet decided that he would go home by the first trip; the thought of leaving, when it forced itself upon him, was very painful. This steamer was the first arrival expected, and the islanders, eager for variety and mails, looked excitedly to see the ice melt or be drifted away. Caius looked at the ice ring with more intense long-ing, but his longing was that it should remain. His wishes, like prayers, besought the cold winds and frosty nights to conserve it for him.

It so happened that the Gaspé schooner arrived before the southern packet, and lay outside of the ice, waiting until she could make her way through. So welcome was the sight that the islanders gathered upon the shores of the bay just for the pleasure of looking at her as she lay without the harbour. Caius looked at her, too, and with comparative indifference, for he rejoiced that he was still in prison.

Upon that day the night fell just as it falls upon all days; but at midnight Caius had a visitor. O'Shea came to him in the darkness.

Caius was awakened from sound sleep by a muffled thumping at his door that was calculated to disturb him without carrying sharp sound into the surrounding air. His first idea was that some drunken fellow had blundered against his wall by mistake. As the sounds continued and the full strangeness of the event, in that lonely place, entered his waking brain, he arose with a certain trepidation akin to that which one feels at the thought of supernatural visitors, a feeling that was perhaps the result of some influence from the spirit of the man outside the door; for when he opened it, and held his candle to O'Shea's face, he saw a look there that made him know certainly that something was wrong.

O'Shea came in and shut the door behind him, and went into the inner room and sat down on the foot of the bed. Caius followed, holding the candle, and inspected him again.

"Sit down, man." O'Shea made an impatient gesture at the light. "Get into bed, if ye will; there's no hurry that I know of."

Caius stood still, looking at the farmer, and such nervousness had come upon him that he was almost trembling with fear, without the slightest notion as yet of what he feared.

"In the name of Heaven——" he began.

"Yes, Heaven!" O'Shea spoke with hard, meditative inquiry. "It's Heaven she trusts in. What's Heaven going to do for her, I'd loike to know?"

"What is it?" The question now was hoarse and breathless.

"Well, I'll tell you what it is if ye'll give me time"—the tone was sarcastic—"and you needn't spoil yer beauty by catching yer death of cold. 'Tain't necessary, that I know of. There's things that are necessary; there's things that will be necessary in the next few days; but that ain't."

For the first time Caius did not resent the caustic manner. Its sharpness was turned now towards an impending fate, and to Caius O'Shea had come as to a friend in need. Mechanically he sat in the middle of the small bed, and huddled its blankets about him. The burly farmer, in fur coat and cap, sat in wooden-like stillness; but Caius was like a man in a fever, restless in his suspense. The candle, which he had put upon the floor, cast up a yellow light on all the scant furniture, on the two men as they thus talked to each other, with pale, tense faces, and threw distorted shadows high up on the wooden walls.

Perhaps it was a relief to O'Shea to torture Caius some time with this suspense. At last he said: "He's in the schooner."

"Le Maître? How do you know?"

"Well, I'll tell ye how I know. I told ye there was no hurry."

If he was long now in speaking, Caius did not know it. Upon his brain crowded thoughts and imaginations: wild plans for saving the woman he loved; wild, unholy desires of revenge; and a wild vision of misery in the background as yet—a foreboding that the end might be submission to the worst pains of impotent despair.

O'Shea had taken out a piece of paper, but did not open it.

"'Tain't an hour back I got this. The skipper of the schooner and me know each other. He's been bound over by me to let me know if that man ever set foot in his ship to come to this place, and he's managed to get a lad off his ship in the noight, and across the ice, and he brought me this. Le Maître, he's drunk, lyin' in his bunk; that's the way he's preparing to come ashore. It may be one day, it may be two, afore the schooner can get in. Le Maître he won't get off it till it's in th' harbour. I guess that's about all there is to tell." O'Shea added this with grim abstinence from fiercer comment.

"Does she know?" Caius' throat hardly gave voice to the words.

"No, she don't; and I don't know who is to tell her. I can't. I can do most things." He looked up round the walls and ceiling, as if hunting in his mind for other things he could not do. "I'll not do that. 'Tain't in my line. My wife is adown on her knees, mixing up prayers and crying at a great rate; and says I to her, 'You've been a-praying about this some years back; I'd loike to know what good it's done. Get up and tell madame the news;' and says she that she couldn't, and she says that in the morning you're to tell her." O'Shea set his face in grim defiance of any sentiment of pity for Caius that might have suggested itself.

Caius said nothing; but in a minute, grasping at the one straw of hope which he saw, "What are you going to do?" he asked.

O'Shea smoothed out the letter he held.

"Well, you needn't speak so quick; it's just that there I thought we might have our considerations upon. I'm not above asking advoice of a gintleman of the world like yerself; I'm not above giving advoice, neither."

He sat looking vacantly before him with a grim smile upon his face. Caius saw that his mind was made up.

"What are you going to do?" he asked again.

t the same moment came the sharp consciousness upon him that he himself was a murderer, that he wanted to have Le Maître murdered, that his question meant that he was eager to be made privy to the plot, willing to abet it. Yet he did not feel wicked at all; before his eyes was the face of Josephine lying asleep, unconscious and peaceful. He felt that he fought in a cause in which a saint might fight.

"What I may or may not do," said O'Shea, "is neither here nor there just now. The first thing is, what you're going to do. The schooner's out there to the north-east; the boat that's been used for the sealing is over here to the south-west; now, there ain't no sinse, that I know of, in being uncomfortable when it can be helped, or in putting ourselves about for a brute of a man who ain't worth it. It's plain enough what's the easy thing to do. To-morrow morning ye'll make out that ye can't abide no longer staying in this dull hole, and offer the skipper of one of them sealing-boats fifty dollars to have the boat across the ice and take you to Souris. Then ye will go up and talk plain common-sinse to madame, and tell her to put on her man's top-coat she's worn before, and skip out of this dirty fellow's clutches. There ain't nothing like being scared out of their wits for making women reasonable—it's about the only time they have their sinses, so far as I know."

"If she won't come, what then?" Caius demanded hastily.

"My woife says that if ye're not more of a fool than we take ye for, she'll go."

There was something in the mechanical repetition of what his wife had said that made Caius suspect.

"You don't think she'll go?"

O'Shea did not answer.

"That is what you'll do, any way," he said; "and ye'll do it the best way ye know how."

He sat upon the bed some time longer, wrapped in grim reserve. The candle guttered, flared, burned itself out. The two men were together in the dark. Caius believed that if the first expedient failed, and he felt it could not but fail, murder was their only resource against what seemed to them intolerable evil.

O'Shea got up.

"Perhaps ye think the gintleman that is coming has redeeming features about him?" A fine edge of sarcasm was in his tone. "Well, he hain't. Before we lost sight of him, I got word concarning him from one part of the world and another. If I haven't got the law of him, it's because he's too much of a sneak. He wasn't anything but a handsome sort of beast to begin with; and, what with drinking and the life he's led, he's grown into a sort of thing that had better go on all fours like Nebuchadnezzar than come nigh decent people on his hind-legs. Why has he let her alone all these years?" The speech was grimly dramatic. "Why, just because, first place, I believe another woman had the upper hand of him; second place, when he married madame it was the land and money her father had to leave her that made him make that bargain. He hadn't that in him that would make him care for a white slip of a girl as she was then, and, any way, he knew that the girl and the money would keep till he was sick of roving. It's as nasty a trick as could be that he's served her, playing dead dog all these years, and coming to catch her unawares. I tell ye the main thing he has on his mind is revenge for the letters she wrote him when she first got word of his tricks, and then, too, he's coming back to carouse on her money and the money she's made on her father's land, that he niver looked to himself."

O'Shea stalked through the small dark rooms and went out, closing the outer door gently behind him. Caius sat still, wrapped in his blankets. He bowed his head upon his knees. The darkness was only the physical part of the blackness that closed over his spirit. There was only one light in this blackness—that was Josephine's face. Calm he saw it, touched with the look of devotion or mercy; laughing and dimpled he saw it, a thing at one with the sunshine and all the joy of earth; and then he saw it change, and grow pale with fear, and repulsion, and disgust. Around this one face, that carried light with it, there were horrid shapes and sounds in the blackness of his mind. He had been a good man; he had preferred good to evil: had it all been a farce? Was the thing that he was being driven to do now a thing of satanic prompting, and he himself corrupt—all the goodness which he had thought to be himself only an organism, fair outside, that rotted inwardly? Or was this fear the result of false teaching, the prompting of an artificial conscience, and was the thing he wished to do the wholesome and natural course to take—right in the sight of such Deity as might be beyond the curtain of the unknown, the Force who had set the natural laws of being in motion? Caius did not know. While his judgment was in suspense he was beset by horrible fears—the fear that he might be driven to do a villainous deed, the greater fear that he should not accomplish it, the awful fear, rising above all else in his mind, of seeing Josephine overtaken by the horrible fate which menaced her, and he himself still alive to feel her misery and his own.

No, rather than that he would himself kill the man. It was not the part that had been assigned to him, but if she would not save herself it would be the noblest thing to do. Was he to allow O'Shea, with a wife and children, to involve himself in such dire trouble, when he, who had no one dependent upon him, could do the deed, and take what consequences might be? He felt a glow of moral worth like that which he had felt when he decided upon his mission to the island—greater, for in that his motives had been mixed and sordid, and in this his only object was to save lives that were of more worth than his own. Should he kill the man, he would hardly escape death, and even if he did, he could never look Josephine in the face again.

Why not? Why, if this deed were so good, could he not, after the doing of it, go back to her and read gratitude in her eyes? Because Josephine's standard of right and wrong was different from his. What was her standard? His mind cried out an impatient answer. "She believes it is better to suffer than to be happy." He did not believe that; he would settle this matter by his own light, and, by freeing her and saving her faithful friends, be cut off from her for ever.

It would be an easy thing to do, to go up to the man and put a knife in his heart, or shoot him like a dog!

His whole being revolted from the thought; when the deed came before his eyes, it seemed to him that only in some dark feverish imagination could he have dreamed of acting it out, that of course in plain common-sense, that daylight of the mind, he could not will to do this.

Then he thought again of the misery of the suffering wife, and he believed that, foreign as it was to his whole habit of life, he could do this, even this, to save her.

Then again came over him the sickening dread that the old rules of right and wrong that he had been taught were the right guides after all, and that Josephine was right, and that he must submit.

The very thought of submission made his soul rise up in a mad tempest of anger against such a moral law, against all who taught it, against the God who was supposed to ordain it; and so strong was the tempest of this wrath, and so weak was he, perplexed, wretched, that he would have been glad even at the same moment to have appealed to the God of his fathers, with whom he was quarrelling, for counsel and help. His quarrel was too fierce for that. His quarrel with God made trust, made mere belief even, impossible, and he was aware that it was not new, that this was only the culminating hour of a long rebellion.

CHAPTER 7. THE WILD WAVES WHIST

Next morning, when Caius walked forth into the glory of the April sunshine, he felt himself to be a poor, wretched man. There was not a fisherman upon the island, lazy, selfish as they were, and despised in his eyes, that did not appear to him to be a better man than he. All the force of training and habit made the thing that he was going to do appear despicable; but all the force of training and habit was not strong enough to make his judgment clear or direct his will.

The muddy road was beginning to steam in the sunshine; the thin shining ice of night that coated its puddles was melting away. In the green strip by the roadside he saw the yellow-tufted head of a dandelion just level with the grass. The thicket of stunted firs on either side smelt sweet, and beyond them he saw the ice-field that dazzled his eyes, and the blue sea that sparkled. From this side he could not see the bay and the ship of fate lying at anchor, but he noticed with relief that the ice was not much less.

There was no use in thinking or feeling; he must go on and do what was to be done. So he told himself. He shut his heart against the influence of the happy earth; he felt like a guest bidden by fate, who knew not whether the feast were to be for bridal or funeral. That he was not a strong man was shown in this—that having hoped and feared, dreamed and suffered, struggling to see a plain path where no path was, for half the night, he now felt that his power of thought and feeling had burned out, that he could only act his part, without caring much what its results might be.

It was eight o'clock. He had groomed his horse, and tidied his house, and bathed, and breakfasted. He did not think it seemly to intrude upon the lady before this hour, and now he ascended her steps and knocked at her door. The dogs thumped their tails on the wooden veranda; it was only of late they had learned this welcome for him. Would they give it now, he wondered, if they could see his heart? As he stood there waiting for a minute, he felt that it would be good, if possible, to have laid his dilemma fairly before the canine sense and heart, and to have let the dogs rise and tear him or let him pass, as they judged best. It was a foolish fancy.

It was O'Shea's wife who opened the door; her face was disfigured by crying.

"You have told her?" demanded Caius, with relief.

The woman shook her head.

"It was the fine morning that tempted her out, sir," she said. "She sent down to me, saying how she had taken a cup of milk and gone to ride on the beach, and I was to come up and look after the girls. But look here, sir"—eagerly—"it's a good thing, I'm thinking, for her spirits are high when she rides in fine weather, and she's more ready for games and plays, and thinking of pleasure. She's gone on the west shore, round by the light, for O'Shea he looked at the tracks. Do you get your horse and ride after, where you see her tracks in the sand."

Caius went. He mounted his horse and rode down upon the western shore. He found the track, and galloped upon it. The tide was low; the ice was far from shore; the highway, smoothed by the waves, was firm and good. Caius galloped to the end of the island where the light was, where the sealing vessels lay round the base of the lighthouse, and out upon the dune, and still the print of her horse's feet went on in front of him. It was not the first time that he and she had been upon the dune together.

A mile, two miles, three; he rode at an easy pace, for now he knew that he could not miss the rider before him. He watched the surf break gently on the broad shallow reach of sand-ridges that lay between him and the floating ice. And when he had ridden so far he was not the same man as when he mounted his horse, or at least, his own soul, of which man has hardly permanent possession, had returned to him. He could now see, over the low mists of his own moods, all the issues of Josephine's case—all, at least, that were revealed to him; for souls are of different stature, and it is as the head is high or low that the battlefield is truly discerned.

Long before he met her he saw Josephine. She had apparently gone as far as she thought wise, and was amusing herself by making her horse set his feet in the cold surf. It was a game with the horse and the wavelets that she was playing. Each time he danced back and sunned himself he had to go in again; and when he stood, his hind-feet on the sand and his fore-feet reared over the foam, by way of going where she wished and keeping himself dry, Caius could see her gestures so well that it seemed to him he heard the tones of playful remonstrance with which she argued the case.

When she perceived that Caius intended to come up to her, she rode to meet him. Her white cap had been taken off and stuffed into the breast of her dress; the hood surrounded her face loosely, but did not hide it; her eyes were sparkling with pleasure—the pure animal pleasure of life and motion, the sensuous pleasure in the beauty and the music of the waves; other pleasures there might be, but these were certain, and predominated.

"Why did you come?"

She asked the question as a happy child might ask of its playmate—no hint of danger.

To Caius it was a physical impossibility to answer this question with the truth just then.

"Is not springtime an answer?" he asked, then added: "I am going away to-day. I came for one last ride."

She looked at him for a few moments, evidently supposing that he intended to go to Harbour Island to wait there for his ship. If that were so, it seemed that she felt no further responsibility about her conduct to him. His heart sank to see that her joy in the spring and the morning was such that the thought of parting did not apparently grieve her much.

In a moment more her eyes flashed at him with the laughter at his expense which he knew so well; she tried not to laugh as she spoke, but could not help it.

"I have been visiting the band of men who were going to murder you the night you came. Would you like to see them?"

"If you will take care of me."

As she turned and rode before him he heard her laughing.

"There," she said, stopping and pointing to the ground—"there is the place where the quicksand was. I have not gone over it this morning. Sometimes they last from one season to another; sometimes they change themselves in a few days. I was dreadfully frightened when we began to sink, but it was you who saved the pony."

"Don't," said Caius—"don't attempt to make the best of me. I would rather be laughed at." He spoke lightly, without feeling, and that seemed to please her.

"I think," she said candidly, "we behaved very badly; but it was O'Shea's fault—I only enjoyed it. And I don't see what else we could have done, because those two French sailors had to watch if anyone came to steal from the wreck, and they were going to help us so far as to go to the sheds on the cliff for boards to get up the cart; but O'Shea could not have stayed all night with the bags unless I had left him my coat as well as his own."

"You might have trusted me," said Caius. Still he spoke with no sensibility; she grew more at her ease.

"O'Shea wouldn't; and I couldn't control O'Shea. And then we had to meet so often, that I could not bear that you should know I had worn a man's coat. I had to do it, for I couldn't drive home any other way." Here a pause, and her mind wandered to another recollection. "Those men we met brought us word that one of my friends was so ill; I had to hurry to him. In my heart I thought you would not respect me because I had worn a man's coat; and because—— Yes, it was very naughty of me indeed to behave as I did in the water that summer. Even then I did try to get O'Shea to let me walk with you, but he wouldn't."

She had been slowly riding through a deep, soft sand-drift that was heaped at the mouth of the hollow, and when they had got through the opening, Caius saw the ribs of one side of an enormous wreck protruding from the sand, about six feet in height. A small hardy weed had grown upon their heads in tufts; withered and sear with the winter, it still hung there. The ribs bent over a little, as the men he had seen had bent.

"The cloud-shadows and the moonlight were very confusing," remarked Josephine; "and then O'Shea made the two sailors stand in the same way, and they were real. I never knew a man like O'Shea for thinking of things that are half serious and half funny. I never knew him yet fail to find a way to do the thing he wanted to do; and it's always a way that makes me laugh."

If Josephine would not come away with him, would O'Shea find a way of killing Le Maître? and would it be a way to make her laugh? With the awful weight of the tidings he brought upon his heart, all that he said or did before he told them seemed artificial.

"I thought"—half mechanically—"that I saw them all hold up their hands."

"Did you?" she asked. "The first two did; O'Shea told them to hold up their hands."

"There is something you said a minute ago that I want to answer," he said.

She thought he had left the subject of his illusion because it mortified him.

"You said"—he began now to feel emotion as he spoke—"that you thought I should not respect you. I want to tell you that I respected you as I respect my mother, even when you were only a mermaid. I saw you when I fell that night as we walked on this beach. If you had worn a boy's coat, or a fishskin, always, I had sense enough to see that it was a saint at play. Have you read all the odd stories about the saints and the Virgin—how they appear and vanish, and wear odd clothes, and play beneficent tricks with people? It was like that to me. I don't know how to say it, but I think when good people play, they have to be very, very good, or they don't really enjoy it. I don't know how to explain it, but the moderate sort of goodness spoils everything."

Caius, when he had said this, felt that it was something he had never thought before; and, whatever it might mean, he felt instinctively that it meant a great deal more than he knew. He felt a little shabby at having expressed it from her religious point of view, in which he had no part; but his excuse was that there was in his mind at least the doubt that she might be right, and, whether or not, his mission just then was to gain her confidence. He brushed scruples aside for the end in view.

"I am glad you said that," she said. "I am not good, but I should like to be. It wasn't becoming to play a mermaid, but I didn't think of that then. I didn't know many things then that I know now. You see, my uncle's wife drowned her little child; and afterwards, when she was ill, I went to take care of her, and we could not let anyone know, because the police would have interfered for fear she would drown me. But she is quite harmless, poor thing! It is only that time stopped for her when the child was drowned, and she thinks its little body is in the water yet, if we could only find it. I found she had made that dress you call a fishskin with floats on it for herself, and she used to get into the sea, from the opening of an old cellar, at night, and push herself about with a pole. It was the beautiful wild thing that only a mad person with nice thoughts could do. But when she was ill, I played with it, for I had nothing else to do; it was desecration."

"I thought you were like the child that was lost. I think you are like her."

"She thought so, too; she used to think sometimes that I was her little daughter grown up. It was very strange, living with her; I almost think I might have gone mad, too, if I hadn't played with you."

It was very strange, Caius thought, that on this day of all days she should be willing to talk to him about herself, should be willing to laugh and chat and be happy with him. The one day that he dare not listen long, that he must disturb her peace, was the only time that she had seemed to wish to make a friend of him.

"When you lived so near us," he asked, "did you ever come across the woods and see my father's house? Did you see my father and mother? I think you would like them if you did."

"Oh, no," she said lightly; "I only knew who you were because my aunt talked about you; she never forgot what you had done for the child."

"Do not turn your horse yet." He allowed himself to be urgent now. "I have something to say to you which must be said. I am going home; I do not want to wait for the steamer; I want to bribe one of those sealing vessels to start with me to-day. I have come to ask you if you will not come with me to see my mother. You do not know what it is to have a mother. Mothers are very good; mine is. You would like to be with her, I know; you would have the calm of feeling taken care of, instead of standing alone in the world."

He said all this without letting his tone betray that that double-thoughted mind of his was telling him that this was doubtful, that his mother might be slow to believe in Josephine, and that he was not sure whether Josephine would be attracted by her.

Josephine looked at him with round-eyed surprise; then, apparently conjecturing that the invitation was purely kind, purely stupid, she thanked him, and declined it graciously.

"Is there no folly with which you would not easily credit me?" He smiled faintly in his reproach. "Do you think I do not know what I am saying? I have been awake all night thinking what I could do for you." For a moment he looked at her helplessly, hoping that some hint of the truth would come of itself; then, turning away his face, he said hoarsely: "Le Maître is on the Gaspé schooner. O'Shea has had the news. He is lying drunk in his berth."

He did not turn until he heard a slight sound. Then he saw that she had slipped down from her horse, perhaps because she was afraid of falling from it. Her face was quite white; there was a drawn look of abject terror upon it; but she only put her horse's rein in his hand, and pointed to the mouth of the little valley.

"Let me be alone a little while," she whispered.

So Caius rode out upon the beach, leading her horse; and there he held both restive animals as still as might be, and waited.

CHAPTER 8. "GOD'S IN HIS HEAVEN"

Caius wondered how long he ought to wait if she did not come out to him. He wondered if she would die of misery there alone in the sand-dune, or if she would go mad, and meet him in some fantastic humour, all the intelligence scorched out of her poor brain by the cruel words he had said. He had a notion that she had wanted to say her prayers, and, although he did not believe in an answering Heaven, he did believe that prayers would comfort her, and he hoped that that was why she asked to be left.

When he thought of the terror in her eyes, he felt sanguine that she would come with him. Now that he had seen her distress, it seemed to him worse than any notion he had preconceived of it. It was right that she should go with him. When she had once done that, he would stand between her and this man always. That would be enough; if she should never care for him, if he had nothing more than that, he would be satisfied, and the world might think what it would. If she would not go with him—well, then he would kill Le Maître. His mind was made up; there was nothing left of hesitation or scruple. He looked at the broad sea and the sunlight and the sky, and made his vow with clenched teeth. He laughed at the words which had scared him the night before—the names of the crimes which were his alternatives; they were made righteousness to him by the sight of fear in a woman's face.

It is one form of weakness to lay too much stress upon the emotion of another, just as it is weak to take too much heed of our own emotions; but Caius thought the sympathy that carried all before it was strength.

After awhile, waiting became intolerable. Leading both horses, he walked cautiously back to a point where he could see Josephine. She was sitting upon the sandy bank near where he had left her. He took his cap in his hand, and went with the horses, standing reverently before her. He felt sure now that she had been saying her prayers, because, although her face was still very pallid, she was composed and able to speak. He wished now she had not prayed.

"You are very kind to me." Her voice trembled, but she gave him a little smile. "I cannot pretend that I am not distressed; it would be false, and falsehood is not right. You are very, very kind, and I thank you——"

She broke off, as if she had been going to say something more but had wearily forgotten what it was.

"Oh, do not say that!" His voice was like one pleading to be spared a blow. "I love you. There is no greater joy to me on earth than to serve you."

"Hush," she said; "don't say that. I am very sorry for you, but sorrow must come to us all in some way."

"Don't, don't!" he cried—"don't tell me that suffering is good. It is not good; it is an evil. It is right to shun evil; it is the only right. The other is a horrid fable—a lie concocted by priests and devils!"

"Suppose you loved someone—me, for instance—and I was dead, and you knew quite certainly that by dying you would come to where I was—would you call death good or evil?"

He demurred. He did not want to admit belief in anything connected with the doctrine of submission.

"I said 'suppose,'" she said.

"I would go through far more than death to come near you."

"Suffering is just a gate, like death. We go through it to get the things we really want most."

"I don't believe in a religion that calls suffering better than happiness; but I know you do."

"No, I don't," she said, "and God does not; and people who talk as if He did not want us to seek happiness—even our own happiness—are making to themselves a graven image. I will tell you how I think about it, because I have been alone a great deal and been always very much afraid, and that has made me think a great deal, and you have been very kind, for you risked your life for my poor people, and now you would risk something more than that to help me. Will you listen while I try to tell you?"

Caius signified his assent. He was losing all his hope. He was thinking that when she had done talking he would go and get ready to do murder; but he listened.

"You see," she began, "the greatest happiness is love. Love is greedy to get as well as to give. It is all nonsense talking about love that gives and asks for no return. We only put up with that when we cannot get the other, and why? Why should we think it the grandest thing to give what we would scorn to take? You, for instance—you would rather have a person you loved do nothing for you, yet enjoy you, always demanding your affection and presence, than that he or she should be endlessly generous, and indifferent to what you give in return."

"Yes." He blushed as he said it.

"Well then, it is cant to speak as if the love that asks for no return is the noblest. Now listen. I have something very solemn to say, because it is only by the greatest things that we learn what the little ought to be. When God came to earth to live for awhile, it was for the sake of His happiness and ours; He loved us in the way that I have been saying; He was not content only to bless us, He wanted us to enjoy Him. He wanted that happiness from us; and He wanted us to expect it from Him and from each other; and if we had answered, all would have been like the first marriage feast, where they had the very best wine, and such lots of it. But, you see, we couldn't answer; we had no souls. We were just like the men on Cloud Island who laughed at you when you wanted them to build a hospital. The little self or soul that we had was of that sort that we couldn't even love each other very much with it, and not Him at all. So there was only one way, and that was for us to grow out of these stupid little souls, and get good big ones, that can enjoy God, and enjoy each other, and enjoy everything perfectly." She looked up over the yellow sand-hills into the deep sunny sky, and drew a long breath of the April air involuntarily. "Oh," she said, "a good, big, perfect soul could enjoy so much."

It seemed as if she thought she had said it all and finished the subject.

"Well," said Caius, interested in spite of himself, "if God wanted to make us happy, He could have given us that kind of soul."

"Ah, no! We don't know why things have to grow, but they must; everything grows —you know that. For some reason, that is the best way; so there was just one way for those souls to grow in us, and He showed us how. It is by doing what is quite perfectly right, and bearing all the suffering that comes because of it, and doing all the giving side of love, because here we can't get much. Pain is not good in itself; it is a gate. Our souls are growing all through the gate of the suffering, and when we get to the other side of it, we shall find we have won them. God wants us to be greedy for happiness; but we must find it by going through the gate He went through to show us the way."

Caius stood before her holding the horses; even they had been still while she was speaking, as if listening to the music of her voice. Caius felt the misery of a wavering will and conflicting thoughts.

"If I thought," he said, "that God cared about happiness—just simple happiness—it would make religion seem so much more sensible; but I'm afraid I don't believe in living after death, or that He cares——"

What she said was wholly unreasonable. She put out her hand and took his, as if the hand-clasp were a compact.

"Trust God and see," she said.

There was in her white face such a look of glorious hope, that Caius, half carried away by its inspiration, still quailed before her. After he had wrung her hand, he found himself brushing his sleeve across his eyes. As he thought that he had lost her, thought of all that she would have to endure, of the murder he still longed to commit, and felt all the agony of indecision again, and suspected that after this he would scruple to commit it—when all this came upon him, he turned and leaned against one of the horses, sobbing, conscious in a vague way that he did not wish to stop himself, but only craved her pity.

Josephine comforted him. She did not apparently try to, she did not do or say anything to the purpose; but she evinced such consternation at the sight of his tears, that stronger thoughts came. He put aside his trouble, and helped her to mount her horse.

They rode along the beach slowly together. She was content to go slowly. She looked physically too exhausted to ride fast. Even yet probably, within her heart, the conflict was going forward that had only been well begun in her brief solitude of the sand valley.

Caius looked at her from time to time with feelings of fierce indignation and dejection. The indignation was against Le Maître, the dejection was wholly upon his own account; for he felt that his plan of help had failed, and that where he had hoped to give strength and comfort, he had only, in utter weakness, exacted pity. Caius had one virtue in these days: he did not admire anything that he did, and he did not even think much about the self he scorned. With regard to Josephine, he felt that if her philosophy of life were true it was not for him to presume to pity her. So vividly had she brought her conception of the use of life before him that it was stamped upon his mind in a brief series of pictures, clear, indelible; and the last picture was one of which he could not think clearly, but it produced in him an idea of the after-life which he had not before.

Then he thought again of the cloud under which Josephine was entering. Her decision would in all probability cut down her bright, useful life to a few short years of struggle and shame and sorrow. At last he spoke:

"But why do you think it right to sacrifice yourself to this man? It does not seem to me right."

He knew then what clearness of thought she had, for she looked with almost horror in her face.

"Sacrifice myself for Le Maître! Oh no! I should have no right to do that; but to the ideal right, to God—yes. If I withheld anything from God, how could I win my soul?"

"But how do you know God requires this?"

"Ah! I told you before. Why will you not understand? I have prayed. I know God has taken this thing in his own hand."

Caius said no more. Josephine's way of looking at this thing might not be true; that was not what he was considering just then. He knew that it was intensely true for her, would remain true for her until the event of death proved it true or false. This was the factor in the present problem that was the enemy to his scheme. Then, furthermore, whether it were true or false, he knew that there was in his mind the doubt, and that doubt would remain with him, and it would prevent him from killing Le Maître; it would even prevent him from abetting O'Shea, and he supposed that that abetting would be necessary. Here was cause enough for dejection—that the whole miserable progress of events which he feared most should take place. And why? Because a woman held a glorious faith which might turn out to be delusion, and because he, a man, had not strength to believe for certain that it was a delusion.

It raised no flicker of renewed hope in Caius to meet O'Shea at the turn of the shore where the boats of the seal fishery were drawn up. O'Shea had a brisk look of energy that made it evident that he was still bent upon accomplishing his design. He stopped in front of the lady's horse, and said something to her which Caius did not hear.

"Have ye arranged that little picnic over to Prince Edward's," he called to Caius.

Caius looked at Josephine. O'Shea's mere presence had put much of the spiritual aspect of the case to flight, and he suddenly smarted under the realization that he had never put the question to her since she had known her danger—never put the request to her strongly at all.

"Come," said Josephine; "I am going home. I am going to send all my girls to their own homes and get the house ready for my husband."

O'Shea, with imperturbable countenance, pushed off his hat and scratched his head.

"I was thinking," he remarked casually, "that I'd jist send Mammy along with ye to Prince Edward." (Mammy was what he always called his wife.) "I am thinking he'll be real glad to see her, for she's a real respectable woman."

"Who?" asked Josephine, puzzled.

"Prince Edward, that owns the island," said O'Shea. "And she's that down in the mouth, it's no comfort for me to have her; and she can take the baby and welcome. It's a fair sea." He looked to the south as he spoke. "I'd risk both her and the brat on it; and Skipper Pierre is getting ready to take the boat across the ice."

Caius saw that resolution had fled from Josephine. She too looked at the calm blue southern sea, and agonized longing came into her eyes. It seemed to Caius too cruel, too horribly cruel, that she should be tortured by this temptation. Because he knew that to her it could be nothing but temptation, he sat silent when O'Shea, seeing that the lady's gaze was afar, signed to him for aid; and because he hoped that she might yield he was silent, and did not come to rescue her from the tormentor.

O'Shea gave him a look of undisguised scorn; but since he would not woo, it appeared that this man was able to do some wooing for him.

"Of course," remarked O'Shea, "I see difficulties. If the doctor here was a young man of parts, I'd easier put ye and Mammy in his care; but old Skipper Pierre is no milksop."

Josephine looked, first alert, as if suspecting an ill-bred joke, and then, as O'Shea appeared to be speaking to her quite seriously, forgetting that Caius might overhear, there came upon her face a look of gentle severity.

"That is not what I think of the doctor; I would trust him more quickly than anyone else, except you, O'Shea."

The words brought to Caius a pang, but he hardly noticed it in watching the other two, for the lady, when she had spoken, looked off again with longing at the sea, and O'Shea, whose rough heart melted under the trustful affection of the exception she made, for a moment turned away his head. Caius saw in him the man whom he had only once seen before, and that was when his child had died. It was but a few moments; the easy quizzical manner sat upon him again.

"Oh, well, he hasn't got much to him one way or the other, but——" this in low, confidential tones.

Caius could not hear her reply; he saw that she interrupted, earnestly vindicating him. He drew his horse back a pace or two; he would not overhear her argument on his behalf, nor would he trust O'Shea so far as to leave them alone together.

The cleverness with which O'Shea drove her into a glow of enthusiasm for Caius was a revelation of power which the latter at the moment could only regard curiously, so torn was his heart in respect to the issue of the trial. He was so near that their looks told him what he could not hear, and he saw Josephine's face glow with the warmth of regard which grew under the other's sneers. Then he saw O'Shea visibly cast that subject away as if it was of no importance; he went near to her, speaking low, but with the look of one who brought the worst news, and Caius knew, without question, that he was pouring into her ears all the evil he had ever heard of Le Maître, all the detail of his present drunken condition. Caius did not move; he did not know whether the scene before him represented Satan with powerful grasp upon a soul that would otherwise have passed into some more heavenly region, or whether it was a wise and good man trying to save a woman from her own fanatical folly. The latter seemed to be the case when he looked about him at the beach, at the boats, at the lighthouse on the cliff above, with a clothes-line near it, spread with flapping garments. When he looked, not outward, but inward, and saw Josephine's vision of life, he believed he ought to go forward and beat off the serpent from the dove.

The colloquy was not very long. Then O'Shea led Josephine's horse nearer to Caius.

"Madame and my wife will go with ye," he said. "I've told the men to get the boat out."

"I did not say that," moaned Josephine.

Her face was buried in her hands, and Caius remembered how those pretty white hands had at one time beckoned to him, and at another had angrily waved him away. Now they were held helplessly before a white face that was convulsed with fear and shame and self-abandonment.

"There ain't no particular hurry," remarked O'Shea soothingly; "but Mammy has packed up all in the houses that needs to go, and she'll bring warm clothes and all by the time the boat's out, so there's no call for madame to go back. It would be awful unkind to the girls to set them crying; and"—this to Caius—"ye jist go and put up yer things as quick as ye can."

His words were accompanied by the sound of the fishermen putting rollers under the small schooner that had been selected. The old skipper, Pierre, had begun to call out his orders. Josephine took her hands from her face suddenly, and looked towards the busy men with such eager hungry desire for the freedom they were preparing for her that it seemed to Caius that at that moment his own heart broke, for he saw that Josephine was not convinced but that she had yielded. He knew that Mammy's presence on the journey made no real difference in its guilt from Josephine's standpoint; her duty to her God was to remain at her post. She had flinched from it out of mere cowardice—it was a fall. Caius knew that he had no choice but to help her back to her better self, that he would be a bastard if he did not do it.

Three times he essayed to speak; he had not the right words; then, even without them, he broke the silence hurriedly:

"I think you are justified in coming with me; but if you do what you believe to be wrong—you will regret it. What does your heart say? Think!"

It was a feeble, stammered protest; he felt no dignity in it; he almost felt it to be the craven insult seen in it by O'Shea, who swore under his breath and glared at him.

Josephine gave only a long sobbing sigh, as one awakening from a dream. She looked at the boat again, and the men preparing it, and then at Caius—straight in his eyes she looked, as if searching his face for something more.

"Follow your own conscience, Josephine; it is truer than ours. I was wrong to let you be tempted," he said. "Forgive me!"

She looked again at the boat and at the sea, and then, in the stayed subdued manner that had become too habitual to her, she said to O'Shea:

"I will go home now. Dr. Simpson is right. I cannot go."

O'Shea was too clever a man to make an effort to hold what he knew to be lost; he let go her rein, and she rode up the path that led to the island road. When she was gone O'Shea turned upon Caius with a look of mingled scorn and loathing.

"Ye're afraid of Le Maître coming after ye," he hissed; "or ye have a girl at home, and would foind it awkward to bring her and madam face to face; so ye give her up, the most angel woman that ever trod this earth, to be done to death by a beast, because ye're afraid for yer own skin. Bah! I had come to think better of ye."

With that he cut at the horse with a stick he had in his hand, and the creature, wholly unaccustomed to such pain and indignity, dashed along the shore, by chance turning homeward. Caius, carried perforce as upon the wings of the wind for half a mile, was thrown off upon the sand. He picked himself up, and with wet clothes and sore limbs walked to his little house, which he felt he could no longer look upon as a home.

He could hardly understand what he had done; he began to regret it. A man cannot see the forces at work upon his inmost self. He did not know that Josephine's soul had taken his by the hand and lifted it up—that his love for her had risen from earth to heaven when he feared the slightest wrong-doing for her more than all other misfortune.

CHAPTER 9. "GOD'S PUPPETS, BEST AND WORST"

All that long day a hot sun beat down upon the sea and upon the ice in the bay; and the tide, with its gentle motion of flow and ebb, made visibly more stir among the cakes of floating ice, by which it was seen that they were smaller and lighter than before. The sun-rays were doing their work, not so much by direct touch upon the ice itself as by raising the temperature of all the flowing sea, and thus, when the sun went down and the night of frost set in, the melting of the ice did not cease.

Morning came, and revealed a long blue channel across the bay from its entrance to Harbour Island. The steamer from Souris had made this channel by knocking aside the light ice with her prow. She was built to travel in ice. She lay now, with funnel still smoking, in the harbour, a quarter of a mile from the small quay. The Gaspé schooner still lay without the bay, but there was a movement of unfurling sails among her masts, by which it was evident that her skipper hoped by the faint but favourable breeze that was blowing to bring her down the same blue highway.

It was upon this scene that Caius, wretched and sleepless, looked at early dawn. He had come out of his house and climbed the nearest knoll from which the bay could be seen, for his house and those near it looked on the open western sea. When he reached this knoll he found that O'Shea was there before him, examining the movements of the ship with his glass in the gray cold of the shivering morning. The two men stood together and held no communication.

Pretty soon O'Shea went hastily home again. Caius stood still to see the sun rise clear and golden. There were no clouds, no vapours, to catch its reflections and make a wondrous spectacle of its appearing. The blue horizon slowly dipped until the whole yellow disc beamed above it; ice and water glistened pleasantly; on the hills of all the sister isles there was sunshine and shade; and round about him, in the hilly field, each rock and bush cast a long shadow. Between them the sun struck the grass with such level rays that the very blades and clumps of blades cast their shadows also.

Caius had remained to watch if the breeze would strengthen with the sun's uprising, and he prayed the forces of heat and cold, and all things that preside over the currents of air, that it might not strengthen but languish and die.

What difference did it make, a few hours more or less? No difference, he knew, and yet all the fresh energy the new day brought him went forth in this desire that Josephine might have a few hours longer respite before she began the long weary course of life that stretched before her.

Caius had packed up all his belongings. There was nothing for him to do but drive along the dune with his luggage, as he had driven four months before, and take the steamer that night to Souris. The cart that took him would no doubt bring back Le Maître. Caius had not yet hired a cart; he had not the least idea whether O'Shea intended to drive him and bring back his enemy or not. That would, no doubt, be Josephine's desire. Caius had not seen Josephine or spoken to O'Shea; it mattered nothing to him what arrangement they would or would not make for him.

As he still stood watching to see if the breeze would round and fill the sails which the Gaspé schooner had set, O'Shea came back and called from the foot of the knoll. Caius turned; he bore the man no ill will. Josephine's horse had not been injured by the accident of yesterday, and his own fall was a matter of complete indifference.

"I'm thinking, as ye packed yer bags, ye'll be going for the steamer."

O'Shea spoke with that indefinable insult in his tone which had always characterized it in the days of their first intercourse, but, apart from that, his manner was crisp and cool as the morning air; not a shade of discouragement was visible.

"I am going for the steamer," said Caius, and waited to hear what offer of conveyance was to be made him.

"Well, I'm thinking," said O'Shea, "that I'll just take the boat across the bay, and bring back the captain from Harbour Island; but as his honour might prefer the cart, I'll send the cart round by the dune. There's no saying but, having been in tropical parts, he may be a bit scared of the ice. Howsomever, knowing that he's in that haste to meet his bride, and would, no doubt, grudge so much as a day spent between here and there on the sand, I'll jist give him his chice; being who he is, and a foine gintleman, he has his right to it. As for you"—the tone instantly slipped into insolent indifference—"ye can go by one or the other with yer bags."

It was not clear to Caius that O'Shea had any intention of himself escorting Le Maître if he chose to go by the sand. This inclined him to suppose that he had no fixed plan to injure him. What right had he to suppose such plan had been formed? The man before him wore no look of desperate passion. In the pleasant weather even the dune was not an unfrequented place, and the bay was overlooked on all sides. Caius could not decide whether his suspicion of O'Shea had been just or a monstrous injustice. He felt such suspicion to be morbid, and he said nothing. The futility of asking a question that would not be answered, the difficulty of interference, and his extreme dislike of incurring from O'Shea farther insult, were enough to produce his silence. Behind that lay the fact that he would be almost glad if the murder was done. Josephine's faith had inspired in him such love for her as had made him save her from doing what she thought wrong at any cost; but the inspiration did not extend to this. It appeared to him the lesser evil of the two.

"I will go with the boat," said Caius. "It is the quicker way."

He felt that for some reason this pleased O'Shea, who began at once to hurry off to get the luggage, but as he went he only remarked grimly:

"They say as it's the longest way round that is the shortest way home. If you're tipped in the ice, Mr. Doctor, ye'll foind that true, I'm thinking."

Caius found that O'Shea's boat, a heavy flat-bottomed thing, was already half launched upon the beach, furnished with stout boat-hooks for pushing among the ice, as well as her oars and sailing gear. He was glad to find that such speedy departure was to be his. He had no thought of saying good-bye to Josephine.

CHAPTER 10. "DEATH SHRIVE THEY SOUL!"

It was an immense relief to stand in the boat with the boat-hook, whose use demanded all the skill and nerve which Caius had at command. For the most part they could only propel the boat by pushing or pulling the bits of ice that surrounded it with their poles. It was a very different sort of travel from that which they had experienced together when they had carried their boat over islands of ice and launched it in the great gaps between them. The ice which they had to do with now would not have borne their weight; nor was there much clear space for rowing between the fragments. O'Shea pushed the boat boldly on, and they made their journey with comparative ease until, when they came near the channel made by the steamship, they found the ice lying more closely, and the difficulty of their progress increased.

Work as they would, they were getting on but slowly. The light wind blew past their faces, and the Gaspé schooner was seen to sail up the path which the steamer had made across the bay.

"The wind's in the very chink that makes her able to take the channel. I'm thinking she'll be getting in before us."

O'Shea spoke with the gay indifference of one who had staked nothing on the hope of getting to the harbour first; but Caius wondered if this short cut would have been undertaken without strong reason.

A short period of hard exertion, of pushing and pulling the bits of ice, followed, and then:

"I'm thinking we'll make the channel, any way, before she comes by, and then we'll just hail her, and the happy bridegroom can come off if he's so moinded, being in the hurry that he is. 'Tain't many bridegrooms that makes all the haste he has to jine the lady."

Caius said nothing; the subject was too horrible.

"Ye and yer bags could jist go on board the ship before the loving husband came off; ye'd make the harbour that way as easy, and I'm thinking the ice on the other side of the bay is that thick ye'd be scared and want me to sit back in my boat and yelp for help, like a froightened puppy dog, instead of making the way through."

Cains thought that O'Shea might be trying to dare him to remain in the boat. He inclined to believe that O'Shea could not alone enter into conflict with a strong unscrupulous man in such a boat, in such a sea, with hope of success. At any rate, when O'Shea, presuming on his friendship with the skipper, had accomplished no less a thing than bringing the sailing vessel to a standstill, Caius was prepared to board her at once.

The little boat was still among the ice, but upon the verge of clear water. The schooner, already near, was drifting nearer. O'Shea was shouting to the men on her deck. The skipper stood there looking over her side; he was a short stout man, of cheery aspect. Several sailors, and one or two other men who might be passengers, had come to the side also. Beside the skipper stood a big man with a brown beard; his very way of standing still seemed to suggest habitual sluggishness of mind or manner; yet his appearance at this distance was fine. Caius discovered that this was Le Maître; he was surprised, he had supposed that he would be thin and dark.

"It's Captain Le Maître I've come for; it's his wife that's wanting to see him," O'Shea shouted.

"He's here!"

The skipper gave the information cheerfully, and Le Maître made a slight sign showing that it was correct.

"I'll just take him back, then, in the boat with me now, for it's easy enough getting this way, but there's holes in the sand that makes drivin' unpleasant. Howsomever, I can't say which is the best passage. This city gentleman I've got with me now thinks he's lost his life siveral times already since he got into this boat."

He pointed to Caius as he ended his invitation to Le Maître. The men on the schooner all grinned. It was O'Shea's manner, as well as his words, that produced their derision.

Caius was wondering what would happen if Le Maître refused to come in the boat. Suspicion said that O'Shea would cause the boat to be towed ashore, and would then take the Captain home by the quicksands. Would O'Shea make him drunk, and then cast him headfirst into the swallowing sand? It seemed preposterous to be harbouring such thought against the cheerful and most respectable farmer at his side. What foundation had he for it? None but the hearing of an idle boast that the man had made one day to his wife, and that she in simplicity had taken for earnest.

Le Maître signified that he would go with O'Shea. Indeed, looked at from a short distance, the passage through the ice did not look so difficult as it had proved.

O'Shea and Caius parted without word or glance of farewell. Caius clambered over the side of the schooner; the one thought in his mind was to get a nearer view of Le Maître.

This man was still standing sleepily. He did not bear closer inspection well. His clothes were dirty, especially about the front of vest and coat; there was everything to suggest an entire lack of neatness in personal habits; more than that, the face at the time bore unmistakable signs that enough alcohol had been drunk to benumb, although not to stupefy, his faculties: the eye was bloodshot; the face, weather-beaten as it was, was flabby. In spite of all this, Caius had expected a more villainous-looking person, and so great was his loathing that he would rather have seen him in a more obnoxious light. The man had a certain dignity of bearing; his face had that unfurrowed look that means a low moral sense, for there is no evidence of conflict. His eyes were too near each other; this last was, perhaps, the only sign by which Nature from the outset had marred a really excellent piece of manly proportion.

Caius made these observations involuntarily. As Le Maître stepped here and there in a dull way while a chest that belonged to him was being lowered into the boat, Caius could not help realizing that his preconceived notions of the man as a monster had been exaggerated; he was a common man, fallen into low habits, and fixed in them by middle age.

Le Maître got into the boat in seaman-like fashion. He was perfectly at home there, and dull as his eye looked, he tacitly assumed command. He took O'Shea's pole from him, stepped to the prow, and began to turn the boat, without regarding the fact that O'Shea was still holding hasty conversation with the men on the schooner concerning the public events of the winter months—the news they had brought from the mainland.

Everything had been done in the greatest haste; it was not twelve minutes after the schooner had been brought to a stand when her sails were again turned to catch the breeze. The reason for this haste was to prevent more sideways drifting, for the schooner was drifting with the wind against the floating ice amongst which O'Shea's boat was lying. The wind blew very softly; her speed when sailing had not been great, and the drifting motion was the most gentle possible.

Caius had not taken his eyes from the boat. He was watching the strength with which Le Maître was turning her and starting her for Cloud Island. He was watching O'Shea, who, still giving back chaff and sarcasm to the men on the schooner, was forced to turn and pick up the smaller pole which Caius had relinquished; he seemed to be interested only in his talk, and to begin to help in the management of the boat mechanically. The skipper was swearing at his men and shouting to O'Shea with alternate breath. The sails of the schooner had hardly yet swelled with the breeze when O'Shea, bearing with all his might against a bit of ice, because of a slip of his pole, fell heavily on the side of his own boat, tipping her suddenly over on a bit of ice that sunk with her weight. Le Maître, at the prow, in the violent upsetting, was seen to fall headlong between two bits of ice into the sea.

"By——! Did you ever see anything like that?" The skipper of the schooner had run to the nearest point, which was beside Caius.

Then followed instantly a volley of commands, some of which related to throwing ropes to the small boat, some concerning the movement of the schooner, for at this moment her whole side pressed against all the bits of ice, pushing them closer and closer together.

The boat had not sunk; she had partially filled with water that had flowed over the ice on which she had upset; but when the weight of Le Maître was removed and O'Shea had regained his balance, the ice rose again, righting the boat and almost instantly tipping her toward the other side, for the schooner had by this time caused a jam. It was not such a jam as must of necessity injure the boat, which was heavily built; but the fact that she was now half full of water and that there was only one man to manage her, made his situation precarious. The danger of O'Shea, however, was hardly noticed by the men on the schooner, because of the horrible fact that the closing of the bits of ice together made it improbable that Le Maître could rise again.

For a moment there was an eager looking at every space of blue water that was left. If the drowning man could swim, he would surely make for such an aperture.

"Put your pole down to him where he went in!" The men on the schooner shouted this to O'Shea.

"Put the rope round your waist!" This last was yelled by the skipper, perceiving that O'Shea himself was by no means safe.

A rope that had been thrown had a noose, through which O'Shea dashed his arms;

then, seizing the pole, he struck the butt-end between the blocks of ice where Le Maître had fallen.

It seemed to Caius that the pole swayed in his hands, as if he were wrenching it from a hand that had gripped it strongly below; but it might have been only the grinding of the ice.

O'Shea thrust the pole with sudden vehemence further down, as if in a frantic effort to bring it better within reach of Le Maître if he were there; or, as Caius thought, it might have been that, feeling where the man was, he stunned him with the blow.

Standing in a boat that was tipping and grinding among the ice, O'Shea appeared to be exercising marvellous force and dexterity in thus using the pole at all.

The wind was now propelling the schooner forward, and her pressure on the ice ceased. O'Shea threw off the noose of the rope wildly, and looked to the men on the vessel, as if quite uncertain what to do next.

It was a difficult matter for anyone to decide. To leave him there was manifestly impossible; but if the schooner again veered round, the jamming of the ice over the head of La Maître would again occur. The men on the schooner, not under good discipline, were all shouting and talking.

"He's dead by now, wherever he is." The skipper made this quiet parenthesis either to himself or to Caius. Then he shouted aloud: "Work your boat through to us!"

O'Shea began poling vigorously. The ice was again floating loosely, and it was but the work of a few minutes to push his heavy boat into the open water that was in the wake of the schooner. There was a pause, like a pause in a funeral service, when O'Shea, standing ankle-deep in the water which his boat held, and the men huddled together upon the schooner's deck, turned to look at all the places in which it seemed possible that the body of Le Maître might again be seen. They looked and looked until they were tired with looking. The body had, no doubt, floated up under some cake of ice, and from thence would speedily sink to a bier of sand at the bottom of the bay.

"By——! I never saw anything like that." It was the remark which began and ended the episode with the skipper. Then he raised his voice, and shouted to O'Shea: "It's no sort of use your staying here! Make the rope fast to your boat, and come up on deck!"

But this O'Shea would not do. He replied that he would remain, and look about among the ice a bit longer, and that, any way, it would be twice as far to take his boat home from Harbour Island as from the place where he now was. The schooner towed his boat until he had baled the water out and got hold of his oars. The ice had floated so far apart that it seemed easy for the boat to go back through it.

During this time excited pithy gossip had been going on concerning the accident.

"You did all a man could do," shouted the captain to O'Shea consolingly, and remarked to those about him: "There wasn't no love lost between them, but O'Shea did all he could. O'Shea might as easy as not have gone over himself, holding the pole under water that time."

The fussy little captain, as far as Caius could judge, was not acting a part. The sailors were French; they could talk some English; and they spoke in both languages a great deal.

"His lady won't be much troubled, I dare say, from all I hear." The captain was becoming easy and good-natured again. He said to Caius: "You are acquainted with her?"

"She will be shocked," said Caius.

He felt as he spoke that he himself was suffering from shock—so much so that he was hardly able to think consecutively about what had occurred.

"They won't have an inquest without the body," shouted the captain to O'Shea. Then to those about him he remarked: "He was as decent and good-natured a fellow as I'd want to see."

The pronoun referred to Le Maître. The remark was perhaps prompted by natural pity, but it was so instantly agreed to by all on the vessel that the chorus had the air of propitiating the spirit of the dead.

CHAPTER 11. THE RIDDLE OF LIFE

The schooner slowly moved along, and lay not far from the steamship. The steamship did not start for Souris until the afternoon. Caius was put on shore there to await the hour of embarking. In his own mind he was questioning whether he would embark with the steamer or return to Cloud Island; but he naturally did not make this problem known to those around him.

The skipper and several men of the schooner came ashore with Caius. There was a great bustle as soon as they reached the small wharf because of what they had to tell. It was apparent from all that was told, and all the replies that were made, that no shadow of suspicion was to fall upon O'Shea. Why should it? He had, as it seemed, no personal grudge against Le Maître, whose death had been evidently an accident.

A man who bore an office akin to that of magistrate for the islands came down from a house near the harbour, and the story was repeated to him. When Caius had listened to the evidence given before this official personage, hearing the tale again that he had already heard many times in a few minutes, and told what he himself had seen, he began to wonder how he could still harbour in his mind the belief in O'Shea's guilt. He found, too, that none of these people knew enough about Josephine to see any special interest attaching to the story, except the fact that her husband, returning from a long voyage, had been drowned almost within sight of her house. "Ah, poor lady! poor lady!" they said; and thus saying, and shaking their heads, they dispersed to eat their dinners.

Caius procured the bundle of letters which had come for him by this first mail of the year. He sauntered along the beach, soon getting out of sight and hearing of the little community, who were not given to walking upon a beach that was not in this case a high-road to any place. He was on the shingle of the bay, and he soon found a nook under a high black cliff where the sun beat down right warmly. He had not opened his letters; his mind did not yet admit of old interests.

The days were not long passed in which men who continued to be good husbands and fathers and staunch friends killed their enemies, when necessary, with a good conscience. Had O'Shea a good conscience now? Would he continue to be in all respects the man he had been, and the staunch friend of Josephine? In his heart Caius believed that Le Maître was murdered; but he had no evidence to prove it—nothing whatever but what O'Shea's wife had said to him that day she was hanging out her linen, and such talk occurs in many a household, and nothing comes of it.

Now Josephine was free. "What a blessing!" He used the common idiom to himself, and then wondered at it. Could one man's crime be another man's blessing? He found himself, out of love for Josephine, wondering concerning the matter from the point of view of the religious theory of life. Perhaps this was Heaven's way of answering Josephine's appeal, and saving her; or perhaps human souls are so knit together that O'Shea, by the sin, had not blessed, but hindered her from blessing. It was a weary round of questions, which Caius was not wise enough to answer. Another more practical question pressed.

Did he dare to return now to Cloud Island, and watch over Josephine in the shock which she must sustain, and find out if she would discover the truth concerning O'Shea? After a good while he answered the question: No; he did not dare to return, knowing what he did and his own cowardly share in it. He could not face Josephine, and, lonely as she was, she did not need him; she had her prayers, her angels, her heaven.

Perhaps Time, the proverbial healer of all wounds, would wash the sense of guilt from his soul, and then he could come back and speak to Josephine concerning this new freedom of hers. Then he remembered that some say that for the wound of guilt Time no healing art. Could he find, then, other shrift? He did not know. He longed for it sorely, because he longed to feel fit to return to Josephine. But, after all, what had he done of which he was ashamed? What was his guilt? Had he felt any emotion that it was not natural to feel? Had he done anything wrong? Again he did not know. He sat with head bowed, and felt in dull misery that O'Shea was a better man than he—more useful and brave, and not more guilty.

He opened his letters, and found that in his absence no worse mishap had occurred at home than that his father had been laid up some time with a bad leg, and that both father and mother had allowed themselves to worry and fret lest ill should have befallen their son.

Caius embarked on the little steamship that afternoon, and the next noon found him at home.

The person who met him on the threshold of his father's house was Jim Hogan. Jim grinned.

"Since you've taken to charities abroad," he said, "I thought I'd begin at home."

Jim's method of beginning at home was not in the literal sense of the proverb. It turned out that he had been neighbouring to some purpose. Old Simpson could not move himself about indoors or attend to his work without, and Jim, who had not before this attached himself by regular employment, had by some freak of good-nature given his services day by day until Caius should return, and had become an indispensable member of the household.

"He's not a very respectable young man," said the mother apologetically to her son, while she was still wiping her tears of joy; "but it's just wonderful what patience he's had in his own larky way with your father, when, though I say it who shouldn't, your father's been as difficult to manage as a crying baby, and Jim, he just makes his jokes when anyone else would have been affronted, and there's father laughing in spite of himself sometimes. So I don't know how it is, but we've just had him to stop on, for he's took to the farm wonderful."

An hour after, when alone with his father, Simpson said to him:

"Your mother, you know, was timorous at night when I couldn't help myself; and then she'd begin crying, as women will, saying as she knew you were dead, and that, any way, it was lonesome without you. So when I saw that it comforted her a bit to have someone to cook for, I encouraged the fellow. I told him he'd nothing to look for from me, for his father is richer than I am nowadays; but he's just the sort to like vagary."

Jim went home, and Caius began a simple round of home duties. His father needed much attendance; the farm servants needed direction. Caius soon found out, without being told, that neither in one capacity nor the other did he fulfil the old man's pleasure nearly so well as the rough-and-ready Jim. Even his mother hardly let a day pass without innocently alluding to some prank of Jim's that had amused her. She would have been very angry if anyone had told her that she did not find her son as good a companion. Caius did not tell her so, but he was perfectly aware of it.

Caius had not been long at home when his cousin Mabel came to visit them. This time his mother made no sly remarks concerning Mabel's reason for timing her visit, because it seemed that Mabel had paid a long and comforting visit while he had been at the Magdalen Islands. Mabel did not treat Caius now with the unconscious flattery of blind admiration, neither did she talk to him about Jim; but her silence whenever Jim's name was mentioned was eloquent.

Caius summed all this up in his own mind. He and Jim had commenced life as lads together. The one had trodden the path of virtue and laudable ambition; the other had just amused himself, and that in many reprehensible ways; and now, when the ripe age of manhood was attained in that state of life to which—as the Catechism would have it—it had pleased God to call them, it was Jim who was the useful and honoured man, not Caius.

It was clear that all the months and years of his absence had enabled his parents to do very well without their son. They did not know it, but in all the smaller things that make up the most of life, his interests had ceased to be their interests. Caius had the courage to realize that even at home he was not much wanted. If, when Jim married Mabel, he would settle down with the old folks, they would be perfectly happy.

On his return, Caius had learned that the post for which he had applied in the autumn had not been awarded to him. He knew that he must go as soon as possible to find out a good place in which to begin his professional life, but at present the state of his father's bad leg was so critical, and the medical skill of the neighbourhood so poor, that he was forced to wait.

All this time there was one main thought in his mind, to which all others were subordinate. He saw his situation quite clearly; he had no doubts about it. If Josephine would come to him and be his wife, he would be happy and prosperous. Josephine had the power to make him twice the man he was without her. It was not only that his happiness was bound up in her; it was not only that Josephine had money and could manage it well, although he was not at all above thinking of that; it was not even that she would help and encourage and console him as no one else would. There was that subtle something, more often the fruit of what is called friendship than of love, by which Josephine's presence increased all his strong faculties and subdued his faults. Caius knew this with the unerring knowledge of instinct. He tried to reason about it, too: even a dull king reigns well if he have but the wit to choose good ministers; and among men, each ruling his small kingdom, they are often the most successful who possess, not many talents, but the one talent of choosing well in friendship and in love.

Ah! but it is one thing to choose and another to obtain. Caius still felt that he dared not seek Josephine. Since Le Maître's death something of the first blank horror of his own guilt had passed away, but still he knew that he was not innocent. Then, too, if he dared to woo her, what would be the result? That last admonition and warning that he had given her when she was about to leave the island with him clogged his hope when he sought to take courage. He knew that popular lore declared that, whether or not she acknowledged its righteousness, her woman's vanity would take arms against it.

Caius had written to Josephine a letter of common friendliness upon the occasion of her husband's death, and had received in return a brief sedate note that might, indeed, have been written by the ancient lady whom the quaint Italian handwriting learned in the country convent had at first figured to his imagination. He knew from this letter that Josephine did not suppose that blame attached to O'Shea. She spoke of her husband's death as an accident. Caius knew that she had accepted it as a deliverance from God. It was this attitude of hers which made the whole circumstance appear to him the more solemn.

So Caius waited through the lovely season in which summer hovers with warm sunshiny wings over a land of flowers before she settles down upon it to abide. He was unhappy. A shade, whose name was Failure, lived with him day by day, and spoke to him concerning the future as well as the past. Debating much in his mind what he might do, fearing to make his plight worse by doing anything, he grew timid at the very thought of addressing Josephine. Happily, there is something more merciful to a man than his own self—something which in his hour of need assists him, and that often very bountifully.

CHAPTER 12. TO CALL A SPIRIT FROM THE VASTY DEEP

It was when the first wild-flowers of the year had passed away, and scarlet columbine and meadow-rue waved lightly in the sunny glades of the woods, and all the world was green —the new and perfect green of June—that one afternoon Caius, at his father's door, met a visitor who was most rarely seen there. It was Farmer Day. He accosted Caius, perhaps a little sheepishly, but with an obvious desire to be civil, for he had a favour to ask which he evidently considered of greater magnitude than Caius did when he heard what it was. Day's wife was ill. The doctor of the locality had said more than once that she would not live many days, but she had gone on living some time, it appeared, since this had been first said. Day did not now call upon Caius as a medical man. His wife had taken a fancy to see him because of his remembered efforts to save her child. Day said apologetically that it was a woman's whim, but he would be obliged if Caius, at his convenience, would call upon her. It spoke much for the long peculiarity and dreariness of Day's domestic life that he evidently believed that this would be a disagreeable thing for Caius to do.

Day went on to the village. Caius strolled off through the warm woods and across the hot cliffs to make this visit.

The woman was not in bed. She was dying of consumption. The fever was flickering in her high-boned cheeks when she opened the door of the desolate farmhouse. She wore a brown calico gown; her abundant black hair was not yet streaked with gray. Caius could not see that she looked much older than she had done upon the evening, years ago, when he had first had reason to observe her closely. He remembered what Josephine had told him—that time had stood still with her since that night: it seemed true in more senses than one. A light of satisfaction showed itself in her dark face when, after a moment's inspection, she realized who he was.

"Come in," she said briefly.

Caius went in, and had reason to regret, as well on his own account as on hers, that she shut the door. To be out in the summer would have been longer life for her, and to have the summer shut out made him realize forcibly that he was alone in the desolate house with a woman whose madness gave her a weird seeming which was almost equivalent to ghostliness.

When one enters a house from which the public has long been excluded and which is the abode of a person of deranged mind, it is perhaps natural to expect, although unconsciously, that the interior arrangements should be very strange. Instead of this, the house, gloomy and sparsely furnished as it was, was clean and in order. It lacked everything to make it pleasant—air, sunshine, and any cheerful token of comfort; but it was only in this dreary negation that it failed; there was no positive fault to be found even with the atmosphere of the kitchen and bare lobby through which he was conducted, and he discovered, to his surprise, that he was to be entertained in a small parlour, which had a round polished centre table, on which lay the usual store of such things as are seen in such parlours all the world over—a Bible, a couple of albums, a woollen mat, and an ornament under a glass case.

Caius sat down, holding his hat in his hand, with an odd feeling that he was acting a part in behaving as if the circumstances were at all ordinary.

The woman also sat down, but not as if for ease. She drew one of the big cheap albums towards her, and began vigorously searching in it from the beginning, as if it were a book of strange characters in which she wished to find a particular passage. She fixed her eyes upon each small cheap photograph in turn, as if trying hard to remember who it represented, and whether it was, or was not, the one she wanted. Caius looked on amazed.

At length, about the middle of the book, she came to a portrait at which she stopped, and with a look of cunning took out another which was hidden under it, and thrust it at Caius.

"It's for you," she said; "it's mine, and I'm going to die, and it's you I'll give it to."

She looked and spoke as if the proffered gift was a thing more precious than the rarest gem.

Caius took it, and saw that it was a picture of a baby girl, about three years old. He had not the slightest doubt who the child was; he stood by the window and examined it long and eagerly. The sun, unaided by the deceptive shading of the more skilled photographer, had imprinted the little face clearly. Caius saw the curls, and the big sad eyes with their long lashes, and all the baby features and limbs, his memory aiding to make the portrait perfect. His eager look was for the purpose of discovering whether or not his imagination had played him false; but it was true what he had thought—the little one was like Josephine.

"I shall be glad to have it," he said—"very glad."

"I had it taken at Montrose," said the poor mother; and, strange to say, she said it in a commonplace way, just as any woman might speak of procuring her child's likeness. "Day, he was angry; he said it was waste of money; that's why I give it to you." A fierce cunning look flitted again across her face for a moment. "Don't let him see it," she whispered. "Day, he is a bad father; he don't care for the children or me. That's why I've put her in the water."

She made this last statement concerning her husband and child with a nonchalant air, like one too much accustomed to the facts to be distressed at them.

For a few minutes it seemed that she relapsed into a state of dulness, neither thought nor feeling stirring within her. Caius, supposing that she had nothing more to say, still watched her intently, because the evidences of disease were interesting to him. When he least expected it, she awoke again into eagerness; she put her elbows on the table and leaned towards him.

"There's something I want you to do," she whispered. "I can't do it any more. I'm dying. Since I began dying, I can't get into the water to look for her. My baby is in the water, you know; I put her in. She isn't dead, but she's there, only I can't find her. Day told me that once you got into the water to look for her too, but you gave it up too easy, and no one else has ever so much as got in to help me find her."

The last part of the speech was spoken in a dreary monotone. She stopped with a heart-broken sigh that expressed hopeless loneliness in this mad quest.

"The baby is dead," he said gently.

She answered him with eager, excited voice:

"No, she isn't; that's where you are wrong. You put it on the stone that she was dead. When I came out of th' asylum I went to look at the stone, and I laughed. But I liked you to make the stone; that's why I like you, because nobody else put up a stone for her."

Caius laid a cool hand on the feverish one she was now brandishing at him.

"You are dying, you say"—pityingly. "It is better for you to think that your baby is dead, for when you die you will go to her."

The woman laughed, not harshly, but happily.

"She isn't dead. She came back to me once. She was grown a big girl, and had a wedding-ring on her hand. Who do you think she was married to? I thought perhaps it was you."

The repetition of this old question came from her lips so suddenly that Caius dropped her hand and stepped back a pace. He felt his heart beating. Was it a good omen? There have been cases where a half-crazed brain has been known, by chance or otherwise, to foretell the future. The question that was now for the second time repeated to him seemed to his hope like an instance of this second sight, only half understood by the eye that saw it.

"It was not your little daughter that came back, Mrs. Day. It was her cousin, who is very like her, and she came to help you when you were ill, and to be a daughter to you."

She looked at him darkly, as if the saner powers of her mind were struggling to understand; but in a minute the monomania had again possession of her.

"She had beautiful hair," she said; "I stroked it with my hand; it curled just as it used to do. Do you think I don't know my own child? But she had grown quite big, and her ring was made of gold. I would like to see her again now before I die."

Very wistfully she spoke of the beauty and kindness of the girl whose visit had cheered her. The poor crazed heart was full of longing for the one presence that could give her any comfort this side of death.

"I thought I'd never see her again." She fixed her dark eyes on Caius as she spoke. "I was going to ask you, after I was dead and couldn't look for her any more, if you'd keep on looking for her in the sea till you found her. But I wish you'd go now and see if you couldn't fetch her before I die."

"Yes, I will go," answered Caius suddenly.

The strong determination of his quick assent seemed to surprise even her in whose mind there could be no rational cause for surprise.

"Do you mean it?"

"Yes, I mean it. I will go, Mrs. Day."

A moment more she paused, as if for time for full belief in his promise to dawn upon her, and then, instead of letting him go, she rose up quickly with mysterious looks and gestures. Her words were whispered:

"Come, then, and I'll show you the way. Come; you mustn't tell Day. Day doesn't know anything about it." She had led him back to the door of the house and gone out before him. "Come, I'll show you the way. Hush! don't talk, or someone might hear us. Walk close to the barn, and no one will see. I never showed anyone before but her when she came to me wearing the gold ring. What are you so slow for? Come, I'll show you the way to look for her."

Impelled by curiosity and the fear of increasing her excitement if he refused, Caius followed her down the side of the open yard in which he had once seen her stand in fierce quarrel with her husband. It had seemed a dreary place then, when the three children swung on the gate and neither the shadow of death nor madness hung over it; it seemed far more desolate now, in spite of the bright summer sunlight. The barns and stable, as they swiftly passed them, looked much neglected, and there was not about the whole farmstead another man or woman to be seen. As the mad woman went swiftly in front of him, Caius remembered, perhaps for the first time in all these years, that after her husband had struck her upon that night, she had gone up to the cowshed that was nearest the sea, and that afterwards he had met her at the door of the root-house that was in the bank of the chine. It was thither she went now, opening the door of the cowshed and leading him through it to a door at the other end, and down a path to this cellar cut in the bank.

The cellar had apparently been very little used. The path to it was well beaten, but Caius observed that it ran past the cellar down the chine to a landing where Day now kept a flat-bottomed boat. They stood on this path before the heavy door of the cellar. Rust had eaten into the iron latch and the padlock that secured it, but the woman produced a key and opened the ring of the lock and took him into a chamber about twelve feet square, in which props of decaying beams held up the earth of the walls and roof. The place was cold, smelling strongly of damp earth and decaying roots; but, so far, there was nothing remarkable to be seen; just such a cellar was used on his father's farm to keep stores of potatoes and turnips in when the frost of winter made its way through all the wooden barns. In three corners remains of such root stores were lying; in the fourth, the corner behind the door, nearest the sea, some boards were laid on the floor, and on them flower-pots containing stalks of withered plants and bulbs that had never sprouted.

"They're mine," she said. "Day dursn't touch them;" and saying this, she fell to work with eager feverishness, removing the pots and boards. When she had done so, it was revealed that the earth under the boards had broken through into another cellar or cave, in which some light could be seen.

"I always heard the sea when I was in this place, and one day I broke through this hole. The man that first had the farm made it, I s'pose, to pitch his seaweed into from the shore."

She let her long figure down through the hole easily enough, for there were places to set the feet on, and landed on a heap of earth and dried weed. When Caius had dropped down into this second chamber, he saw that it had evidently been used for just the purpose she had mentioned. The seaweed gathered from the beach after storms was in common use for enriching the fields, and someone in a past generation had apparently dug this cave in the soft rock and clay of the cliff; it was at a height above the sea-line at which the seaweed could be conveniently pitched into it from a cart on the shore below. Some three or four feet of dry rotten seaweed formed its carpet. The aperture towards the sea was almost entirely overgrown with such grass and weeds as grew on the bluff. It was evident that in the original cutting there had been an opening also sideways into the chine, which had caved in and been grown over. The cellar above had, no doubt, been made by someone who was not aware of the existence of this former place.

To Caius the secret chamber was enchanted ground. He stepped to its window, framed in waving grasses, and saw the high tide lapping just a little way below. It was into this place of safety that Josephine had crept when she had disappeared from his view before he could mount the cliff to see whither she went. She had often stood where he now stood, half afraid, half audacious, in that curious dress of hers, before she summoned up courage to slip into the sea for daylight or moonlight wanderings.

He turned round to hear the gaunt woman beside him again talking excitedly. Upon a bit of rusty iron that still held its place on the wall hung what he had taken to be a heap of sacking. She took this down now and displayed it with a cunning look.

"I made it myself," she said, "it holds one up wonderful in the water; but now I've been a-dying so long the buoys have burst."

Caius pityingly took the garment from her. Her mad grief, and another woman's madcap pleasure, made it a sacred thing. His extreme curiosity found satisfaction in discovering that the coarse foundation was covered with a curious broidery of such small floats as might, with untiring industry, be collected in a farmhouse: corks and small pieces of wood with holes bored through them were fastened at regular intervals, not without some attempt at pattern, and between them the bladders of smaller animals, prepared as fishermen prepare them for their nets. Larger specimens of the same kind were concealed inside the neck of the huge sack, but on the outside everything was comparatively small, and it seemed as if the hands that had worked it so elaborately had been directed by a brain in which familiarity with patchwork, and other homely forms of the sewing-woman's art, had been confused with an adequate idea of the rough use for which the garment was needed. Some knowledge of the skill with which fishermen prepare their floats had also evidently been hers, for the whole outside of the garment was smeared or painted with a brownish substance that had preserved it to a wonderful extent from the ravages of moisture and salt. It was torn now, or, rather, it seemed that it had been cut from top to bottom; but, besides this one great rent, it was in a rotten condition, ready to fall to pieces, and, as the dying woman had said, many of the air-blown floats had burst.

Caius was wondering whether the occasion on which this curious bathing-dress had been torn was that in which he, by pursuing Josephine, had forced her to cease pushing herself about in shallow water and take to more ordinary swimming. He looked around and saw the one other implement which had been necessary to complete the strange outfit; it, too, was a thing of ordinary appearance and use: a long pole or poker, with a handle at one end and a small flat bar at the other, a thing used for arranging the fire in the deep brick ovens that were still in use at the older farmsteads. It was about six feet long. The woman, seeing his attention directed to it, took it eagerly and showed how it might be used, drawing him with her to the aperture over the shore and pointing out eagerly the landmarks by which she knew how far the shallow water extended at certain times of the tide. Her topographical knowledge of all the sea's bed within about a mile of the high-water mark was extraordinarily minute, and Caius listened to the information she poured upon him, only now beginning to realize that she expected him to wear the dress, and take the iron pole, and slip from the old cellar into the tide when it rose high enough, and from thence bring back the girl with the soft curls and the golden ring. It was one of those moments in which laughter and tears meet, but there was a glamour of such strange fantasy over the scene that Caius felt, not so much its humour or its pathos, as its fairy-like unreality, and that which gave him the sense of unreality was that to his companion it was intensely real.

"You said you would go." Some perception of his hesitation must have come to her; her words were strong with insistence and wistful with reproach. "You said you would go and fetch her in to me before I die."

Then Caius put back the dress she held on the rusty peg where it had hung for so long.

"I am a man," he said. "I can swim without life-preservers. I will go and try to bring the girl back to you. But not now, not from here; it will take me a week to go and come, for I know that she lives far away in the middle of the deep gulf. Come back to the house and take care of yourself, so that you may live until she comes. You may trust me. I will certainly bring her to you if she's alive and if she can come."

With these promises and protestations he prevailed upon the poor woman to return with him to her lonely home.

Caius had not got far on his road home, when he met Day coming from the village. Caius was full of his determination to go for Josephine by the next trip of the small steamer. His excuse was valid; he could paint the interview from which he had just come so that Josephine would be moved by it, would welcome his interference, and come again to nurse her uncle's wife. Thus thinking, he had hurried along, but when he met Day his knight-errantry received a check.

"Your wife ought not to be alone," he said to Day.

"No; that's true!" the farmer replied drearily; "but it isn't everybody she'll have in the house with her."

"Your son and daughter are too far away to be sent for?"

"Yes"—briefly—"they are in the west."

Caius paused a moment, thinking next to introduce the subject which had set all his pulses bounding. Because it was momentous to him, he hesitated, and while he hesitated the other spoke.

"There is one relation I've got, the daughter of a brother of mine who died up by Gaspé Basin. She's on the Magdalens now. I understood that you had had dealings with her."

"Yes; I was just about to suggest—I was going to say——"

"I wrote to her. She is coming," said Day.

CHAPTER 13. THE EVENING AND THE MORNING

Josephine had come. All night and all the next day she had been by her aunt's bedside; for Day's wife lay helpless now, and death was very near. This much Caius knew, having kept himself informed by communication with the village doctor, and twenty-four hours after Josephine's arrival he walked over to the Day farm, hoping that, as the cool of the evening might relax the strain in the sick-room, she would be able to speak to him for a few minutes.

When he got to the dreary house he met its owner, who had just finished his evening work. The two men sat on wooden chairs outside the door and watched the dusk gathering on sea and land, and although they did not talk much, each felt glad of the other's companionship.

It was nine years since Caius had first made up his mind that Day was a monster of brutality and wickedness; now he could not think himself back into the state of mind that could have formed such a judgment When Caius had condemned Day, he had been a religious youth who thought well of himself; now his old religious habits and beliefs had dropped off, but he did not think well of himself or harshly of his neighbour. In those days he had felt sufficient for life; now all his feeling was summed up in the desire that was scarcely a hope, that some heavenly power, holy and strong, would come to his aid.

It is when the whole good of life hangs in a trembling balance that people become like children, and feel the need of the motherly powers of Heaven. Caius sat with Day for two hours, and Josephine did not come down to speak to him. He was glad to know that Day's evening passed the more easily because he sat there with him; he was glad of that when he was glad of nothing that concerned himself.

Day and Caius did not talk about death or sorrow, or anything like that. All the remarks that they interchanged turned upon the horses Day was rearing and their pastures. Day told that he had found the grass on the little island rich.

"I remember finding two of your colts there one day when I explored it. It was four years ago," said Caius dreamily.

Day took no interest in this lapse of time.

"It's an untidy bit of land," he said, "and I can't clear it. 'Tisn't mine; but no one heeds the colts grazing."

"Do you swim them across?" asked Caius, half in polite interest, half because his memory was wandering upon the water.

"They got so sharp at swimming, I had to raise the fence on the top of the cliff," said Day.

The evening wore away.

In the morning Caius, smitten with the fever of hope and fear, rose up at dawn, and, as in a former time he had been wont to do, ran to the seashore by the nearest path and walked beside the edge of the waves. He turned, as he had always done, towards the little island and the Day Farm.

How well he knew every outward curve and indentation of the soft red shelving bank! how well he knew the colouring of the cool scene in the rising day, the iridescent light upon the lapping waves, the glistening of the jasper red of the damp beach, and the earthen pinks of the upper cliffs! The sea birds with low pathetic note called out to him concerning their memories of the first dawn in which he had walked there searching for the body of the dead baby. Then the cool tints of dawn passed into the golden sunrise, and the birds went on calling to him concerning the many times in which he had trodden this path as a lover whose mistress had seemed so strange a denizen of this same wide sea.

Caius did not think with scorn now of this old puzzle and bewilderment, but remembered it fondly, and went and sat beneath baby Day's epitaph, on the very rock from which he had first seen Josephine. It was very early in the morning; the sun had risen bright and warm. At that season even this desolate bit of shore wag garlanded above with the most lovely green; the little island was green as an emerald.

Caius did not intend to keep his present place long. The rocky point where the red cliff ended hid any portion of the Day farm from his view, and as soon as the morning was far enough advanced he intended to go and see how the owner and his household had fared during the night.

In the meantime he waited, and while he waited Fate came to him smiling.

Once or twice as he sat he heard the sound of horse's feet passing on the cliff above him. He knew that Day's horses were there, for they were pastured alternately upon the cliff and upon the richer herbage of the little island. He supposed by the sounds that they were catching one of them for use on the farm. The sounds went further away, for he did not hear the tread of hoofs again. He had forgotten them; his face had dropped upon his hands; he was looking at nothing, except that, beneath the screen of his fingers, he could see the red pebbles at his feet. Something very like a prayer was in his heart; it had no form; it was not a thing of which his intellect could take cognizance. Just then he heard a cry of fear and a sound as if of something dashing into the water. The sounds came from behind the rocky point. Caius knew the voice that cried and he rose up wildly, but staggered, baffled by his old difficulty, that the path thither lay only through deep water or round above the cliff.

Then he saw a horse swimming round the red rocks, and on its back a woman sat, not at ease—evidently distressed and frightened by the course the animal was taking. To Caius the situation became clear. Josephine had thought to refresh herself after her night's vigil by taking an early ride, and the young half-broken horse, finding himself at large, was making for the delicacies which he knew were to be found on the island pasture. Josephine did not know why her steed had put out to sea, or whither he was going. She turned round, and, seeing Caius, held out her hand, imploring his aid.

Caius thanked Heaven at that moment It was true that Josephine kept her seat upon the horse perfectly, and it was true that, unless the animal intended to lie down and roll when he got into the deep grass of the island, he had probably no malicious intention in going there. That did not matter. Josephine was terrified by finding herself in the sea and she had cried to him for aid. A quick run, a short swim, and Caius waded up on the island sands. The colt had a much longer distance to swim, and Caius waited to lay his hand on the bridle.

For a minute or two there was a chase among the shallow, rippling waves, but a horse sinking in heavy sand is not hard to catch. Josephine sat passive, having enough to do, perhaps, merely to keep her seat. When at length Caius stood on the island grass with the bridle in his hand, she slipped down without a word and stood beside him.

Caius let the dripping animal go, and he went, plunging with delight among the flowering weeds and bushes. Caius himself was dripping also, but, then, he could answer for his own movements that he would not come too near the lady.

Josephine no longer wore her loose black working dress; this morning she was clad in an old habit of green cloth. It was faded with weather, and too long in the skirt for the fashion then in vogue, but Caius did not know that; he only saw that the lower part of the skirt was wet, and that, as she stood at her own graceful height upon the grass, the wet cloth twisted about her feet and lay beside them in a rounded fold, so that she looked just now more like the pictures of the fabled sea-maids than she had ever done when she had floated in the water.

The first thing Josephine did was to look up in his face and laugh; it was her own merry peal of low laughter that reminded him always of a child laughing, not more for fun than for mere happiness. It bridged for him all the sad anxieties and weary hours that had passed since he had heard her laugh before; and, furthermore, he knew, without another moment's doubt, that Josephine, knowing him as she did, would never have looked up to him like that unless she loved him. It was not that she was thinking of love just then—that was not what was in her face; but it was clear that she was conscious of no shadow of difference between them such as would have been there if his love had been doomed to disappointment. She looked to him to join in her laughter with perfect comradeship.

"Why did the horse come here?" asked Josephine.

Caius explained the motives of the colt as far as he understood them; and she told how she had persuaded her uncle to let her ride it, and all that she had thought and felt when it had run away with her down the chine and into the water. It was not at all what he could have believed beforehand, that when he met Josephine they would talk with perfect contentment of the affairs of the passing hour; and yet so it was.

With graver faces they talked of the dying woman, with whom Josephine had passed the night. It was not a case in which death was sad; it was life, not death, that was sad for the wandering brain. But Josephine could tell how in those last nights the poor mother had found peace in the presence of her supposed child.

"She curls my hair round her thin fingers and seems so happy," said Josephine.

She did not say that the thin hands had fingered her wedding-ring; but Caius thought of it, and that brought him back the remembrance of something that had to be said that must be said then, or every moment would become a sin of weak delay.

"I want to tell you," he began—"I know I must tell you—I don't know exactly why, but I must—I am sorry to say anything to remind you—to distress you—but I hated Le Maître! Looking back, it seems to me that the only reason I did not kill him was that I was too much of a coward."

Josephine looked off upon the sea. The wearied pained look that she used to wear when the people were ill about her, or that she had worn when she heard Le Maître was returning, came back to her face, so that she seemed not at all the girl who had been laughing with him a minute before, but a saint, whose image he could have worshipped. And yet he saw then, more clearly than he had ever seen, that the charm, the perfect consistency of her character, lay in the fact that the childlike joy was never far off from the woman's strength and patience, and that a womanly heart always underlay the merriest laughter.

They stood silent for a long time. It is in silence that God's creation grows.

At length Josephine spoke slowly:

"Yes, we are often very, very wicked; but I think when we are so much ashamed that we have to tell about it—I think it means that we will never do it again."

"I am not good enough to love you," said Caius brokenly.

"Ah! do not say that"—she turned her face away from him—"remember the last time you spoke to me upon the end of the dune."

Caius went back to the shore to get the boat that lay at the foot of the chine. The colt was allowed to enjoy his paradise of island flowers in peace.

Made in the USA
Middletown, DE
25 June 2021